THE SEA OF STARS

BOOK TWO THE TWINS OF MOON

FRANK P. RYAN

SWIFT
PUBLISHERS

A SWIFT BOOK

First published by Swift Publishers 2022

1 3 5 7 9 8 6 4 2

Copyright © Frank P. Ryan 2022

The rights of Frank P. Ryan to be identified as the Author of this Work have been asserted by him in accordance with the Copyright, Designs and Patents Act 1988

A catalogue record for this book is available from the British Library

ISBN 978-1-874082-85-9

Cover art by Mark Salwowski

Typeset by Word-2-Kindle

Praise for Frank P. Ryan's writing

"Undoubtedly the best fantasy novel I've ever read."

Glenda A. Bixler, Authorsden

"It works well as a magical adventure and will appeal to fans of traditional fantasy and those that fancy some well-crafted escapism."

Catherine Mann, The British Fantasy Society

"His main characters are brilliantly depicted, as are the weird and wonderful adventures they embark on – it's hard to imagine either teen or adult not being enthralled . . ."

Shelley Marsden, *Irish World*

"A fast-paced, action-packed and truly fantastical journey."

Pamela Luke, *Fantasy Book Review*

"Fantasy fans will find a rich, immersive world and carefully handled characters."

Stacey Comfort, Booklist on Line

Other Fantasy Titles by Frank P. Ryan

The Twins of Moon Trilogy

The Twins of Moon

The Three Powers Quartet

The Snowmelt River

The Tower of Bones

The Sword of Feimhin

The Return of the Arinn

Other Fiction Titles by Frank P. Ryan

The Doomsday Genie

Goodbye Baby Blue

Sweet Summer

Tiger Tiger

I would like to thank Laura Hane for her diligent correction of my peccadilloes. My thanks as always to my friend and artist, Mark Salwowski, for his magnificent cover art.

Contents

THE SCUTTLEBUTT

The spray struck Eefa full in the face. Wiping it from her eyes with half-frozen fingers, she took a firmer grip of the prow rail to steady herself against the rolling of the ship. How she had come to love the sea in the few weeks they had been aboard. It just felt so alive to be here. From day to day, sometimes from moment to moment, it sprang surprises on you. Right now, in the glimmering light of a new morning, she leaned out as far as she dared over the rail so that her nostrils were filled with ozone. Blinking the salty spray from her eyes, she peered down into the depths and glimpsed there something new, something strange, perhaps even wonderful, something quick-moving by them, absorbed with its own being and survival, just beneath the churning froth of the waves. Even at night, when she was perched in this selfsame spot, she had found herself imagining the mysteries in those inky depths, glimpsing flashes of movements flickering with phosphorescent light, like ghosts of the deeps.

Of course, she shouldn't allow her imagination to run away with her. It didn't do, as Bird Woman had warned her more than once, to let this happen. Nevertheless, there were real dark powers out there, searching for her and her twin brother, Magio – enemies that, for reasons she couldn't fathom, were determined to put an end to them. Only recently she and Magio had been so threatened that, had it not been for Quimbre and Bird Woman, they would never have escaped from their home in Warren on the island of Moon. The memory of all that was still so close, so terrifying, that even now Eefa felt her heart wilt inside her chest, her mouth go uncomfortably dry. The familiar sense of fear made her want to blank it out, to pretend it hadn't happened. But it wasn't easy to do so. Oh . . . it wasn't easy at all!

Even as Eefa was lost in her memories, two hands appeared from behind to close off her eyes. 'Trade you a secret for a wish.'

She could smell the owner of those large, brawny hands.

'Quimbre!'

She could feel the damaged fingers where Bird Woman had splintered the broken bones after Quimbre's brave fight with the Hunter. Quimbre had been prepared to die to save her and Magio. Eefa knew why he was hugging her now. He was trying to give her courage after so many terrifying adventures. Right now, gazing out into the waves, Eefa needed all the courage she could find.

Quimbre laughed, rotating her around by the shoulders so he could look at her.

'Gave me the run around, you did. All those times Magio tried to persuade me you were real. And all the while I couldn't believe him. Yet here you are as real as this creaky old brig. Hey, you got to allow a hoary old mariner time to get used to you.'

It was so strange now to hear Quimbre actually talking to her – something she had, instinctively, avoided throughout her childhood. She knew now that she had let her own fears block out the possibility of anyone other than Magio and Gran from knowing that she actually existed. Now, looking back, it seemed a strange thing to have done, something too foolish to comprehend. And yet her instincts had been so overwhelming – even if they had been brought about by some kind of irrational fear.

'I know I did, Quimbre. I'm sorry – I suppose it will take us a little while to get used to one another.'

'Forget about it, Kiddo. We have other things to worry about.'

'What do you mean?'

'The danger hasn't gone away. This is the Sea of Stars. You can't even imagine how unpredictable these waters are. The normal rules don't apply here.'

'I like surprises.'

'Hah!' Quimbre threw back his head and laughed. He lifted her effortlessly off the deck, then twirled her around as if she weighed no more than a cork, all the while still guffawing with laughter.

'My dear young lady – since a young lady is what you now assuredly are – be aware that every living creature has its secrets. If you but studied the tiniest creatures on the sea floor, stealing shells to hide in – or the shock-eels hiding in their burrows – or the birds that lay their eggs in the nests of others – all have their secrets. And no world is more riddled with secrets than the eldritch sea we now blithely sail. Magic is all about us here. It hides in the wind that billows the sails above you, in the isles that abound in every direction, and all the more does it lurk in the deeps beneath our keel.

Eefa leaned her head back and gazed up enraptured into the sky of whirling clouds. Oh, she was already coming to realize that those waves about them were nothing like the friendly surf at Warren where she had so loved to play. These were roiling monsters, slow-rolling walls of water that struck the ship as if they wanted to devour it. But still, and perhaps even more so, she relished the wonder of it all, the unknown places all about them, and the new discoveries they would soon be experiencing.

'Oh, Quimbre – I know you're worried about the ship.'

'Alas,' he hesitated, 'she's a poor old scuttlebutt with a single mainsail, and all the while I can hear her clinkered timbers squeaking and shuddering as they cringe from all that pounding.'

A poor old scuttlebutt.

Eefa laughed inside at Quimbre's words. And even as she did so, she realized that he had unwittingly given the ship her name.

So that's it – we're sailing the Sea of Stars aboard the poor old Scuttlebutt.

She lifted her chin to gaze up at the Scuttlebutt's single great sail, only now growing visible in the dawn, its belly bowed by the wind, and the two smaller triangular sails on the prow side of the mast.

'Why did you choose her, Quimbre?'

'It was all I could find seaworthy in that accursed graveyard, given our numbers and the short shrift we had for escaping that monstrous shore.'

His words caused Eefa to blink too rapidly and for her heart to pitter-patter too rapidly in her breast: *that monstrous shore.* They evoked a memory that she would rather forget – a terrifying memory.

Eefa shuddered to recall the Beach of Bones, where the Lady of the Shore had been imprisoned. How she hated to be reminded of that terrible place, the iron shackles that had tethered the goddess there, held fast to the monstrous shack of unyielding iron plates, doorless and windowless, that had been her only shelter. Now, thinking back, Eefa recalled how

Bird Woman had explained, even as they fled from the hunter, how strange it was that the Beach of Bones was not truly off the northwest coast of the island of Moon, but lost in some in-between place, a mysterious location half-way between the real world that ordinary folks lived in and the heavens that contained the undying. That strange in-between world was called Dromenon.

Dromenon . . .

It was an impossible concept even to think about, just one of many bizarre things that had happened along the way in their escape from Moon. For example, it had taken the wings of a dragon to snatch them from extreme danger and then ferry them to the Beach of Bones. The memory of that extraordinary escape was emblazoned on her memory. Looking back, it was all a confusion of dread, power, and the strangest things – magic beyond their understanding. They had been forced to accept that there was nowhere left for them on Moon. Quimbre had been forced to search for a seaworthy craft from the litter of wrecks that had ended up on the Beach of Bones.

Eefa closed her eyes tightly shut for several moments.

When she opened them again, she found herself confronted by Quimbre's bewhiskered face, that grey-haired head lifted at the sky, his dark brown eyes squinting at the movements of the clouds, his nostrils agape. Eefa knew that he had once been a pirate. Perhaps only a pirate could have spirited them away from such a terrible place in such impossible circumstances. Right now, the sea around them was increasingly choppy and, here in the exposed prow, the spray was directly in their faces and in their hair.

Magio's shout rang out from behind. 'Oh, stop tormenting Quimbre – you know he did his best!'

Her brother must have overheard them talking, and now he joined them, piping up in defense of Quimbre.

Out of the corner of her eye, Eefa saw that Bird Woman was approaching. She too must have overheard Eefa's conversation with Quimbre, since it was to their captain that she now addressed her caution. 'It would appear that your best has put us at risk from squall to squall.'

'Have a care, Woman, with that whiplash of a tongue. You do not know this patch of sea. She has her moods and will turn on those that do not pay her sufficient respect.'

Magio weighed in to support Quimbre. 'He's telling you what you know to be the truth, Bird Woman.'

Bird Woman sighed. All three of them, Eefa, Bird Woman, and Magio, knew that Magio was right. Quimbre had saved them all, at terrible risk to himself, in their escape from Moon. And now he was their only hope of surviving in this leaking old brig.

Eefa cut through the tension to blurt out, 'Quimbre has given the ship a name. We are sailing the Sea of Stars on the good ship Scuttlebutt.'

Magio cheered. 'Hey, Quimbre – did you really call her that?'

'Methinks your sister had a hand in naming her.'

'Britzy!'

'Britzy my foot!' Bird Woman wrinkled her lip in scorn. 'I presume he chose the name to suggest we are set to sink to the bottom in her?'

Quimbre showed his teeth in a grin. 'Well, such is likely if we just worry ourselves to death and meanwhile do nothing about it. But we won't be scuttling anytime soon – not if I can help it.'

Bird Woman pressed him. 'Then, you have a plan?'

'Well – that might better be described as a hope and a prayer.'

'Even so, let's all hear it.'

'Very well! I promise you all that we'll get together a proper meeting of minds to discuss it.' Quimbre looked from one of the twins to the other. 'What do you say, Kiddos – are we agreed?'

'Agreed!' They chorused.

Later the same day, Eefa found herself thinking back to Quimbre's words – *a hope and a prayer* – as she found herself once again in her favorite spot at the prow rail, and the Scuttlebutt dipped and rose again through another devastating sway. It seemed to her that all of her life had been spent running from terrifying forces.

None of them, not even Magio, could imagine what it was like to have been invisible from birth. The torment of that had so scarred her childhood that, were it not for her brother's love, it would have been unbearable. But now here she was, feeling the thrust of the winds on her body, the cold wet spray on her cheeks. What must surely be no more than a nuisance to the others was a source of delight to her. How everyday experiences made her feel truly alive. For a moment, she was back there, racing Magio the beach at Warren, her feet running on the warm white sand, heading for their den.

She was flooded by the realization that the simple, wonderful, childhood game was gone now.

Gone forever.

Buffeted by the wind and rain, she strained every muscle to press herself forward – enjoying, if only for a fleeting moment, her sense of becoming an integral part of the prow of the ship.

Eefa felt immensely saddened at the loss of that world of childhood. But now she must put it aside and no longer think back. The beach at Warren was gone, lost forever. In its place was this new wonderland. She inhaled its briny smell deep into her nostrils, her whole being enchanted by the realization that she here she was, aboard the good ship Scuttlebutt, sailing the enchanted Sea of Stars.

An Emergency

'Well now! So, you would all have me explain in more detail why I chose this clinkered old island hopper in preference to all the others?'

From Quimbre's exasperated expression, it was obvious that he was still mightily annoyed by Bird Woman's criticism. 'Perhaps I should remind you of the choice facing us among those wrecks that littered the shoreline of that terrible locality. I was obliged to look out for a cog fast in her jib while also small enough to be managed by a motley crew such as we witness here.' Quimbre lifted his bushy eyebrows to gaze at the three of them in turn. I gather Eefa has given the brig a name. The Scuttlebutt, she has decided. So, Scuttlebutt it is. You ask me why I chose the Scuttlebutt of the scatter of wrecks that abounded on that sordid beach's shore. First and foremost, she was the only one with a mainsail light enough to be winched aloft by a couple of pups when I, as skipper, might be caught up in managing any likely crisis.'

They were gathered amidships in the fading light of evening. Quimbre was standing by the wheel, his muscular arms holding steady their course, with Magio and Eefa seated cross-legged on the deck at his feet. Meanwhile Bird Woman had her back to them, her hands on the rail, while she stared out at the sea. A strong breeze filled the mainsail and it thrummed in the lines high above them, as an angry

Quimbre continued to explain the vagaries of his choice of ship. Magio was blinking hard, the sun coming at his eyes in varying angles, because of the rolling of the deck. He knew Quimbre well enough to acknowledge that this was not the time to interrupt him. Moreover, he suspected that there was something else on their captain's mind. Magio's shoulders were tense with anxiety as he found himself watching that glowering face.

Eefa's voice cut through Magio's ruminations. 'Nobody blames you for picking the Scuttlebutt, Quimbre. We trust you. But we need to put that behind us and think ahead. We've been at sea for several weeks. Surely, we've left behind any pursuers. But it feels as if we don't really know where we're heading. Bird Woman is quite right. We must have a plan.'

Quimbre looked down at Eefa, as if startled by her suggestion. Nodding his head, he spoke thoughtfully. 'What you suggest is sensible. And mayhaps I do have a plan of sorts.'

'Out with it then, man.' Bird Woman insisted. 'What ails you? I know there's a problem – but you refuse to talk about it?'

Quimbre scowled at being confronted by her yet again. He looked tired. It was hardly surprising. The company of four had traveled as far and as fast as they could from Moon, under sail continuously night and day, aiming to put distance between them and their home island. It was little wonder that they were all feeling tired.

Magio shrugged. 'Oh, Quimbre – I know you must surely have some idea of where we're headed. You must have some place in mind?'

Quimbre shook his head. 'Given the aid of the stars, I have put us on a heading of sorts. But we can follow no hard and fast line. You're not on land now, Kiddo. The sea lies beneath your feet. And there's nothing above and around you other than the immeasurable sky.'

Bird Woman refused to be placated. 'But even the sea, tricky as it is, can be somewhat measured and navigated.'

Quimbre rested his elbows against the wheel. 'Woman – think on! You're talking about the Sea of Stars. Do you imagine that these waters are predictable?'

'But surely there must be a compass or such to guide us?'

Quimbre barked a laugh. 'In ordinary waters, mariners take comfort from the aid of lodestones. But no lodestone will see you through these temperamental waters.'

'How do you know?'

'Once I shared that same illusion.'

The ship was now rocking violently and Bird Woman was forced to turn around and face them, sliding down so her back was against the rail.

Quimbre took a deep breath, then spoke urgently. 'You, above all – you with your witchery – should know what I am talking about. There is bewitchment galore in these waters. Places where lodestones will spin and rattle like a flibbertigibbit – as like to lead a mariner into a whirlpool as to guide him to sanctuary.'

'What,' a wide-eyed Magio exclaimed, 'is a flibbertigibbit?'

Bird Woman leaned forward into the doorway of the wheelhouse cabin to pat Magio on his dark brown curls, meanwhile continuing to press Quimbre. 'Well, if lodestones are so unreliable, how are we to find our way?'

'You're going to have to trust an old sea-dog's instincts – my experience with winds and currents, and perhaps that oldest of compasses, the night sky. And we must hope that the demons of chance do not catch a whiff of our difficulties before we have had the opportunity to improve the odds.'

Magio's eyes widened at Quimbre's words.

'Of course, it's asking for trouble, even for a seasoned mariner to discover himself sailing the Sea of Stars in a leaking old brig, with one serviceable sail, and the galley fast running out of drinking water.'

Magio's eyes lifted above them and into a sky with fast-moving thunderous clouds and to the sudden appearance of what appeared to be wheeling flocks of birds. He was immediately on his feet and out of the wheelhouse, so he could stare excitedly into the sky.

'Hey, look!' he shouted back to the company. 'Everybody! Look up there – there's something going on.'

They all joined him in staring up at the gamboling forms that flashed into focus between the dark rolling clouds.

Bird Woman shook her head. 'They're not birds, Magio.'

'What do you mean?'

'Look more closely and you'll see that they have scales on their bodies where birds would have feathers. See how their jaws have teeth.'

Magio was staring up into the sky, agog. 'Wow – jinxy!'

Eefa's eyes were equally wide with excitement as she exclaimed, 'What are they then? Are they flying lizards?'

Quimbre was growling in the bottom of his throat. Magio saw how his upraised face had become a mask of suspicion. 'They're neither birds nor lizards. Storm riders – or at least that's what we mariners call 'em.'

'Storm riders – does that mean we're in for a storm?'

'Aye – happens it does. They're a bad omen and no mistake. And we'll soon discover what they portend.'

Magio followed Quimbre's gaze into the distance to witness a sea-hugging mist that was fast approaching. There were twinkles of light that appeared like glittering diamonds throughout the dark and rapidly thickening clouds. Was Quimbre sensing something that none of the others were capable of sensing? Magio thought it very likely he was. Meanwhile the thickening gloom now caused him to shiver.

Eefa snuggled closer to Bird Woman. 'Quimbre is really worried, isn't he? What is he so afraid of?'

'He thinks we'll struggle to cope with a storm.'

Quimbre snorted. 'A storm is nightmare enough. But it might be the least of our worries. If my senses judge it aright, we are about to face a gale. If you would know what has been worrying me of late, it's the fact that we're taking in water faster than we can bail it. And yet, maybe, the weight of that water building up in the hold might be the very thing we need to counter the gale.'

Magio looked into Quimbre's worried face. 'That's what you've been worrying about, all along? The hold is flooding?'

'I'm afraid so, Kiddo. These clinkers desperately need recaulking. We just can't afford to take on further damage.'

Magio gazed at the encroaching clouds and he felt his heartbeat double in his chest. Already the afternoon was dark as dusk. The flashes he had glimpsed in the bellies of the clouds were clearly flashes of lightning. Suddenly it began to pour with rain, a hard, heavy rain, rattling against the deck and drenching Magio and Quimbre and everything about them.

'What can we do, Quimbre?'

Quimbre leaned down closer to his ear to be heard above the roar of the rain. 'Well, now! There is a place where we could repair the hull. That place is known as the Isle of Tar.

But first we need to get there. We need to ride out the coming ill weather. The plan, therefore, is we reef sail to half way, so as to retain a measure of control over the ship, meanwhile dampen the stresses on the mainmast.' Quimbre put his right hand on Magio's left shoulder. 'If I judge it aright, the next few hours will be a close-run thing.'

'What do you want me to do?'

'I need to know the direction the gale is headed. That will be your job, Magio. You will need to go aloft and find that direction.'

Quimbre was already heading for the ropes as Magio glanced back to witness the drenched Eefa and Bird Woman, who were watching their progress. Quimbre had to shout at the top of his voice to be heard. 'You, madam – if you would do what you can to help – lock yourself and Eefa in the shelter of the wheelhouse.'

'You think we're in for no ordinary storm?'

'Use those eldritch senses of yours. And don't you pretend you don't know what I mean.'

She replied angrily. 'You assume that I am a witch, given to superstition, to spells, omens, curses, and the like?'

'Just do it.'

With a soft-spoken curse, the grey eyes in Bird Woman's lean and wrinkled face confronted the equally implacable brown eyes under Quimbre's bristling eyebrows.

'I know your nature, woman. Much as a child I came to know the temperament of this accursed sea. I sense the wiles and wilful antics of her, and her wayward cruelty. She delights in being unpredictable. Thus, might she be every bit as like to direct a ship towards harbor as to the bottom of the sea.'

'Are you saying that the storm is bewitched?'

'So I now wonder!'

Magio felt the weight of Quimbre's protective hand still on his shoulder. 'Get yourself aloft to the lookout, Kiddo, and keep a watch on high. Be careful! This no normal storm. It may become somewhat rough up there, so – take my belt. Use it to strap yourself securely to the mainmast so you don't get thrown overboard.'

Magio grabbed the heavy leather belt, winding it so that it traveled twice around his slim waist.

'Watch out for what?'

'Keep an eye on the storm – and those accursed storm riders.'

Magio followed Quimbre's gaze up at the clouds of whirling bird-like shapes that seemed to be hugging the very heart of the storm.

'Why – what should I be looking out for?'

'I wouldn't risk sending you up there if the situation were not so perilous. Those buzzards are said to ride the storm because it takes them where they want to be going. That's why I need you in the lookout. I need to know where this gale is heading.'

Magio nodded. 'Britzy!'

'Get up there and anchor yourself to the mainmast. Take no unnecessary risk. Shout down anything you happen to see.'

With a growl, Quimbre took a firm hold of the rail as he made his way back to the lines, ready to trim sail. Meanwhile, he shouted back over his shoulder to the outraged Bird Woman, 'Have you failed to notice that this accursed gale is already blowing us in an unwanted line of travel?'

A barefooted Magio was already sprinting up the rope, ignoring the fact that the bucking of the ship, combined with the lashing of the rising gale, made him spin like a top. Within half a minute, he was already beyond the spar that supported the mainsail and, clambering above it to get deep into the rigging. His heart was already racing madly in his breast. He took a moment to recover his bearings, glancing down to see the rolling deck of the ship and then staring above him into the black-bellied clouds that filled the storm-maddened sky. That vision terrified him. He had to clench his eyes shut, while now climbing further out into the rigging using a mixture of feel and instinct, his face and body buffeted by the howling winds. For a single precarious moment, he clung to the rigging with his white-knuckled hands, his head full of the dizzying feeling that he was spinning between the sea and the sky.

He laughed. Magio couldn't help himself. He opened his eyes wide to the rain and he stared again into that maelstrom of sky, those same storm winds pressing against his face and eyes.

There was some mad demon within him that didn't give a jot about the danger any more. He shouted his glee to the world, uncaring that the words were instantly whipped from his throat.

'*Yeeeeehaaaaah!*'

Somehow, buffeted by the storm of winds, he made his way to the simple crosspiece that was the lookout, his left arm tightly wrapped around the top of the mainmast and his bare feet planted on the lookout. He uncoiled Quimbre's thick leather belt, refastening it around his waist and buckling himself tight to the mast. Only then did he have the courage to stare up into the roiling clouds. The storm riders wheeled and screeched much closer to him, with bodies that no longer looked like birds and soaring with what now appeared to be enormous wings. Those strange shapes appeared to be everywhere about him, and coming closer to him by the second. Instinctively, Magio clutched at his amulet, dangling on a leather cord from his neck. He clasped it tight within his fist while at the same time he squeezed his eyes shut.

Storm Riders

When Magio dared to open his eyes again, he was confronted by a daunting sight. The storm clouds were billowing about him. He could see boiling movements at their very hearts, twisting and twirling furiously. His heartbeat had never come down out of his throat since climbing up here to the lookout and now the sight of what appeared to be rampaging mountains of black air and clouds, all massing and tumbling about him, filled his terrified vision.

He heard Quimbre's shout from below. 'What direction is the storm heading, Kiddo?'

He hollered back, 'I've no idea. It's circling all about us.'

Peering down, Magio caught a glimpse of Quimbre's burly face, ringed by his beard, looking grim. 'Damn it to hell! If we keep our present course, it will likely send us to the deeps.'

'Magio – get back down here now.' Eefa shouted from a chink of opening in the door of the wheelhouse.

'I can't.' He shouted down. 'I daren't move an inch. You should see what's going on up here. The storm riders – oh, Eefie, they're amazing. Honestly! I think they're singing to one another. It's like I'm in the middle of a choir of them. Oh, look! Oh britzy, britzy, briiiiiitzyyyyyyy!'

His eyes were dazzled by their rainbow sheens. Magio was gazing spellbound at an impossible brilliance of colors, wheeling everywhere around him.

Quimbre roared back, 'That's enough, Kiddo. Do as your sister tells you. Get down onto the deck right now.'

But Magio was too excited to heed Quimbre's caution. 'I can't come down – not yet. Oh, Quimbre, you wouldn't believe what's happening. The storm riders – there must be hundreds, maybe even thousands, of them.'

A powerful gust of wind flattened his hair to his skull. Then a second gust struck the Scuttlebutt amidships, so the mainmast rocked wildly from side to side. Magio, still tethered to the mainmast, saw Eefa cringing under the arm of Bird Woman as the changing winds rose to a howling and the sea was lashed by the rising maelstrom. The mainmast was now whipping from side to side with such violence that Magio prayed it wouldn't snap. In those same minutes the sky appeared to turn black, and the winds tore the breath from his lips. All the while he clung to the mast, thinking, maybe, this might be the moment he would die.

He closed his eyes tight shut once again. If this was his fate, it was of his own doing. He couldn't stop thinking of Eefa, how terrified she must be down in the bowels of the ship. She had suffered so much from being invisible throughout her childhood. He had no idea how he would have coped with that. In growing up, there had been such a closeness between them – the feelings and even the awake-dreams they often shared. He knew that right now Eefa was terrified for him, knowing he was up here lashed to the mast.

But then, unexpectedly, it was Gran's face that came into his mind, Gran scolding him, as she so often had done after his numerous pranks had resulted in cuts and bruises.

'Stop feeling sorry for yourself, Magio. One day you will need to grow up and become a man.'

Become a man!

He was clinging to the mast with his arms in addition to his being lashed to it by Quimbre's belt. He was losing his foothold on the slippery beam of the lookout because his bare feet were soaked with brine, meanwhile the entire ship was wheeling and whipping about in the gale.

He recalled Quimbre's warning, 'It isn't a normal storm.'

'No!' He spoke his thoughts aloud, blinking furiously with the full weight of the realization of what Quimbre had really implied. 'This isn't a normal storm.'

You're right. It really isn't.

Magio just heard those words inside his head. That wasn't his voice – he wasn't thinking those words aloud. Yet the voice sounded gentle, unthreatening.

'Did I really hear that?'

Yes, you heard me, Magio.

'Who are you?'

Have you forgotten me so soon? Did you and Eefa journey out from Moon into the Sea of Stars entirely alone?

'What!'

The rising gale flattened his ears to his head as he struggled to think beyond the screeching of the circling storm riders in the sky directly overhead.

In the tribulations that now challenge you, have you forgotten the amulet that dangles about your neck?

Magio was so bewildered, he didn't know what to think.

Right then he heard a plaintive wail.

Schree-schree-schree!

It sounded as though something very young was terrified, begging the world for help. The urgency of the voice overwhelmed his senses, even though he was surrounded by the developing storm.

'What – what is it? Who are you?'

There was no reply.

I have lost the advantage of the storm. Darkness is everywhere. I cannot find the way. If you care for honor and justice, please help me.

Magio had no more time to think of the strange wailing before the storm once more enveloped him. It appeared to him that the entire globe of sky had burst open. He realized a moment later that it had been a lightning bolt striking somewhere perilously close, and so bright that he was temporarily blinded.

He huddled down into himself, once again squeezing his eyes shut.

His vision came back in fits and starts, with overly sparkling images of the lowering sky, and the intermittent gleam of the moon on the waves – waves that now appeared far too huge for any ship to sail through.

He also heard the song of the storm riders, now so close he could make out their shapes, wheeling and tossing in the tormented air above him.

The first voice re-entered his mind. *Take care, special one of the undying.*

'Who are you?'

Have you forgotten what happened on the Beach of Bones?

No! He shook his head, repeatedly. How in the world could he have possibly forgotten that!

Your sister, Eefa, was not abandoned by the Lady of the Shore.

No – he remembered. A single spark of gold had detached itself from the rest, a being he had no understanding of, and yet a Queen of her kind – Woll!

'Is it you? Are you Woll?'

At last, the foolish Magio comes to his senses.

'Oh, Woll! I don't pretend to understand anything of what is happening here. I just want to save us from the storm. But I have no idea what to do.'

We must face it together and deal with it as it happens. I'm afraid that your enemy knows that you are a threat now.

'What enemy?'

The same immortal enemy that imprisoned the Lady of the Shore on the Beach of Bones.

'Oh, jinxy!'

It was inevitable, given the circumstances of your escape. And he's a very dangerous enemy, Magio. We must pursue our quest with the greatest urgency.

'Quest – what quest? I thought we were just running away?'

So you – and thus we – are. But no purpose is served by merely running away. Run to where? Find sanctuary where? What sanctuary would protect you from such a powerful enemy? No, Magio, we cannot be content with merely running away.

Magio stared up into the spiraling black clouds. His ears were full of the sound of the waves, enormous waves from the sounds of it, crashing against the creaking timbers of the ship.

'What quest are you talking about?'

I shall duly explain. But not in this perilous moment. We need to focus all of our attention on your survival.

Eefa let Bird Woman hold onto her in her slender, raw-boned hands, as they tottered against the violent rolling of the deck, hauling themselves back to the wheelhouse, leaving Quimbre to furl what was still aloft of the mainsail. The Scuttlebutt was being spun around and whipped from side to side by the gale. Here, in what small shelter they found in the wheelhouse, they clung to one another, Eefa clinging onto her guardian, their backs pressed against the hull wall. She could hear the clinkered oak planks creaking loudly and, no doubt letting in even more water. Eefa was grateful, as so often when she had needed it in their escape from Warren, for the comforting arm of the strange woman, with her smoky grey eyes in that gaunt, wrinkled face – a woman who had proved so resourceful and kind in helping her and her brother, Magio, to escape from their terrible pursuers.

Bird Woman was so wonderful in her knowledge of nature. How strange she was, really. To somehow be able to communicate with birds. And yet was that any stranger than the fact that, until very recently, Eefa had herself been invisible to all, other than her twin brother, Magio.

Oh, crazy Magio!

Her wilful brother was still up there in the rigging, caring nothing for his own safety in the storm, which was tossing the entire ship from side to side. He seemed as content as those strange flying creatures riding the storm, with their dark blue scaly bodies and membranous wings.

'Bird Woman, what are the storm riders? Are they wanderers, lost and fleeing the world? Lost and fleeing . . . like us?'

Bird Woman merely held her close with her one free hand. 'They are not wanderers. No more are they lost, like us. We must try to be patient. Somehow, we must keep faith in that confounded pirate.'

Eefa wasn't sure she had that much faith within her.

She was reminded of the fact that Bird Woman sometimes appeared capable of reading her mind. 'Won't you tell me how you saw me? Back then – when we first met. I was invisible to everybody other than Magio. It really startled me at the time that you could see me.'

Bird Woman merely shook her head. 'I doubt that I saw you quite so clearly as your brother. I sensed you, and through sensing, I . . . well I suppose that I felt something of the reality of you.'

Eefa thought about that, her eyes clenched shut against another fierce burst of the gale force wind.

'Oh, come on, Bird Woman! Please tell me more. Tell me how you sensed me when nobody else could?'

That encircling arm hugged her a little tighter. 'You are so determined to discover more about me.' She laughed. 'Perhaps you look too hard. There is little that is special about me. I am so very ordinary.'

'You talk to birds.'

'I am not so special. I have some small sensibility to the natural world. I suspect that many share it with me.'

Eefa shook her head. 'I know you have some special sense – even Quimbre feels it. You have something magical about you.'

Bird Woman inclined her head and laughed. 'Quimbre would no doubt call it eldritch.'

'Are you a witch?'

'A witch – my goodness! I think we have had this conversation – or at least something resembling it – more than once back on Moon.'

'I'm sorry. Oh, I really am. If I have upset you . . .'

'Don't be sorry. The world is a very confusing place for one as young and sensitive as you – even for one as time-worn as me.'

'Oh, but you truly appear magical to me. You're not at all like the other people I met back on Moon.'

'I suspect there is a little magic in everybody. It is a gift that should be cherished. But, alas, it is often frowned upon by those who do not understand. What they don't understand frightens them, and, thus, they despise it.'

'Oh!'

Eefa reached up and hugged the slim muscular arm to her breast. She didn't want to let Bird Woman go. At that moment a bolt of forked lightning burst upon the deck, illuminating the ship brighter than daylight, causing Eefa to scream and clench her eyes shut.

The Eye of the Maelstrom

Quimbre swore, fighting his way forward against a solid wall of wind, uncoupling and recoupling the rope that tethered him to the starboard rail, to get to a place where he could trim the sail to half mast. But even as he did so, the ship was caught by another fierce blast that caused it to slew at something approaching thirty degrees. He knew that behind him, within the wheelhouse, Bird Woman was clinging protectively to Eefa with one arm, her other wrapped around the stanchion that held the wheel.

He knew he had to do something.

But what to do?

Coughing and retching in the brine-laden gale, Quimbre made slow progress further aft, where he reached the winches and began to reduce the enormous pressure on the mainsail. He trimmed as much as he dared. Any more and he would lose control of the ship. Even as he racked his brain to think what more he could do, a second immense blow provoked such a wave that it flooded the deck and knocked him off his feet, trapping his feet in a mesh of fallen rigging. Clutching wildly about himself for a purchase, Quimbre found himself sliding sternwards, clinging desperately to any projecting spur of rail or rope that might prevent him from being pitched overboard.

He heard Magio's excited cry from the lookout. 'Watch out! Watch out everyone. The encroaching storm is a wall of black from sea to the very heavens, aflame with lightning strikes.'

Quimbre hauled himself onto his feet, fighting for anything that would give him a purchase. He struggled back to the winches, above which the mainsail was now stretched to breaking point.

He heard Bird Woman's wail from within the wheelhouse. 'I can't believe it has built up like this, in such a short space of time."

He shouted back. 'Help Eefa to hold on while I further trim the mainsail. Keep a hold on her, Woman, for dear life.'

Quimbre muttered to himself. 'Aye – for what good it will likely do you, Eefa, or any one of us. We're good as done for in this demon of a gale.'

'No – not so, Quimbre.' He heard Eefa's shriek from the wheelhouse. Damn, but she had overheard his very whisper. 'Don't give up on us now. Magio is calling out to me. He says we're not done yet.'

Quimbre curled a line fast around his left wrist, fixing his position so he wasn't cast overboard, meanwhile attempting to listen to what Magio was screaming down to Eefa. But he had difficulty in making out their conversation in the shrieking winds.'

'What is it, Eefa? What's going on?'

'Magio has an idea. He admits it's a crazy idea.'

Quimbre couldn't help but laugh. A crazy lad seized by a crazy idea in a world that had already gone further than mere crazy.

Quimbre cursed under his breath. 'What idea?'

'He wants you to make full sail.'

Quimbre lifted his head to peer up at the lookout. 'Then he's gone crazy, Eefa. What in the world is he thinking?'

Magio's voice reached him, sounding no more than a piping reed in the gale, but Quimbre could make out his words. 'I'm so close to them – the storm riders. Hey, you should see how they really do it – how they actually ride the storm. They hurl themselves right into it and then wheel up, at lightning speed, high, high. Oh, britzy! They ride it way up into the sky, with their skins making glittering rainbows. Oh, Quimbre, it's absolutely crazy. But, oh! Just absolutely britzy! It's as if they are one with the winds and waves. Like . . . gee, I just don't know how to describe it. Like they're one with the gale.'

'Get your head back in gear, Kiddo. We're in a terrible pickle.'

'I know. Oh, I know, Quimbre. But – oh, britzy, I think I can see how they ride the storm. What it is, they don't fight it. It's the most fantastic thing you could imagine. At first, I couldn't see what they were up to. But now! Oh, wow, now I get it! They're all massing and flapping and wheeling about. But now I see that they're all getting it together, sort of as if they were getting in tune with it. Hey, britzy! Oh, wow, they become one with the storm instead of fighting it.'

Quimbre cursed under his breath. What was Magio raving about? The lad was surely losing his wits. Even as Quimbre shook his head with consternation, his left arm, gripping the line, was almost pulled out of its socket by another howl of wind.

Still Magio was raving up there in the rigging.

Quimbre had to listen hard to hear that distant piping reed of voice . . . 'Oh, Quimbre! There are so very many of them. Oh, britzy! Far more than just hundreds. More like thousands. It's downright crazy. They're all wheeling together, all flapping together . . . Like . . . oh, wow! It's like they're all part of one great cloud.'

Quimbre paused to think, all the while panting for breath. 'You mean, they're finding some way of running with it? Hauling the storm?

'No – not hauling it. That's what I thought at first. But now I think – oh, britzy! Somehow, they're controlling it. They're controlling the storm.'

Quimbre shouted back, 'You're crazy.'

'Yeah! I can see that it looks crazy. But, honestly, Quimbre, they're very skillful at it – like they're born to it.'

Bird Woman, who had been listening in throughout, shouted out to Quimbre, 'What if Magio is right? What if the storm riders really do direct storms for their own purposes? They would gain far more than merely being carried by them. It would help explain events that were previously inexplicable. Some sages have proposed that storms are not always wild turbulences but potentially purposive. Have not mariners like you acquired lore from winds and currents that enable you to take advantage of both?'

Quimbre exhaled, making no effort to hide his skepticism. 'It all sounds like witchcraft to me.'

But Bird Woman stood her ground. 'Why would the storm riders devote such immense energy and risk to following storms if there were no gain? Perhaps what Magio is witnessing is a similar instinctive understanding between the storm riders and the storm.'

In a lull of the winds, Quimbre had managed to haul himself back to the mainmast again, so he was within reach of the winches.

'What use is such gobbledygook to our situation?'

'What if Magio is right! Perhaps in his chance discovery, we can make use of that lore to help ourselves?'

Quimbre shook his head. Such considerations were beyond him. He shouted to Magio, 'Hey, Kiddo, I hope you've been listening all the while you've been admiring the bird's colors and their acrobatics?'

'I have been listening – and I agree with Bird Woman.'

'And what strategy does that offer us?'

'The way I figure it, the storm riders have some way of encouraging the winds to take them where they want to go.' Magio had to pause to catch his breath. 'Oh, Quimbre, just think about it. If only it is true.'

Quimbre glared back up through the cataract of rain at the bedraggled figure up there in the sheets. The old tar swore to himself, all the while clinging to whatever was at hand as the ship creaked and heaved beneath his feet, wondering if the lad had gone entirely mad. But then he felt Bird Woman's bony hand fall on his shoulder. He heard her urgent whisper in his ear.

'What if Magio is right?'

'Do you know what you're asking of me, woman? Throw ourselves on the mercy of the storm? This leaky old brig will be torn apart.'

'Surely we're doomed unless we discover a solution, however implausible.'

Quimbre shook his head. 'Even if we keep full sail and haul to windward – if I do what that mischievous lad urges and run with it – we lose all control of direction. We leave our fate entirely open to the whims of the winds.'

'What do we have to lose?'

Quimbre glared at the woman, his eyes aghast.

Those eyes confronted his own. 'We'll lose everything anyway if we don't try.'

Quimbre shook his head. 'Control the storm? I've never heard so downright crazy in my life.'

'Can you suggest an alternative?'

'I'll be damned if I can.' Quimbre sighed deeply, working himself close enough to grab the winch. He so wanted to trim even more, but he just couldn't make himself do it. Against every instinct, he raised full sail. 'I have such an ominous feeling – such a dreadful sense of doubt. But at least we'll not have long to discover the outcome.'

Magio stared into a darkening sky in which he could see no immediate evidence to confirm he was right. The storm riders wheeled and screeched above him, soaring on their enormous wings. The same winds that supported those wings flattened his hair to his head. Then another fierce gust struck the Scuttlebutt amidships and rocked it furiously from side to side. Magio glimpsed Eefa welcoming back Bird Woman into the wheelhouse, then cringing under her protective arm as the winds rose to a scream and the sea became a maelstrom. The mainmast was whipped from side to side with such violence that, had it not been for Quimbre's stout belt, Magio would have most certainly have lost his purchase and been tossed into the storm-lashed sea.

In desperation, he clenched his hands around the amulet that was dangling on its cord around his neck. Within minutes the sky had turned black, and the very air was whipped from his nostrils, as if defying him from taking a breath. All the while. tethered to the mast, he attempted to think past the desperation of their situation, to figure out something he could do, something to save his sister, Eefa, terrified down below. Always there had been such a common and intimate link between them. At times, in growing up, there had been so many feelings, thoughts, dreams, they had shared. When they had spoken of such things to Gran, she had merely nodded her grey-haired head, as if such was to be expected between twins. Strange things sometimes happened – things you would never be able to explain in logic. Magio knew the truth of Gran's affirmation right now. He knew, with absolute certainty, that here and now, in this situation of terrible danger, Eefa would sense, feel, know, exactly what he was experiencing. She would see everything he was seeing and she would feel everything he was feeling up here on the lookout.

In all the frenzy of storm and its effects on the ship, he heard Eefa's whisper inside his head. 'Follow your instincts, Magio.'

The rising winds tore at his ears as he attempted to think beyond the louder squealing – it actually sounded more like screaming – of the storm riders above him.

You should heed your sister, Magio. In the tribulation that challenges you, you should remember the source of your power.

Magio recognized the voice of Woll again. But he was already so bewildered and terrified by the growing storm that he had difficulty in thinking through Woll's advice. What power was she referring to?

Just then he heard that screech again, this time much louder. It came from somewhere close above him, somewhere in the tangle of rigging.

'Schree—schree—schree!'

What could it possibly mean?

Magio had no more time to think before the storm intensified. It appeared to him that the entire globe of sky about him had ruptured. He realized a moment later that it had been a lightning bolt striking somewhere close, and so bright that the explosion of light had temporarily blinded him.

He huddled into himself, blinking furiously, hoping against hope for the return of his eyesight.

Vision came back, in fits and starts, with strange colors sparkling here and there, and then recognizable images, though they appeared overly bright. He recognized the lowering sky, and the intermittent gleam of starlight above the gale – and waves below that were monstrously huge in relation to their normal selves. He also heard the screams of the storm riders, now so close he could make out the finer details of their scaly skins, wheeling and tossing in the tormented air above.

Woll's voice had returned to his mind. *Take care, special one.*

Magio was too bewildered to understand the message.

Have you forgotten what happened on the Beach of Bones?

No – how in the world could he have possibly forgotten that?

Your sister, Eefa was not abandoned by the Lady of the Shore.

No – he remembered what had happened. How a single spark of gold had detached itself from the rest, a spark of gold that was the frost sprite queen, Woll.

Magio held on to the mainmast, while gazing up into the now totally black sky. The world appeared to have gone mad. He clenched his eyes shut against the return of the lightning, his ears deafened by recurring thunder, mixed with the background roaring of the waves, enormous waves, crashing against the prow of the ship.

UNCHAINED

In her memory she watches the chosen slip over the horizon before she abandons the Beach of Bones and wades into the sea. The recollection of pain, both physical and mental, rises like a scream throughout her being. Her pain is assuaged by the vision of the small clinkered ship, with the gruff dusky-skinned Quimbre in charge, raising the single mainsail to catch the wind. On reflection, her plan inevitably involved such terrible risks, but the prevailing situation has never allowed for certainties. Indeed, the game remains the same – there are no certainties. Only degrees of peril.

Escape – escape . . .

This need presses upon her mind. In this present emotion-laden moment, it remains all that matters.

Once lost in the deeps, it is easier to escape detection. As it closes around her, she senses it as a closing fist about the arid beach that was once her prison, and that cold, ungiving structure of rusting plates of iron, windowless and doorless. How ironic that, when you have long been tormented by darkness, another darkness should now become your opportunity. It is as vital for her to put distance between herself and that monstrous place as it is for the chosen to flee from the sorceress that would destroy them. She so cares for them – mere children who were subjected to such terrible risk for her sake. And now, at last, it is such a comfort to know that sailing with them is the bosom of her heart – the indomitable queen of the frost sprites.

Woll, the wise.

The chosen will have need of Woll's resourcefulness and wisdom in their flight the perilous archipelago of islands that is the Sea of Stars.

Aahhhh!

The delight of freedom is flowing once again throughout her being. The joy of it is already so intense that she is in danger of losing herself in the consummation. A final glance back at that terrible beach that has held her fast for so many eons. How her whole being is a glory of delight to be free of it – no longer at the whim of his hatred.

Why then does a shiver still run through her, an overwhelming feeling that is synonymous with danger?

An instinct that gives her pause . . .

In this new situation she cannot hope for the infinite freedom of what had once been the normality of her world of sea and shore. No more can she freely return to the domains of the undying. Her nemesis has grown too powerful even in that realm – unchallenged even as he has become so relentlessly cruel.

I must think anew.

Soon he will focus his will on searching for her anew. He will bring to that search all the malignant determination she has come to know of him. Even so, she has friends in the world of the undying that will help her if they can – friends who will also rejoice in the knowledge that she has escaped his clutches. But those friends will be careful to hide their allegiance, given his malice.

She cannot skulk forever in the deeps of the sea. She must become proactive in her own defense. Discover new allies in places that he might not anticipate.

But how to proceed?

She cannot resist a brief return to the surface, choosing a starless night so she can gaze up into the violet labyrinth of space. Stars glitter and galaxies whirl. Her vision is at once all-embracing. It feels so wonderful to be physically and spiritually released merely to enjoy such a beautiful vision. But now she is faced by difficult decisions. Foremost in her mind is revenge. How she seethes at the prospect of revenge. Long and agonizing has been her suffering. But she is not so foolish as to rush into some hopeless strike. She must consider, in the cold light of night, the precise nature and formidable strengths of her nemesis.

Such power.

She cannot suppress an involuntary shiver as she recalls the ease with which he had captured her – captured and then held her for would likely have been forever – in that hellish prison. The thought of it even now causes her to shiver. Yet surely the answers to her dilemma are to be found in that single question:

How did her nemesis come to acquire such power?

Ooooh, I must rest a while and consider that key question.

She is all too aware of the fact that she remains vulnerable. To make an ill-considered move now would be exceedingly foolish. She would likely end up with an even worse fate than before.

Where then, might I look? Where might I find succor?

Those formally friendly to her cause must surely be scattered, frightened, in hiding. She closes her eyes to think more clearly.

Perhaps I too should go into hiding?

Her spirit disdains the thought. But the memory of that dreadful, long-suffering experience on the Beach of Bones, bades caution.

How do I begin?

As if in answer, a voice, unfamiliar to her, enters her mind.

Come – the time is at hand!

She hesitates, baffled, only to harken to another unknown voice.

Caution! Caution! Caution!

Suddenly myriad voices assail her spirit, all speaking at once, all equally frightened, worried, terrified.

We dare not.

He is so powerful.

He is so cruel.

He controls the Lore.

Her head is dizzy with so many discordant opinions.

It would appear that a variety of spirits are calling to her, searching for her, all the while disagreeing with one another. They appear to be sympathetic but uncertain. Some might welcome her. Others might likely hate her and might even be in league with her nemesis. Her instincts reach out to that single, different voice, the voice that suggests an answer to her question . . .

He controls the Lore.

Is this true? Is it the explanation of how her former husband and nemesis has become so powerful? Is it because he controls the Lore?

If so, it would make him far too dangerous to openly challenge. Yet, for the sake of all that is just – for the sake of the restoration of the sacred balance – he must surely be challenged – challenged, confronted, cast out from power.

I will do so. I must do so. I must find a way for all that is just and true to triumph.

Then, the voice of Woll within her mind as sure as if the frost sprite queen were hovering in her immediate vision,

Be wary, My Lady. He might be listening – even to your very thoughts.

A fairy voice, a voice of such sweetness it brings tears to her eyes, a voice of hope, of concern for her, promise of eternal support. Woll, her parting gift to the twins, on their mission as they sailed from Moon and headed for the Sea of Stars.

How the Lady of the Shore would welcome that golden spark beside her now. The very thought gives her pause, with her lips at the level of the lapping waves. She cannot deliberate any longer. It is time for her to steel herself, heart and spirit, for a journey into a much stranger domain. In that moment, she abandons her beloved sea for the deeps of Dromenon, opening wide her very being to it, her arms outstretched, her eyes wide open, glissading through the nothingness that is its waters.

Her passage through the domain of nothingness, which both links and separates the worlds of the mortals and immortals, provokes a disorientation that is daunting even for an undying. Yet here, in this strange in-between world, she has the comfort of being invisible to the probing senses of her nemesis. She has been so long incarcerated that she needs this arid solace to reorientate. Yet even now, while allowing her spirit to become lost in Dromenon, she remains ever vigilant, ever uncertain.

Could it really be over? Could she really be free of that hideous prison? Or is this merely a new trick, some new horror, like the many other tricks her nemesis had invented to torment her during her imprisonment?

No!

There is safety while ever she remains hidden here. But she cannot stay in Dromenon forever. That would merely replace one prison with another.

But a spell in Dromenon will afford her time to reflect. Her tormentor will surely be aware of her escape. He will follow her passage into the sea, and further – he will figure the destination of her escape. Dromenon cannot forever provide a haven. Its very nothingness will become a hell as lonely as the Beach of Bones. She must, somehow, discover a better haven. But she is too exhausted by her eons-long torment, to bring her mind and spirit into a sharp enough focus to consider it further. She must rest both heart and soul for the blessed moment. She must embrace the soothing nothingness that is Dromenon.

A Strange Prophecy

Eefa was comforted by Bird Woman's raw-boned arm around her shoulder as they tottered along the violently-rolling deck. They managed to haul themselves to midships, where they flopped down outside the wheelhouse, their backs pressed against the sodden rail. Eefa could see the exhausted Quimbre, whose arms were wrapped around the wheel, all control lost with the violence of the gale. She could feel the very timbers below her groaning and creaking. Given Quimbre's earlier warning, Eefa was in no doubt that the hull was copiously leaking water, the bilge flooding. She felt grateful, as so often in the past, for the protection of the strange woman beside her, with her smoky grey eyes in that gaunt, wrinkled face. How remarkable Bird Woman truly was – the savior who had turned up completely out of the blue back on Moon, and who had proved so resourceful in helping her and her brother, Magio, to escape from their terrible pursuers! Eefa felt at home with Bird Woman's earthy smell, a blend of herbs and spices, now that she had taken over the galley.

Even now, being tossed about and drenched with every wave that struck the Scuttlebutt, Eefa was unable to ignore how strange Bird Woman was in reality. To be capable of communicating with birds! Bird Woman had proved even more wonderful in her wider understanding of nature. But, then, given Eefa's own situation, was that any stranger than the mystery that, until very recently, Eefa had been invisible to all, other than her twin brother, Magio, and of course the redoubtable Gran.

Oh, Gran! How Magio and I have missed you.

With the loss of Gran, there remained so many things in both their lives that would never entirely make sense. And now that same thought reminded Eefa of Gran's earthy commonsense. It had been dear old Gran who, when Eefa had pressed her with bothersome curiosity, had warned her about the danger of thinking too much about things.

But Gran wasn't here on this gale-racked ship. And Magio was high above them, up there in the rigging, regardless of the storm that was tossing the entire ship from side to side, as if it were an empty bottle. Her brother was fascinated by those strange flying creatures riding the storm, with their iridescent bodies and great sweeping wings. That surely was another bothersome curiosity that Eefa should probably not think too much about. But she was unable to suppress her curiosity.

She had to raise her voice, half-shouting for Bird Woman's to hear, 'What are they, really? What are those storm riders?'

Bird Woman merely held her close with her one free hand. 'I suppose that, in a way, they're wanderers, just like us.'

Eefa could only shake her head, as the Scuttlebutt rose and fell in the grip of yet another mountainous wave. She was no wiser as to the mystery of Bird Woman than when they had first set out on this extraordinary adventure.

'Won't you tell me more of how you sense things?'

That encircling arm hugged Eefa a little tighter. 'You're a cunning minx, and no mistake. You draw upon my protective feelings meanwhile attempting to winkle secrets from me.' Bird Woman laughed. 'Your curiosity is only natural. But it is difficult for me to explain the mystery of things other than to say that, perhaps, we are two of a kind.'

'I don't think we are two of a kind.'

'You never do give up, do you. Perhaps you know more than enough of me already? For example, you know that I have a special sensitivity to the living world, a sense that is . . .' Bird Woman shrugged. 'Perhaps I should call it instinctive?'

'A sense that is more like magical?'

Bird Woman laughed again and hugged her closer to her. 'Perhaps a heightened sensibility when compared to most people.'

'Are you what Quimbre says?'

'A witch? Oh, Eefa! I think we have had this conversation, or at least something resembling it, more than once back on Moon.'

'I'm sorry if I've upset you.'

'Don't be sorry. The world can be a very confusing place for one as young and sensitive as you. It can, at times, confuse even the likes of me.'

'Oh, but you are not at all like the other people I met back on Moon, not even the older, wiser, folk.'

'I suspect there is a little magic in everybody. Where such a gift is found, it is a wonder worth cherishing. Alas, it is all too often discouraged.'

'But why do folks discourage it?'

'I don't know, Eefa.' Bird Woman made ready to get back onto her feet, clearly intending to go below.

Eefa reached up and hugged the slim muscular arm to her chest. She didn't want Bird Woman to go below. At that moment a bolt of forked lightning burst upon their eyes, illuminating the ship brighter than daylight.

'Down we go.' Bird Woman insisted. 'Quimbre needs our assistance. We had better get busy bailing water.'

Eefa reluctantly followed Bird Woman down into the hold, but she was too excited to think about bailing water. Her imagination was full of the visions coming to her from the head of her adventure-loving brother, a phantasmagoria of rainbow-hued specters criss-crossing the livid storm-crossed sky.

Pitching from side to side by the gale-force winds, Magio recalled Quimbre's warning about the unreadiness of the ship. Its lack of seaworthiness in the perilous and unpredictable Sea of Stars had always been close to a death warrant. They had struggled, day and night, to keep her afloat ever since their desperate flight from the Beach of Bones.

The Beach of Bones . . .

With dread, Magio recalled that horror. He would never forget the sight of the manacled woman on that terrible beach, her limbs tethered by chains to a hulking shack of rusting iron, a monstrosity that filled his mind with an absolute sense of horror – the notion of such neverending damnation.

So much had followed their arrival onto the Beach of Bones that now, just thinking about it, Magio simply did not understand it. All he knew was that they had, somehow, saved the woman, who was not really a woman at all. When they had helped to free her from her shackles, she had changed into a beautiful goddess. The frost sprites had called her The Lady of the Shore. Then she in turn had helped them flee from the Beach of Bones, warning them to flee the island of Moon.

Now Magio recalled Quimbre's hurried search along the rocky beach, and his despairing words in a soft whisper to Bird Woman,

'Wrecks there are a plenty on these inclement shores, but most are ruined beyond repair. I have found but a single brig, with a salvageable mainsail, that might last a month or so without the necessary caulking.'

That search had resulted in the Scuttlebutt. And now here they were, after more than a month at sea in that leaking old brig, in this hopeless flight. At least they had left their dreadful pursuers far behind. Surely, they would be safe at last from their attentions, if they could only keep the ship afloat long enough to find a shore where they could put in some desperately needed repairs?

'*Magio – ahoy!*'

Quimbre's roar, muted by the gale, jarred him to attention. He must stop his moping and pay attention to why he was up here on the lookout. Everybody was depending on him to find a way out of the growing maelstrom.

'*Schree--shree—schree!*'

That dreadful shrieking again! It came from nearby in the gloom, drawing his attention to something threshing in the rigging overhead, a mess of ropes that attached the mainsail to the spar that Quimbre called the yard. Peering up, Magio could make out some misshapen body of sorts, which was flapping about in the tangle of ropes. Peering more closely, saw two large black eyes that were staring down at him in absolute panic.

'Hey – what the jinxy?'

The schree—schree—schree had started up again, louder than ever.

Magio could see that one of its legs was caught in the rigging. The creature was dangling there, upside down, staring back at him, all the while shrieking and flapping.

Magio shouted down to Quimbre, 'I think it's one of the storm riders. It's got itself caught up in the lines.'

'Get away from it, Kiddo. Don't you go near it. You'd better get straight back down here and join your sister below decks.'

But those shrieks, which were rising in terror, wouldn't allow him to just abandon the poor creature. Magio looked up again and saw such a pleading look in its huge black eyes. He could just about imagine it, in that medley of bright colors, gamboling about up there in the eye of the storm. He released the leather belt that had been his savior and crawled out of the lookout, inching his way across the thick spar, called the yard, which supported the mainsail.

Quimbre was roaring at him against the thunder of the storm. 'Kiddo, get your backside back on the lookout. Go tether yourself to the mast. Wait there for me. I'm coming to haul you down.'

Magio didn't want to upset Quimbre but at the same time he couldn't resist crawling out further along the yard, his clothes now blown against his skin by the fury of the gale.

The ship lurched as it caught a big wave, the prow rising ten feet, to be followed by an almighty plunge. There were shrieks from below as well as above him. Magio shouted, 'Don't come up, Quimbre. It's britzy. I know what I'm doing.'

A new bolt of lightning erupted so very close that it caused a fierce clutching in his gut, meanwhile five or six more bolts were descending out of the storm-laden sky to strike in every direction at once. Geysers of brine were crashing over the prow each time the Scuttlebutt dipped. Magio could smell the acrid stench of the ozone lingering in the air after the bolts had struck, taking his breath away. The wind tore at him, tore even more furiously at the mast, causing the entire ship to veer from side to side, then whirling it around, directionless, the blow so fierce that he thought that the mainmast would snap, or the entire hull would just rip apart.

He clenched his eyes shut.

When he reopened them, he found himself within touching distance of the trapped creature.

'Here!' he shouted. 'Let me untangle you.'

'What the hell game are you playing?' Quimbre hollered from part way up the mainmast.

'I'm setting it free.'

'Get down here.'

'Magio – Quimbre is right.' Bird Woman's shout now added to the warning. 'The storm riders are dangerous. They're not birds.'

In that moment a new bolt of lightning erupted from within the billowing wrack of clouds overhead, illuminating Magio and the frightened storm rider, in stark lucidity. He saw every detail of its being. Those eyes, widened in his direction, were terrified orbs of midnight. And there were no feathers. Its brilliantly hued skin was covered in scales and that entangled leg ended in claws, huge black claws. The unduly long head, with those huge beseeching eyes, was now staring directly at him.

'Well,' Magio spoke to himself, 'you're certainly no kind of bird. So, what in the world are you?'

He had been thinking that, maybe, it was some bat-like thing, only bigger. But bats didn't have scales. Bats had hairy skin. The creature was no more a bat than it was a bird. He had no idea what it might be, other than the fact it was utterly unlike anything he had ever seen before.

'Hey.' He spoke softly to it, through the neverending gale, hugging the yard and clinging to one of the rope tethers. By now he was close enough to reach out and touch the struggling creature. His closeness caused it to thrash all the more.

'Hush your screeching. I'm trying to free you.'

It was tricky sliding along those remaining few feet of yard drenched with spray, and treacherous with ropes and tethers. The creature eyed him back with that same wide-eyed panic as Magio himself, his legs straddling the thick oak spar, negotiated the obstacles of lines and tethers.

He could see exactly how the rider's leg was hopelessly snagged. But it didn't look as if it had broken any limb or wing in struggling to escape. Hugging the yard with his encircling thighs, and reaching up, he held the trapped claw with one hand and wriggled free the tangle of rigging with the other. Then he offered his forearm as a hold for the creature's freed leg, to let it so it could rest its weight on his arm and avoid crashing down onto the deck.

It wasn't nearly as heavy as he thought it might be. He was able to lower it down to the stout timber of the yard, where it fluttered its enormous wings and stepped here and there over the tethered ropes, all the while screeching at the top of its lungs.

Only now did it occur to Magio how that screeching was reminiscent of how a frightened chick might screech out for a parent when it felt endangered.

That thought expanded in Magio's mind.

He followed the direction of the released creature's uplifted eyes to discover that a much larger creature was hovering overhead, resisting every tossing of storm and ship, to remain close to the youngster trapped in the rigging. Now, as he stared up at that larger shape, it belatedly occurred to Magio that there was a new danger, one even more threatening than the battening gale.

'Quimbre!' he shouted.

'I'm coming, Kiddo.'

But it was all happening too quickly, the situation changing in seconds, and Quimbre was only a third of the way up the mainmast.

At that moment, the ship plunged again, a huge dip of the prow, followed by an equally huge rise up, causing Magio to cling to the rigging.

The mother creature was within yards of him, close enough for him to see that its mouth was nothing like a beak. Its gaping jaws were lined by razor-sharp teeth. In a swoop, the adult descended into the rigging, huge claws settling on the yard just feet away from Magio. For the moment, it appeared to be fussing about the offspring.

This close, the mother had a body that was half as tall again as Quimbre and it was perched on the yard a mere arm's breadth from Magio. Its scaly skin, which had appeared a dark greenish grey at first sight, now appeared to glisten and change hue, depending on how it caught the light. Its eyes, which were the same glistening black as the youngster's and veined with bright carmine, were staring directly at Magio. In their glittering mirrors he glimpsed the reflection of his own terrified face. The wind howled, stealing the breath out of his mouth and nostrils, but it appeared not to trouble the creature, whose sinewy body weathered it without a flicker. It was staring directly at him, its eyes confronting his own, that long mouth parted to reveal those rows of dagger-like teeth.

Magio felt faint, his heartbeat throbbing in his throat.

Even as he watched, the creature slithered closer along the yard to come to within mere feet of him.

Panic began to play tricks inside Magio's head. Strange noises were forcing their way into his mind, noises perhaps that might even be words – though they were unlike any words that he recognized. Gargling and hissing, if they truly were communications, they were the strangest, most unnatural, uttering he had ever heard. Yet he had the feeling that the mother creature was searching for some means of communication between beings that nature had never intended. The realization was one of the most terrifying notions he had ever experienced.

The mother creature was now so close that he could smell the rancid fishy smell of the breath that was coming from that terrifying maw.

He tried to withdraw back along the yard. But his limbs were frozen with panic. Those reptilian eyes observed his struggle, no doubt recognizing his weakness. It began to inch closer along the yard. He saw a snake-like forked tongue emerge, a bright blue against the fleshy pink tunnel deep to those vicious rows of fangs. Those peculiar communications inside his head were louder, even more insistent. The thoughts coming out of that reptilian brain were somehow molding themselves closer to human words that he could understand. He saw its eyes blink, as if shocked by the alien notion of human words . . .

Magio attempted to shout for help. But his tongue, like his fingers, was frozen. His mouth could not form the words.

It was edging still closer – close enough now to lunge for him.

Don't be afraid, Magio.

A voice coming from somewhere close to him. A whispering voice – speaking directly to him mind-to-mind.

'Woll!'

Did you think I had abandoned you?

A sense of relief flooded his senses.

'Oh, Woll! I'm so terrified. I think the mother creature wants to kill me. I don't know what to do. I need to get out of here.'

Be calm.

Magio returned his attentions to the younger rider. He sensed its desperate need to be up there, in the air. He lifted the creature up, unwieldy as it was, struggling to be free of him every inch of the way. But then as he raised it into the air, he saw how its eyes widened, and then he was almost blind-sided by the vigorous clapping of its wings. He guessed that it was testing out the wing that had been trapped. In a moment it was aloft, whisked away by the gale force wind.

'Oh, Woll!'

Magio had expected that the mother creature would follow its offspring. But she made no move to do so. Instead, the guttural noises came once again from her throat, such a strange amalgam of harsh, hissing noises. But this time . . . oh, jinxy . . . this time, he understood those alien words.

Mageling brat. There is no power in you that might challenge me.

'I – I don't understand.'

In that instant the fanged mouth darted towards him, as if to take a bite out of him. But an expanding cloud of gold sealed the air between them.

Mother of Storms, hold your venom.

Magio's own eyes were widened as far as they knew how.

The huge creature turned its back on him, as if startled. But then it suddenly swung its neck back around, with those black eyes confronting his own, and filled with malice.

Even you, Winter Witch, cannot protect this brat.

Have you forgotten how he rescued your offspring, at risk to himself?

A young mage, with barely the down of youth on his cheek. You presume too much. What debt of honor could we owe to such a stripling?

Yet he nevertheless demands satisfaction of your debt.

What in the world was going on? Magio's thoughts were racing, lost in bewilderment. But even as he struggled to grasp what was happening, a torrential wave crashed against the starboard bow, rocking the ship into a crazy angle, and even as it began to right itself, it was followed by dozens of lightning bolts striking the sea all about them. The stink of ozone was overwhelming.

Magio could feel that heartbeat in his throat again. He could even hear its stricken pounding inside his ears.

'Woll . . .!'

The storm was worsening. Any moment, the ship might be torn asunder by the gale. The pounding of his own heart was distracting his very thoughts. Yet he knew he must, somehow, do something.

'Pardon me. Please pardon me, Storm Mother, or whatever Woll called you. You can repay your debt by helping me to save the ship.'

Those reptilian eyes, mere inches away, were staring into his own.

We thought so. From the instant the whelp pretended sympathy. Even as it entered our mind, we knew it could only have been for that single, selfish, purpose.

'What purpose?'

Do not deny it, human. You have trapped us here, by fate's own chains. You will restore our freedom only if we bend to your will.

'I have no idea what you mean?'

Do not dissemble. You know that we, in our joy, direct the storm. Thus, would you have us, our very nature abandoned, follow your selfish purpose.

Woll spoke calmly once more.

Do not be cowed by her aggressive posturing. She knows she is indebted to you for saving her offspring. You must insist that she pays you in satisfaction of that debt.

Magio had no idea what Woll was instructing him to do. A rising nausea had him retching. He was already perilously dizzy from the wheeling of the mast, as the ship tossed and turned in the heart of the gale.

The Mother of Storms doesn't just ride the storm. She directs its eye.

Panting for breath after another bout of retching, Woll's words were only slowly registering in Magio's confused mind. What did they mean? What was Woll actually telling him to do? In the time he was thinking, there was a cracking sound from below, as if the Scuttlebutt was on the brink of breaking apart.

Magio struggled to grasp what Woll might truly mean. What was the eye of a storm? And why was it so important?

'Woll, what are you saying?'

She controls the direction of the gale.

He realized now what Woll was telling him. The mother creature was its eye. She controlled the storm. He thought about it but had no idea whatsoever how that could happen. But then, in his abysmal ignorance, he knew nothing of storms, or their eyes for that matter. He exhaled, attempting to get his confused thoughts in order. He took a deep breath to try to stop his stomach reacting . . . And then, recalling

Quimbre's intention, he understood what Woll was trying to tell him.

'Woll, tell the mother creature that what I did for the trapped young creature will be redeemed if it directs the storm to the Isle of Tar.'

Woll followed his counsel, hovering unwaveringly in the storm-tossed air, and remaining perfectly calm, as she passed his instruction to the creature.

The Mageling will see the debt repaid if the Mother of Storms directs us to the Isle of Tar.

The creature took off from the yard and rose, wheeling into the sky. There she made clear by her shriek, and wheeling display in the wrack of clouds above, that she did not care for the deal. But she descended again to hover over Magio, those great luminescent wings beating over him, those dark eyes fixed on Magio's own, as if studying him anew.

So, then, will the bargain be struck between us, vainglorious youth. Yet though we are presently indebted to pander to your need, we curse you and all of your kind.

Magio closed his eyes, his heartbeat once again in his throat. But Woll appeared to be entirely unperturbed.

Curse as you will, Mother of Storms. The mage child is blessed by powers greater than you. What he will seek has neither legs to strut nor wings to soar, yet his quest will bring hope, such that your arrogance might reflect in wonder.

Magio had no idea of what Woll's words could possibly mean. But even as he clung on for dear life to the yard and its spidersweb of rigging, he witnessed the widening of shock invade the storm rider's eyes.

An Eldritch Guide

The world was a whirling confusion. There was a commotion around him, which merely added to it. Magio found himself blinking too rapidly, struggling to figure out what was happening. Nothing made immediate sense. He had to force himself to remember exactly what had happened to him. He knew he had been brought down onto the deck by Quimbre. But when he tried to remember what exactly had happened, panic caused him to tremble. Even so, he insisted on looking about himself to discover that he was lying on the narrow bunk he normally slept in below decks. It was difficult to focus his thoughts with the huge jolting of his surroundings. He felt the comforting reassurance of his sister, Eefa, who was sitting on her bunk nearby.

'What's happening, Eefie?'

'We're still in the eye of the storm.'

The eye of the storm . . .

That rang a bell in his mind, one that felt important. But what did it mean? There was no sudden awakening of consciousness.

His head hurt. Every muscle in his body ached.

'Oh, jinxy!'

Eefa mopped his brow with a damp rag. 'Stop it, Magio! You have to stop thinking about it.'

But he couldn't stop. He couldn't even stop himself from trembling. His entire skin had erupted with goosebumps.

'Quimbre carried you down from the lookout on his shoulder. He said you'd slipped out of his belt, the belt that should have tethered you to the mainmast. When he found you, you were out in the rigging, with nothing to keep you safe other than threads of what looked like gold, threads that dissolved to nothing before his eyes.'

Magio shook his head, not daring to recall. His tongue felt as dry as an old empty sack inside his equally dry mouth.

'Woll was there. She helped me.'

'When Quimbre brought you down, you were raving. Bird Woman gave you a potion. You've been asleep. Oh, Magio, you've been raving in your bunk for two whole days.'

'I think I'm too scared to remember. That mother creature. I recall that she had a rainbow-colored body and scaly wings. Oh, Eefie, she somehow got inside my head. She spoke to me, in the weirdest way, mind-to-mind.'

But now that his memories were returning to him, he knew that he wasn't telling Eefa the whole truth. He wasn't altogether clear himself of the full truth of the memories he was now recalling.

'Eefie,' he whispered her name, shaking his head.

The cabin around him rose hugely and then fell back equally hugely, causing Eefa to cling to him, as he clung to her. Magio shook his head. It was time he stopped worrying about the strangeness of what he had encountered. But he just couldn't get it out of his mind.

'Woll came to me. She saved me. She told me what to do, what to say to the creature. She really did, Eefa. Woll saved us.'

Even as Magio remembered the strange events that had happened atop the rigging, the oak-timbered cabin spun and yawed again through a huge rise and fall. The air crackled with lightning, illuminating every crevice of the dark bunkroom, and thunder boomed so close, the hull shook with its vibration.

'The storm riders . . . you won't believe it, anymore than I did.' Magio hesitated, breathing deeply to settle his fright. 'They don't just ride the storm. They control it, Eefa. The mother creature – she directs the eye of the storm.'

Eefa patted his brow again. 'You've been dreaming, Magio. The storm still rages about us. But Quimbre thinks it's abating.'

'No, it isn't. You don't understand.'

'What don't I understand?'

'The storm riders – they are directing the ship. They are heading us to where Quimbre wanted to go.'

'You're still dreaming.'

'No! You really don't understand. I did what Woll told me to do. That terrifying creature . . . she was the mother of the trapped one. But she wasn't at all what you might imagine. Oh, Eefa, she wasn't what you think she is. But I had freed her offspring. Because of that, she was obliged to me. So, I just did what Woll told me to do. I . . . I told her, the mother creature . . . I ordered her to take us to the Isle of Tar.'

'Don't be silly.'

Magio stared at Eefa wide-eyed. 'Talk to Bird Woman. Maybe we both should talk to Bird Woman. Maybe she can make you understand.'

'The storm riders are not birds.'

'Heck, no. But they do have flying in common. If you don't believe me, go ahead and call Bird Woman down here. Ask her if she's noticed something unusual.'

'Calm down, Magio. We've all seen plenty that seemed unusual. Quimbre has been muttering about never understanding these eldritch waters. Even Bird Woman has been talking strangely. Muttering things, looking up at the sky.'

'Everything I told you is true. Talk to Bird Woman. She must have some inkling of what is really going on.'

'I wish I knew what you're talking about, Magio.'

'I remember it clearly . . . how it strange it seemed. Woll knew who she was. She called her the Mother of Storms. Oh, jinxy, she was scary. She had such huge claws and teeth. She lunged at me. But Woll protected me. I knew it was her, because she came like a golden spark of light, a spark that turned into a golden cloud between the creature and me. Woll saved me, and very likely all of us. It was thanks to her that the mother creature didn't kill me up there in the rigging.'

'Now you're raving.'

'I'm not crazy. The mother creature spoke to me, mind-to-mind.'

Eefa still did not believe him. She looked at him in that skeptical way of hers. 'You should talk to Bird Woman, Magio. Explain it all to her. See what she makes of it.'

Magio was utterly fed up with trying to explain things. He tried to get out of the bunk, but he was so jiggered he tottered back down to a sitting position. 'Maybe you should call her now, Eefa.'

'I'll do just that.'

He must have dozed off for a while, but when he came to Bird Woman was dabbing his face with a damp towel. Eefa was still there, close beside her, a worried expression on her face. Immediately he got himself into such a lather of excitement, he sat bolt upright and, once sitting up, he couldn't keep still.

'Where have you been, Bird Woman? I've been trying to explain to Eefa . . . but she won't believe me.'

Bird Woman smiled at him, sitting on the edge of the bunk. 'Calm yourself, Magio. I'm here. Quimbre was very worried about you.'

Magio sighed. 'Quimbre is an idiot.'

'Now, hold on, Magio. He said he had seen it all. You were lucky to escape with your life.'

'He doesn't listen to me. I tried to tell him . . .'

'He said you were rambling.'

'I was not rambling. I was excited. I admit that I was excited. But I was just trying to tell him what had happened.'

'Calm down. You're still groggy. I gave you a potion to help you sleep. Let me give you its antidote, so you don't feel so groggy.' Bird Woman found a powdery philter, with what appeared to be tiny kernels of some plant, in one of her pockets. She mixed it with a small amount of water in a cup and handed the cup to Magio.

'Drink it down.'

'How do I know it isn't the same thing that knocked me out?'

'Magio! Do you really believe that I would lie to you, stop protecting you?'

Magio hesitated, gazing at her, face to face. Then he closed his eyes and swallowed the potion.

Bird Woman nodded to him, taking back the empty cup. 'Take time to recover yourself. Eefa and I can wait. Give you time to recover your senses.'

Magio looked at them suspiciously, took a deep breath. 'Haven't you noticed – hasn't any of you noticed – the storm is continuing because the ship is all the while being carried along by the movement of the eye. The storm riders control the storm.'

Bird Woman put her hand on his shoulder. 'I can see what Quimbre might have thought of that. But I really need you to explain what you mean.'

He swallowed, still tasting the potion. 'The storm riders,' he attempted once more to explain what he didn't fully understand himself, 'they don't just follow the storm, gamboling around it. They control the direction of the storm by controlling the eye. You won't believe me. But it was Woll who told me. She explained it to me.' Magio's eyes fell. 'But I don't expect any of you to believe me.'

Bird Woman squeezed his shoulder, reassuringly. 'Well, perhaps I do accept that you had an unusual experience up there in the rigging. Strange things have been happening. Yes, I do believe there is something in what you are saying, Magio.'

'Honestly, I just did what Woll told me to do. I had to bargain hard with the mother creature, just as Woll told me to. I forced her to direct the eye of the storm so it would take us where Quimbre wanted to go – to the Isle of Tar.'

Eefa exclaimed, 'What were you thinking?'

'Hush, Eefa. Please allow Magio to explain.'

'Woll! She told me what I had to do to save the Scuttlebutt.'

'Woll – the frost sprite queen from back in the mountains of Moon?'

'Yes.'

Bird Woman reared back, astonished. She put her hand on her brow and rubbed it, then sat next to Magio on the bunk, silent for several minutes.

'I think that I am beginning to understand. You saw a golden spark, which is likely how she might materialize.'

'I knew it was her. And then she spoke to me.'

Bird Woman hesitated. 'I'm beginning to think that you're right, Magio. Now I consider it, of course she would have intervened. Was she not entrusted to take care of you by the Lady of the Shore?'

'Oh, Bird Woman, it was so terrifying. I heard the weird sounds that were coming out of the creature's mind.'

'And that's what I want to hear more about. We have little time to tarry. Quimbre needs all the help he can get to haul us to safety. But I must know every detail of whatever it was that happened up in the rigging.'

Magio did his best, in the heaving and rolling cabin, to recount what he had witnessed.

'The creature – the full-grown mother creature – was huge. Much bigger than I thought when they were flying above in the air.'

'Quickly, Magio – before you begin to forget exact details – tell me all that you witnessed and sensed.'

'I . . . I suppose that I was wondering just what was going through its mind. All I gathered, at first, was a mess of garbled confusion. But then, bit by bit, it began to make some kind of sense. I have no doubt that Woll had a hand in it. The garbled mess turned into real words that were coming into my mind.' Magio recounted every word that he recalled of that strange and terrible encounter, including Woll's final words to the mother creature. 'Oh, Eefie! Woll! She said such strange things.'

Eefa stared wide-eyed at Magio, then spun around to question Bird Woman. 'What could it mean?'

'We all need time to think about it, Eefa.'

'Don't tell me that those terrible forces that hunted us everywhere we traveled through Moon are still hunting us. Please don't tell us that we haven't escaped.'

Bird Woman could only shake her head, as if bewildered herself at Magio's words, before she and Eefa left him exhausted on his bunk.

In fact, Magio himself remained confused by it all. A little later, left alone in the pitching and rolling cabin, aware of the parlous condition of the ship, he could not shake off the terror he had felt when confronted by that huge creature up there in the rigging. He reached under his bunk to discover his amulet. Bird Woman must have removed it from around his throat when they put him into the bunk. Now he stared anew at the strange shape of it, curled up like a small nautilus shell, but shaped more like a dragon. He felt the familiar thrill of holding it. He hugged it to his breast as he had when he had first discovered it en route for the Beach of Bones. Back then, a spirit being had appeared before him, as if by magic. She had been as diaphanous as a ghost. Yet she wasn't like he would have imagined a ghost. Her hair was salt-grimed and windblown. She had injuries and scars all over her body, as if night creatures had been feeding on her flesh.

Back then he had spoken his fears into the amulet. And that spirit had spoken gentle words back to him, reassuring words that had comforted him, guided him. He had felt the spirit's slim, cold finger pressed against his lips.

'Ask no more questions. Show me your treasure.'

Now, just as then, he held his dragon amulet aloft.

'It is beautiful. I can see why you would treasure it. Make sure you do not lose it when you are compelled to run.'

As the ship reared and fell with the fury of the storm, Magio clung to his treasure, hugging it close to his breast. He knew now that they were still running, all of them — him, Eefa, Bird Woman and Quimbre. He felt himself sink into his own mind, as a comfort, but all he found there was a discomforting glare of whiteness. His mind was baffled by the whiteness. It was as if he were staring into a fathomless void.

Then, as if from a dreamy distance, he heard Quimbre's triumphant shout.

'Land ahoy!'

An Unnatural Vista

Everybody rushed to the foredeck, where Quimbre was standing, with his bare feet astraddle the planks and his gaze fixed on the distant horizon. In the filmy light of early dawn, Eefa was shocked to witness that the sea had settled down into the normal swell of the waves. The black clouds, with their wheeling storm riders, were still overhead, but they were drifting away from them. Blinking in surprise, she attempted to focus her confused mind on Quimbre's pointing finger, where she saw something that resembled a flat raft of the faintest green on the distant horizon.

'What is it, Quimbre?'

'Even the least experienced mariner would recognize that line of green. We are approaching the Isle of Tar.'

With a chill of shock, Eefa remembered Magio's words. 'I forced her to direct the eye of the storm so it would take us where Quimbre wanted to go . . .'

'How do you know it's Tar?'

'You will see how – and indeed why – as we near it.'

There was a new tension in Quimbre's voice, and now that she looked at him, she saw that same tension in his posture.

'What is it, Quimbre?'

'I have warned you all, and now I make no apology for warning you again, that we are sailing the Sea of Stars where nothing is ever quite as it seems.' He put a heavy hand on her shoulder, before quickly removing it. Maybe Quimbre was not yet comfortable with her presence? Perhaps he had not entirely forgiven her for concealing her invisibility from him for so long? Though she couldn't blame him, she felt a stab of resentment that he might harbor any bitterness when that same invisible spell, put upon her by the Lady of the Shore, had caused such deep hurt in her everyday life.

Of course, Quimbre had been a pirate. No doubt he had done many wicked things in his life. But he had helped Gran, in spite of Gran's incessant grumbling, and then he had risked his life to save her and Magio. She realized now that, for perhaps the first time in her life, she was trying to understand the real person that was Quimbre. She found herself deep breathing through her nose, with her eyes closed, for several seconds. And when she opened her eyes again, she found it very difficult even to think of how she might make amends to Quimbre. It seemed incredible to her now to realize that she had never really attempted to discover the real Quimbre.

She just blurted out, 'How did you come to be a pirate?'

Quimbre stiffened.

He was silent for a moment or two, still staring out at that approaching line of green on the horizon. Then, when he spoke, he did so with a sigh.

'You draw your lot when you are born into the world. I was born to a family of pirates. I could no more help being a pirate than you could help being invisible.'

This was followed by a moment's silence between them. Quimbre was still breathing hard, through his nose.

'Please, don't be angry with me.'

'Angry?' He laughed. 'There are many things that anger old Quimbre, but not you, young lady. I shouldn't have spoken to you like that. Though young, you are more sensible than anyone I have ever met. Now, even in the short while I have known of your existence, I have seen how you have matured to become a young woman.'

While comforted by Quimbre's words, Eefa could not help staring at that line of green on the horizon, which was slowly growing in size as it drew nearer.

'Of course, I care for both you and Magio! It has been difficult for me to come to terms with the fact that I largely reared your brother as what I saw as a son. And all the while there was this mysterious twin sister, Eefa – a sister whose very existence was denied to me for so many years.'

'I know this now. And I'm very sorry.'

Quimbre guffawed. 'You asked about me. I grew up in a family where it was assumed that we, the men folk, went to sea. Back then I had a naïve perspective, not unlike that of your brother, that the sea was an exciting adventure. That younger me sure did long for adventure. Who knew, but it seemed to me that in the many mysteries of the Sea of Stars there must be wonders galore. For the eldest son of a pirate captain, that meant plunder aplenty. But sailing that same sea, I learnt a more brutal, if also vital, lesson.'

'You did?'

'I surely did. I learnt that the Sea of Stars, and the wider ocean that it is but a small part of, is too treacherous to be understood. It took me half a lifetime to realize that what really matters is getting on with the day-to-day stuff of life – the things we take for granted. Most important of all is family. Family – the thing we most take for granted – is the only adventure that really matters.'

Eefa wondered if Quimbre thought of her and Magio as his family, even as she watched how the line of green grew enormously in size and height as the Scuttlebutt approached it. It was a strange vision for a girl who had grown up in the desert world of Moon.

She spoke, soft as a whisper. 'But . . . but now it seems that whatever Magio did up there, in the rigging, has led us here?'

'It surely feels like a miracle.'

Eefa closed her eyes at the word, miracle. She was thinking about all her brother had been telling her, and it frightened her.

She felt tears fill her eyes.

A silent Quimbre put an arm around her shoulders.

'Take no notice of me. I've been invisible for so long, it's hard to believe that I have felt the stormy wind in my hair. I still can't quite believe that I am a part of things, a part of it all, the sky, the wind, the ship, the very sea all about us. When you are invisible, you feel at times – oh, you feel it so terribly – that maybe you don't really exist at all.'

Quimbre said nothing. He pondered their slow approach to the island for several minutes before he spoke again. 'We are aboard a very simple but stoutly built island hopper. But I knew that her caulking was gone, leaving the hull as leaky as an old sieve. It's a miracle we made it this far.'

'Oh, Quimbre!'

'What is it?'

'I suddenly have such a feeling inside me. To me, it feels as if the Isle of Tar knows we are approaching. It appears to be cloaking itself with mists even as we approach it in the morning light.'

Quimbre nodded. 'Tar is no ordinary isle. And those are no ordinary trees. When we disembark, beware both those mists and trees.'

Magio, who had come to stand by them, would normally be cheering what he would regard as a great adventure. But now, having overheard Quimbre's warning, he spoke in an urgent whisper, 'What are you planning to do, Quimbre?'

'The old-time sailors had the saying, "By Tar no sailor should tarry." They were right. Unfortunately, we can't sail on by. We have needs that must be seen to.'

'You want me to furl sail?'

'Aye! But not till the very last moment. We need to keep a close eye on wind and tide – so we come in at full tide. There's but a single cove and its beach is pebbled – deep and treacherous. We need to pick up speed to beach her high up on that pebbly beach. It'll be a tight judgment, Kiddo.'

All of a sudden, time was racing along with every beating heart aboard the ship. The mainsail was stretched full and taut. The hull timbers were creaking with the surge of speed that Quimbre had somehow conjured up. And now, as though aware of their approach, the mist that had cloaked the island appeared to thin, and then to fritter away, revealing a sight that took their breath away.

Bird Woman was unable to restrain her wail. 'Merciful spirits!'

Eefa and Magio shared her consternation, gazing open-mouthed at the same vista that was now fully in view. They knew that Tar was a forested island, but never in her wildest dreams would Eefa have imagined such a forest.

She shrieked, 'They're giants.'

Quimbre merely grunted, holding steady the wheel with a determined grimace. 'Giants, they most certainly are. And all the more daunting the closer we get.'

Bird Woman made no attempt to hide her apprehension. 'I sense great danger here. What dire situation have you drawn us into?'

'I have no choice. The hull was leaking even before the storm. Now it is beyond redemption. We recaulk her here or we sink with her.'

'You raving lunatic!'

Quimbre grimaced, through a beard soaked with spray. 'Likely, I am. But even lunatics gather a little wisdom through a lifetime of misadventure.'

'Stop criticizing Quimbre, Bird Woman,' Magio scolded her. 'Have you forgotten how he risked his life for us back on Moon?'

Bird Woman stared wild-eyed at him, her hair matted to her head with spray. 'I shall accept your rebuke if we are alive at the close of this disaster.'

Eefa spoke softly to Bird Woman. 'Whatever you think about Quimbre bringing us here to Tar, we no longer have a choice but to trust him.'

'Twice do I find myself rebuked.'

Quimbre shook his head. 'We should all calm down. From hereon, let me warn you all – and this includes you, Woman – you must follow my directions to the letter. We are about to beach the Scuttlebutt at a quarter into the ebbing tide, and it is my intention to bury her keel deep amid those pebbles.'

Eefa headed for the stern, but Quimbre halted her with a shout. 'Inside the wheelhouse with you, and keep your knees pulled up and your back pressed against the forward wall. The same goes for you, Magio.'

But Magio refused. He insisted on twining his body around the rope Quimbre called the halyard, intent on watching every move that Quimbre made. Bird Woman gave up cajoling him and joined Eefa against the wheelhouse wall.

The shock of the keel striking the beach was bone-jarring, jerking every loose object forward, and Magio found himself swung halfway back to horizontal. Quimbre grunted with pain, his chest crushed against the wheel. The shock of contact continued as the Scuttlebutt rose higher onto the beach, accompanied by a prolonged juddering as the keel cleaved a deep furrow through the pebbles, jarring every bone, joint and sinew of Eefa's body.

But even as she was shaking her giddy senses back to clarity, Quimbre was already making preparations.

'Magio, help me furl sail.'

They all tottered to their feet and joined the melee about the ropes. Even as they were falling over one another to complete the task, Eefa couldn't drag her gaze away from the terrifying sight that now loomed over them. They were confronted by a solid wall of giants, trees with trunks like ascending pillars that soared for hundreds of feet into the air. Where one might have anticipated the usual open spaces between separate trees, allowing space for the expansion of branches and foliage, these were massed too close together for there to be any room for foliage other than in the lofty canopy. As Eefa gazed monstrously high above their heads, she saw that the branches, when branches did finally appear, were thicker than any tree trunk she had ever seen, appearing more like interlocking arms. The impression was one of giants enfolding one another's shoulders, as if fashioning a gargantuan, impregnable barrier. This forest, if forest it truly was, more resembled a monstrous cliff face.

She whispered, 'Bird Woman, they terrify me. I can't help feeling that they know we're here – and they watch our every movement.'

Quimbre shook his head. 'We have no time to wonder. We have a single day to do what must be done. It will begin with fixing the wider cracks in the hull. Fortunately, the old shipwrights who built the Scuttlebutt used only the finest oak. Dried as old prunes it might be, yet still those planks are good and the leaks can be mended. For that, Magio, we are going to need a fire. You two, Bird Woman and Eefa, will gather the driftwood and seaweed. Chose the driest you can find from the highest levels of the beach. Now if I can leave that to you, I need you, Magio, to follow me below decks and help me bend and rove some rivets.'

The Age of Vengeance

Queen Pittaquera gazed about the port of Wart, which was no longer recognizable as the town that had only recently been captured by the Ursascogan army. Other than the encircling stone walls, with the massive breach in the region of the former main gate, nothing remained of its famous old stone square and winding cobbled streets. Those very cobbles had been put to re-use, flooring a ramshackle miscellany of woodworking sheds and furnaces from which arose a thunderous cacophony of heavy carpentry and the roaring maws of bronze and iron smelting furnaces, the latter filling the night air with a multi-hued spark-glowing smoke. As she wandered, intent on observing all that was happening, Pittaquera snorted at the spectacle of incense being sprinkled on burners atop linden altars by the figures of linen-garbed priestesses.

What a wicked pretense!

As if a show of dancing and scented flame would protect the spirits of the ancestors from the contaminating evil of unnatural and fiendish lore being put to work here. Of course, it was all a lie, a towering duplicity.

So, she would have advised the king, had her husband given her the opportunity to advise him. But these days Wirgnatha took no counsel from his wife. Instead, he was led by the nose by that demon-witch, Lustfera. The very thought of what her husband and that fiend were planning provoked a tightness in Pittaquera's chest that caused her to pause in her peregrinations. All she saw was such a sickening realization of the evil afoot that she needed to pause and recover her composure. Holding her fearful self still, Pittaquera sniffed at the air, suspicious that intoxicants might have been added to the priestesses' incense. She took care to inhale as little as possible from this witches' brew that drifted in clouds, penetrating everywhere.

All the same, she had to admit that some good had come from the transformation of Wart. A vast gathering of Ursascogans, attracted by news of the town's conquest by Wirgnatha's army, was now encamped outside the walls. To the queen the nation was the pillar of her life. To witness this return of the kindred – fragmented families of many lineages – deeply touched her. Oh, how blessed was this gathering of the lower ranks, folks who had trekked here from every corner of Moon to find sanctuary at Wart. She had not dared to visit the gathering in person, being warned by the wizar of the risk of the rice-water flux that had found a fertile soil in such insanitary conditions. Instead, the queen felt she must concentrate all of her energies on the upcoming folly.

Heading for the harbor, and a welcome fresh breeze blowing ashore from the sea, she was confronted by a monstrous assemblage of heavy oak beams currently being erected around a newly cut channel leading into the bay. Working with axes of bronze and two-handled iron saws, the shipwrights had made short work of an entire forest of oak trees, so that a vast scaffold was emerging amid the furnaces, smoke and bedlam. Certainly, there was nothing new in Ursascogans erecting and launching a ship of oak. But this construction was cloaked in mystery and it was larger than any she had seen before.

Was the mystery bound to the unusual tattoos decorating the broad shoulders and chests of warriors working closely with what appeared to be a small army of Iron Smiths? Pittaquera held up a jewel-bedecked hand, halting a group of one-plus-eight – the sacred number of the brother unit. All nine stood to attention, bathed in sweat, still bearing the weight of a huge oblong of sheet iron in their muscled arms.

'Your tattoo – I do not recognize it.'

'Our clan is new-formed, Your Majesty.'

'A new-formed clan?'

'Yes, Majesty. We are the Clan of Iron Shipwrights.'

'But we have never heard of such a clan.'

The one in charge bowed his head and, with it duly lowered, asked in a clear calm voice, 'Might Your Majesty permit us to rest our burden while we speak?'

'You may.'

'We are indebted to you, Majesty. The new clan is a sub-unit of the Clan of Iron. It was deemed an honor by our beloved king. Indeed, if I be permitted to explain the wonder of it in appropriate detail, your Majesty?'

'You may.'

An explosion distracted her attention.

Pittaquera felt the ground shift beneath her feet in what felt like a minor earthquake. It was all she could do to remain standing when all about her was shuddering to its very foundation.

She whispered, with her eyes clenched shut, 'My goodness, it's like the end of the world.'

'Not quite, Majesty.'

The interrupting voice was a familiar one, coming from behind her. Pittaquera sensed his presence even before she turned to discover she had been joined by the wizar, Khakhov.

Before either of them could speak, the sky was illuminated by flares of magenta and yellow, accompanied by roaring red flames.

'What in the world?'

The wizar appeared to struggle for words. When he did speak, his voice was shaky, as if struggling with a lump in his throat. 'My Queen! All common sense appears confounded in this rush to still more conflict.'

'I'm afraid that I fail to connect with any of it.'

Their conversation was interrupted by a river of crackling red-hot iron flowing over a slope of sand, all the while showering a cataract of rubicund sparks far and wide into the night sky.

'Your Majesty, they are constructing a battleship of iron.'

'I have never heard of such a thing.'

'It is a ship the like of which has never been seen in all of the centuries of conflict in the Sea of Stars.'

'Do you, Wizar, understand an iota of it?'

'No, Majesty. I do not.'

In a clearing amid the bedlam of sparks and smoke, her eyes caught a flurry of movement. Hundreds of figures were rolling red-glowing iron plates forward into the bizarre construction. In that same moment, her attention was drawn to the figure, highlighted within a ring of torches. It was the king, Wirgnatha, a figure she no longer recognized as the husband she had married. His manly form was unchanged. But his behavior of late, the staring look in what currently appeared his red-reflecting eyes, confirmed her suspicion that an alien nature had invaded his being. And close at hand Pittaquera glimpsed the she-devil that was responsible for this change in her husband, in the tall and ever-metamorphosing shadow of darkness at the center of the torches, yellow-flaring furnaces, and the never-ending mushrooms of red-hot splinters of iron.

Tall and stately, King Wirgnatha was now addressing the gathering of his people, the deep rumble of his voice steady, rhythmical, insistent. 'They treated us as slaves. They forced us to skulk beneath the earth, we whose labors constructed in stone the halls of those who flaunted themselves as our masters. Today that subservience ends.'

Wirgnatha raised his hand to quell the cheers before they became too enthusiastic. 'Yes, my beloved people! Thus, do I deliver you, on this prophetic occasion, the liberation we have longed for through the ages of suffering and ignominy. The time has come for the Ursascogans to assert our rightful hegemony.'

The answering cheers, and the thunder of feet against the rocky ground, were as deafening as the previous hammering of the Iron Smiths. Pittaquera hated how her familiar world was changing in root and stem, from the world of pedigree and etiquette that had reigned not merely for centuries but for millenia. In spite of Wirgnatha's frequent references to the history of her people, and the numerous indignities they had suffered, she sensed no real connection with that dignified past. The very clan of Iron Smiths, which had been more active than all the others in the construction of the monstrosity, had been dignified for ages past with royal patronage and honor. These changes in her familiar world, all happening so very quickly, bewildered Pittaquera. She could not help but wonder where all of this was leading her, and her beloved Ursascogan people.

She spoke her mind to the elderly wizar. 'The very notion of constructing a sea-going battleship of iron.' It was impossible for the queen even to contemplate such foolishness. 'Surely, it will sink like a stone?'

'Indeed, so it would seem to me, Majesty. And yet, or so we are assured, it has been designed to float.'

'I refuse to believe it.'

Such was her astonishment that she was determined to keep her vigil, observing all that was unfolding, hour-by-hour, as monstrosity after monstrosity was being assembled, until at last a triumphant Clan of Iron Shipwrights, amid a bedlam of trumpeting, drumming and cheering, slid the gigantic construction into the foreshore.

There was an almighty splash.

Queen Pittaquera could not help her eyes blinking repeatedly, her hands drawn to her lips, her body frozen with shock. The air was filled with what sounded like the neverending pealing of thunder. The lurid red of furnaces aglow, no longer to melt iron but to celebrate the occasion, now lit up the night sky.

The construction, in the shape of a great iron-plated ship, failed to sink, as Queen Pittaquera had expected. It floated.

Pittaquera felt close to fainting, feeling the wizened hand of the aged wizar touch her shoulder, the old man as astonished as she, both of them refusing to believe what was happening before their very eyes.

'Am I imagining it?'

'No, Highness. The iron ship is confounding logic. It is floating just as would a ship of oak.'

The rousing cheers, accompanied by the stamping of thousands of feet, were enough to overwhelm the roars of dozens of open furnaces and the continuous clattering and clanging of wheeled trolleys and iron chains.

'What's happening now?'

'They appear to be hauling forth another of that creature's monstrosities – the weapon that destroyed the gates of Wart.'

'The Leviathan?'

Pittaquera stared in open astonishment as a small army of heavily-muscled warriors slowed the slide of the gigantic weapon as it descended, amid a chaos of roars and trumpeting, guiding it directly onto the floating monstrosity.

The Wizar slowly shook his head.

Pittaquera felt deeply disturbed in both mind and spirit. She must somehow force her trembling heart to settle. Nothing appeared to make sense. But what if it made extraordinary sense? Her eyes searched the dark once more to discover the shadowy figure astride the Leviathan, a glimmering silhouette of darkness against the explosions of light from torches, furnaces and sparks. She continued to watch the shadowy being make ready to welcome the Leviathan onto the iron plates that made up the deck of the monstrosity.

'It's utter madness.'

'Majesty! Might it not be prudent to bide one's thoughts.'

The ground vibrated again as choirs sang the sacred litanies in sonorous plainchant. Pittaquera was bewildered again. Who was singing? Where were they situated? Normally they would be supplicant before her. But here all that mattered was being kept at a distance from her humble vantage, a punishment, as she must now presume, for her failure to commend the coming military expedition. She had to suppress a rising sense of alarm. At the same time, she could not deny the shiver of pride as she saw her husband stand majestically erect above the scene, then turn to face the natural shelf that stood at the very lip of the sea, and upon which, she must assume the necessary sacrifice would be offered.

'I see it all.' She whispered up close to the Wizar's ear. 'Yet I fail to understand anything of what is happening.'

'As far as I can see the Clan of Oak have constructed a template of sorts. This has given them a scaffold that will bear its weight. And now they feel empowered to maneuver the Leviathan onto the structure.'

'But no ship, whether of oak or iron, could bear such an added weight.'

'Certainly not, Majesty. Her ambition knows no bounds. But do not fear. Surely such an overly ambitious scheme will conclude with a plummet of both ship and Leviathan to the bottom of the sea?'

Pittaquera's eyes lifted to the shadow that was preening itself upon the very prow of the monstrosity, the being from hell who called herself Lustfera. It was difficult for Pittaquera to focus on that hated figure, tall as her husband, but ethereal in its being, a triad of serpents that appeared to be constantly metamorphosing within its very being, with those alien green eyes unchanging. Those same eyes appeared to discover the deepest secrets hidden in the heart of each and every being they encountered.

The Star of Mourning indeed.

Pittaquera dropped her gaze as she heard a sudden roar.

What now? Her gaze lifted again, her eyes searching through the torch-illuminated dark in an attempt to discover what was happening.

There was a sudden focus on the slope down onto the shore. Shouts . . . A clarion trumpeting . . . roar after roar from the assembled crowds . . . Then Pittaquera made out the huge shape of the extraordinary weapon, the Leviathan, as it was maneuvered down a ramp and onto the forward deck of the iron ship. A great cheer erupted from the multitude as the shee-warg climbed astride it, seating herself astride the gigantic maw as it was pulled and pushed to ensure that the barrel peered directly out through the prow. It was clear the fiend now rode the weapon with not a jot of fear of sinking to the sea floor along with her titanic monstrosity?

Pittaquera's faltering sense of reality was rescued by the familiar voice of her husband, ringing out from a platform that surmounted the scene.

'We, the First Folk, are prepared to stake our claim of hegemony over these lands, beyond the Isle of Moon to the totality of these islands, to claim our birthright – to rule all that is bounded by the Sea of Stars.'

The Weeping Trees of Tar

As Eefa joined Bird Woman in fixing a rope around an iron cleat, and lowering the two capacious baskets they would need, she wondered why they had to complete their task by nightfall. Quimbre had so doggedly insisted on this that it puzzled her. Eefa wondered if she should question Bird Woman about it while down on the beach. But the arguments that had already taken place between Bird Woman and Quimbre decided her against it. She decided it would be wiser to stay silent. Together with Bird Woman, she clambered down the rope ladder to alight onto a beach of slippery pebbles. She sensed that Bird Woman became immediately tense.

'What is it?'

'I don't know, Eefa. But I have been feeling troubled about our coming to this Isle, and now that we are here, I feel more apprehensive still.'

'But you don't know why?'

'No! I'm afraid I don't. But, given our instructions from that old pirate, we must collect enough dry material for a fire.'

They dragged their baskets closer to the tree line, where they were surrounded by mounds of dried-out flotsam and seaweed, more than enough for them to fill their baskets in no time at all. But now, as they turned to haul their laden baskets back to the ship, Eefa couldn't avoid raising her eyes to that gigantic wall of trees that towered over them like a malignant cliff.

Bird Woman put a hand on her shoulder, as if drawing Eefa closer so she could whisper, 'I have such an ominous feeling here.'

'What is it?'

'I confess I do not know.'

A baffled Eefa began to drag her heavy basket, but she was forced to stop, seeing that Bird Woman was hesitating.

'What is it?'

'I don't want to frighten you.'

'I insist that you tell me.'

It astonished her when Bird Woman left her basket and gave Eefa a sudden, close hug. As she did so, she whispered into her ear, 'Look closely around you. Look down at that very shingle you're standing on – poke around in it with your toe and see what you can see for yourself.'

Eefa poked around in the pebbles with her right foot for no more than a moment or two. 'No! I daren't. I'm too frightened of what I might find. Please tell me what it is that you sense?'

Bird Woman widened her eyes at her. 'Do it! See if you agree with me. Poke about in the pebbles.'

Eefa squatted down and brushed aside the pebbles with her fingers. She stopped immediately, discovering shapes among them that had strange angles and edges – edges sharp enough to prick the skin of her fingers.

Bird Woman had her hand to her mouth. 'Perhaps I'm growing too suspicious. I've been so disturbed with all that has recently developed that, mayhaps, I am beginning to imagine things.'

Eefa blinked with surprise at Bird Woman's words. She took a deep breath through her nostrils. 'Are we to carry on filling the baskets?'

'Yes! Let's do that.'

Eefa returned to filling her basket with the dry flotsam, but now she was wondering about two separate mysteries. The first was the reason why Quimbre wanted to get away from here by morning. And the second, triggered by Bird Woman's strange behavior, was what in the world had she discovered among the pebbles.

Magio was too impatient to sit and wait while Quimbre was searching for something down in the hold. He followed him down there, descending thick oak steps as steep as a ladder, to discover him, waist high in bilge water amid the floating rubbish, and searching with his bare feet for something submerged in the filthy water.

'Hey, Quimbre, what are you looking for?'

'First answer me, Kiddo. Are they good and busy – that witch woman and Eefa – out there on the beach?'

'Yeah, they certainly are.'

'Good!'

'What are you up to?'

'Something I don't want that crazy woman to know about until I'm ready. Something that might or might not be here. But if we find it – well, it could help our chances of escaping this accursed island.'

Magio watched Quimbre wading about in the flooded bilge, poking and prying, and here and there. 'Hey, tell me what you're looking for. I want to help you.'

'You just need to keep a lookout for me. Make sure that interfering old witch doesn't haul herself up the ropes and poke her nose where it's not wanted.'

'You're worried we mightn't get away from Tar?'

'One thing that crazy woman got right is the fact that this is no resting place. The Isle of Tar is perilous, Magio – more so than even she suspects.'

Magio's eyes widened. 'But Eefa is out there with her. Why did you bring us here if it's so dangerous?'

'Devil or the deep blue sea, Kiddo. I chose the devil.'

Quimbre was tearing slime-coated pots, wooden planks, ropes and pulleys, and rolls of filthy wet sailcloth out of the depths. 'Damn, but I reckon it's got to be here. Every island hopper had one aboard.'

'Hey, let me help you. Just tell me what we're looking for.'

'Hooray!'

'What is it?'

'I think we've got her, Magio.'

'What is it?'

'Felt the shape of her with my foot. Hah! What's that word you got for it, Kiddo? Britzy! Britzy – bloodywell britzy!'

'What is it?'

Quimbre guffawed. 'Why, let's say I came across a familiar old friend. Help me now to haul her out of this stinking bilge. Then we can set up a pulley to hoist her on deck.'

Magio climbed out of the hold, fixed the winch to a convenient tether, and then dropped the heavy iron hook down into the hold. A short while later, Magio found himself studying the monstrosity of bronze that was appearing out of the water-logged hold, trailing mud and splinters of oak from the steps, to be maneuvered onto the aft deck. Here, as Quimbre deluged it with buckets of seawater, Magio witnessed something bulky and awkward, shaped somewhat like the firing mechanism of Quimbre's flintlock, only massively bigger, and attached to a big round barrel, whose bore was almost as wide as it was long. It was bolted to a carriage of heavy oak, with two rusted-up wheels of iron.

'What in the world . . .?'

Quimbre threw his arms around Magio's shoulders and had him join in little jig of triumph.

'I warrant that you have never seen such a piece or ordinance in your entire life. But at your age I was altogether familiar with it. No captain in the entire Sea of Stars went without one o' these Drawer Wetters whenever they set sail.'

Magio was blinking rapidly, his eyes never leaving the amazing object. 'But what is it? What do we do with it?'

Quimbre cackled. 'Between you and me, I reckon it will wet some drawers here on Tar.'

Magio studied the awkward-looking thing, not knowing what Quimbre meant by it all. But he helped him wash and oil the heavy frame, so the barrel sat comfortably in good clean oak, after which they scraped clean and oiled the iron wheels, so the Drawer Wetter could be rolled, albeit creakingly, to the very prow of the Scuttlebutt.

'Nicely done, Kiddo. All we need to do for now is moor her, good and ready. Meanwhile we throw a tarp over her. Keep her secret for the moment.'

Quimbre straightened up, yawned, and then extended his back with a groan.

'Remember what I said. Not a word to the gals down there on the beach. The find is our little secret.'

Magio stood erect and saluted his captain.

With a guffaw, Quimbre looked closely into the sky, as if assessing what little was left of the daylight.

Magio sped down the deck to the stern, peering over the starboard rail, where he saw that Bird Woman and Eefa were taking a rest after filling their baskets. Looking down at them now made him feel somewhat guilty, especially so since Quimbre was clearly up to something. Magio hesitated, tempted to brag about all that he and Quimbre had been up to. But he said not a word.

'Okay! Time to call the women folk up with whatever they've gathered.'

Magio called out to Eefa and Bird Woman, struggling to contain his glee.

But Bird Woman called back up, 'I thought we were to light a fire down here on the beach?'

'No!' Quimbre shook his head at her. Then he winked knowingly at Magio. 'It's time to come back up. Let's get all that you've gathered up here on the deck.'

There was some muttering between Bird Woman and Eefa as they tethered their baskets to the towlines. Quimbre winched the baskets aboard as the beach-combers clambered back up the rope ladder, to join them aboard.

'What's all this about?' Bird Woman demanded, as she confronted Quimbre on the deck, next to their piles of kindling.

Magio was still very excited about their discovery and was desperate to talk about it. But he kept his word to Quimbre, who was explaining what he was thinking. 'There is but an hour left of daylight. We have that long, and not a minute more, to finish what is now necessary to be done.'

'You talk in riddles, man.'

'I know, Woman, though you don't speak of it, you will have delved into what lies beneath those pebbles.'

'As a matter of fact, I did delve. And you know that what I discovered was bones. I did not speak of it, not wanting to frighten Eefa. But then you already knew that the beach is a veritable graveyard of human remains.'

'And now you demand that this lunatic pirate should explain such a mystery?'

'You old scoundrel. What are you not telling us?'

'Perhaps you should use those overlarge ears and listen more carefully?'

At that moment they heard a peculiar sound from high among the trees, which, as they listened, appeared to grow louder.

'What is it? What is going on? For goodness's sake, tell us, man.'

'The forest of Tar is ever hungry. It is as sharp as the eagle in the sky, more voracious than the shark below our keel, and more patient than the spider. It lures sailors onto its shore, offering the pitch sorely needed for re-caulking . . .'

'Pitch – what pitch?'

'You witness it in the black of the trunks. Why do you think the isle is known as Tar? But, of course, it is assuredly a trap. Tar does not give up its black lifeblood willingly or lightly. As ever in nature, blood will fight for blood.'

Bird Woman's face went through a series of expressions. 'What madness possessed you to lead us here?'

'It was our only chance.'

'How so like the thinking of a pirate!'

'I now caution you, woman, that we are wasting time. Vital seconds are now running through our fingers while you wring your hands and whine. Magio and I have been working a plan to wrest us out of this perilous situation. Am I not right, Kiddo?'

Magio stared at them both, shaking his head in amazement.

'You fool. I cannot credit the fact that you have placed us in such mortal danger.'

Quimbre gazed into the sky, which was fading into the first shades of evening. Even as he did so, there was a susurration all around them. It appeared to emanate from the beach. Everybody aboard stiffened to hear it. Then they rushed to the rail to witness what was happening down there, in the now shadowy light,

Bird Woman exclaimed, 'The pebbles are moving.'

Magio took a deep breath, as he confirmed her words. At first it looked as if the pebbles were writhing all by themselves. But then root-like tentacles appeared, sprouting and then rearing and springing up as numerous secondary spike-like tentacles, which were rapidly spreading, like searching snakes.

Quimbre yelled, 'Magio – all of you – get yourselves away from the rails. Quickly now, Magio, help me direct the Drawer Wetter into that black cliff wall.'

Bird Woman exclaimed, 'What's the devil are you up to?'

Both Eefa and Bird Woman were now staring, open-mouthed, at what looked like a squat heavy cannon with an enormous mouth that Quimbre and Magio were busily directing at the cliff-face of trees.

Quimbre was ensuring that the barrel was clean of debris. Then he waved at Magio, who, without understanding anything of what he was doing, followed Quimbre's instructions, filling the cannon with all that he could find of the unused copper rivets, washers, and iron nuts and bolts. Quimbre then stuffed the barrel with a mattress of the dried flotsam collected from the shore, ramming it into a solid plug with the blunt end of an oar.

'Get you all good and ready.'

Bird Woman broke into a fury. 'You maniac. What mad gamble has taken control of your senses?'

'A gamble that improves the odds against providing food for that treacherous forest. And now that night is falling, I suggest we take the opportunity of a brief rest, mayhaps even grab a wink of sleep. We can do nothing more than await the incoming tide.'

Nobody aboard was likely to sleep, given what was happening all about them. Night had fallen but an hour or two when a new sound began to fill the air, a keening sound, more threatening than before. Beside her, Eefa saw that Bird Woman had closed her eyes. But she made no pretense of sleeping. She was holding Eefa close to her, refusing to join Quimbre in keeping watch on the trees and the beach. Eefa couldn't keep her eyes off their pirate captain, as he calmly sat back beside his strange squat weapon, with his left hand curled reassuringly about Magio's shoulder.

She heard Quimbre whisper into Magio's ear, 'It's a matter of choosing the moment, Kiddo. Timing is the key.'

Her brother was wide-eyed with excitement. Eefa clenched her teeth with fear, watching as Magio now joined Quimbre in climbing to his feet, then helped him with getting ready the squat Drawer Wetter in the prow.

What in the world were they up to?

Still watching Magio, standing by the cannon, she saw him nodding to Quimbre, as if he understood something she didn't.

Right then she felt the entire ship shudder. It was followed by a grinding sound of the keel against the pebbles. Another shudder, a much bigger one this time, and the Scuttlebutt righted itself. The tide was coming in.

In that same moment the Drawer Wetter burst into flame. There was a thunderous explosion, following which the weapon rocked back in its heavy oak cradle, then shot back along the deck, the iron wheels screeching, until it crashed into the base of the mainmast. Bird Woman, whose eyes jerked wide open, moaned aloud.

Meanwhile Magio was jumping up and down and shrieking, 'Yeeeeehaaaaah! Yeeeeehaaaaah!'

Eefa wondered what he was so pleased about. She saw that Quimbre was bustling about the deck, though she had no idea what he was up to. Even as she was climbing back onto her feet, she heard him command,

'Now – Magio – stand ready by the wheel.'

Bird Woman still had her eyes firmly closed and she appeared to be praying. She whispered, 'I beg you, from the bottom of my heart, please, O beloved undying, you must help us.'

Eefa could hardly breathe. But still she kept her eyes wide open to watch in the moonlight what Quimbre and Magio were up to. She rushed to the prow, demanding of Magio. 'What is it – what's Quimbre up to?'

'He's saving us.'

Eefa shook her head in bewilderment.

The wailing of the trees was rapidly changing to a horrifying screeching. It was so thunderous it was shaking the boards of the deck.

'Magio – tell me what's happening.'

'Look for yourself – you can see it in the moonlight. Look at the trees – see what's happening.'

Eefa looked into that terrible wall of trees. She saw an emerging darkness, like a pulsating river that was flowing out of the trunks. Blinking with astonishment, she leaned out over the rail to peer more closely.

'Oh, Magio!'

A river of darkness was pouring out of the cliff wall of tree trunks. That was what the Drawer Wetter had been aimed at. The river of darkness was the life blood of the trees. Suddenly, with astonishment, she understood everything.

'The trees are weeping their lifeblood onto the beach.'

'Of course, they are! How do you think the island got its name? Didn't you hear Quimbre tell us so? The life blood of those monstrous trees is tar.'

Eefa was still too bewildered to immediately take it all in.

'Quimbre – he planned this?'

'The ship was leaking on so many of the clinkered seams. He found a desperate solution to a desperate situation.'

Eefa's mind was spinning.

'But . . .'

Even as she was speaking, she felt the ship shift. Extraordinary as it seemed the ship was being lifted up on the river of tar pouring out of the giant tree trunks.

Magio punched the air and cheered again.

Then she heard Quimbre's voice, their captain who was now taking control of the wheel. 'Forgive old Quimbre, Kiddos. The risk was such that I felt unable to worry you with explanations.'

Eefa felt breathless with astonishment. 'Oh, Quimbre, what is really going on?'

'Look over the rail.'

Eefa did so and was so astonished she closed her eyes in a prolonged blink, then reopened them and looked again to be sure of what she was seeing. There was a river of tar running down over what had previously been the pebbly beach, and it was lapping everywhere about the clinkered hull of the ship, rising to within a few feet of the rails.

She just stared at it with disbelief, watching the black tar paint the entirety of the hull, caulking every seam and joint of its timbers, even as the ship was now beginning to slide back seawards over the pebbles.

'Oh . . . oh, it's a miracle.'

'A miracle engineered by Quimbre,' Magio shouted proudly.

Eefa was dizzy with the awareness that everything was in motion. It was so astonishing to see – to sense and feel. But there was no time for wonder. The wailing of the trees was now as loud as the previous gale winds. When she dared to peer once more over the rail, she saw enormously thick roots, writhing like a seething tangle of snakes, attempting to clamber up the hull. But they were slipping back down because of the lubricating coating of tar.

She took a huge breath.

'I feel sorry for the trees.'

'Spare a thought for the unwitting souls who slept exhausted on that same beach. Their life blood was leached from them by those roots, and their bones have been pounded and ground to provide the pebbles you just trod on.'

'Oh, Quimbre!'

Eefa's head was spinning, even as she had turned to gaze back at that dreadful wall of trees.

Magio's excited voice burst upon her flailing thoughts. 'Never mind thinking about it. This is no time for panicking. We need to let Quimbre concentrate on the wheel, so he can turn us into the wind when we are afloat.'

'What can we do to help him?'

'We can take over the halyard between us – hoist the mainsail.'

The screaming of the trees was deafening, meanwhile the ship was slithering, its old timbers groaning, as it slewed from one side to another. Eefa had to forgo her concerns and simply do what Magio had impressed on her. She put every effort into helping him work the winches that hauled up the heavy mainsail, with them breathless from the effort, and being thrown all about as everything was juddering to and fro.

Then there was a sudden wheeling lurch, ripping their hands from the winches as the ship dipped to a crazy angle, and whirled about like a top.

She could not believe her ears as her crazy brother screeched at the top of his lungs, 'Yeeeeehaaaaah!'

Eefa was thrown against the side rail, where she felt too jarred to dare open her eyes. Then she heard Quimbre shout.

'We did it, Kiddos. It was the craziest of notions – as crazy as that confounded woman will no doubt remind us. But yet it worked.'

Eefa staggered back to her feet and then she gazed about them, where all she could see was the great wide sea, and overhead the twinkles of stars in the inky gloom of night.

'Oh, Quimbre!'

'I know. I know, Kiddos both.'

Eefa hugged Magio, hugged him so hard that she felt she would never again let him go, even if he insisted on shrieking.

'Yeeeeehaaaaah!'

A Frightening Dream

By the second evening after they had fled Tar, an exhausted Eefa clutched at the prow rail of the Scuttlebutt as it cut its furrow through a restless Sea of Stars. She and Magio had slaved in the hold in a bucket-passing passing relay, together with Quimbre and Bird Woman above decks, to get the stinking bilge water out and over the rail. To begin with, it had been as high as Eefa's chest, but now at last the exercise was over. Behind her, as she day-dreamed, the hatches had been opened wide so the hull timbers could finally dry out. The effect on the small ship was reinvigorating. They had doubled their speed, cleaving through the sea with a satisfying bow-wave, and Quimbre had been delighted to furl sail to three-quarters. A relieved Eefa gazed ahead through scattered banks of mists that hung over the waves as if clouds had descended out of the sky. In between mists she glimpsed streamlined shapes leaping and coursing on either side of them, like spirited guardians.

'Oh, my! They're dolphins – dolphins gamboling along with us so wild and free. Oh, you lucky, lucky, dolphins!'

She so felt like joining them. How she would have loved her spirit to gambol wild and free, just like them.

'I wish I could join them.'

But then an alien voice had broken into her thoughts, causing every muscle in her body to tense.

Not so, my dear!

'What? Who are you?'

The dolphins you envy are not coursing by you in delight. They are fleeing in terror to escape a predator that seeks to devour them.

Whose voice was talking to her inside her head? Who was intruding upon her in such an intimate fashion, invading her very thoughts?

But there was no time to think further because Quimbre, in the wheelhouse, was shouting out a warning to Magio, above in the lookout. 'Damn these winds! Damn them to hell! Hey, Magio, keep a ready eye on the horizon! My mariner's instincts tell me that we're drifting off-course.'

Eefa had to gather up what courage she had to focus herself into the here-and-now. She shouted back to Quimbre.

'What's going on?'

'Naught to worry your head about, girl.'

Yet still, his reply just vexed her. 'You were worrying about our direction of travel?'

'What you need to grasp is the fact we're sailing a clinker, and that has its disadvantages but also its advantages. The winds are pushing us off course. But I figure if we ply a crafty zigzag, which is better done in a clinker-built, we can still make slow but steady headway. And hey, Kiddo!' He gave her a thumbs-up. 'Old Quimbre will soon have us headed in the right direction.'

Eefa trusted Quimbre. She returned to the prow to watch, with admiration, how he caused the Scuttlebutt to zigzag, all the while edging southwards. South had been the direction he had chosen after Tar, because of those same piratical instincts. She was impressed by what turned out to be a patient exercise on Quimbre's part in what seemed to her a curious dance with winds and sea.

In the days that followed, the water was increasingly greened by shoals of seaweed that spread far and wide about them. The air remained saturated with mist so they might as well have been sailing through a continuous light shower of rain. There was little that Eefa could contribute to their passage, spending most of her time just observing from the prow. She found herself getting to know Quimbre a little better. Not that he told her much of his piratical background.

It was just another day, like so many before it, with Quimbre's burly shape hunched over the wheel, the usual droplets of condensation glinting in his bearded face. But then, on an occasion when Eefa looked back, she saw that he had left the wheelhouse and was leaning out to peer out over the starboard rail, his graying hair blown about by the winds and a worried expression on his face. A moment or two later, she heard a shout from Magio up in the lookout,

'What is it, Quimbre? Where do you think we're headed?'

Quimbre shouted angrily back, 'Towards the Isle of Mists. That's where we're headed!'

Eefa hurried back to talk to Quimbre. 'You sound worried?'

'We don't want to go there.' He glanced her way, with a slow shake of his head. 'Damn it to hell! We're closer to that eldritch island than I would care to be.'

'Eldritch!' The very thought of something eldritch interested Eefa. 'What's eldritch about the island?'

'Nothing to worry about. I'm sorry I've put such silliness into your head. The Sheeoguers, as your Gran would have called them, haunt that place. As weird a folk as ever populated your Gran's fairytales. And they don't welcome visitors.'

Eefa's eyes widened. 'Sheeoguers!'

Quimbre snorted. 'Witcher folk. The like of which you don't want to meet.'

'But why would they be interested in us? Are they pirates?'

'Nothing so respectable.' Quimbre laughed at the expression on Eefa's face.

Magio, who was ear-wigging this conversation, shouted down excitedly. 'Hey, are they cannibals, Quimbre?'

Quimbre stepped out of the wheelhouse to reply to him. 'I doubt they have any taste for human flesh, or for that matter anything human. But there are rumors aplenty. If half the rumors be true, they're best avoided.'

Eefa's hands gripped the mist-drenched rail beside their captain. 'Oh, Quimbre, now you're scaring me.'

'That's all to the good. Fear is your ally in hostile territory. But not to worry. There's a thing in our favor.'

'What's that?'

'It's not yet morning. And, if the rumors be true, these eldritch creatures don't care for the light of day.'

As Quimbre returned to the wheelhouse, Bird Woman emerged from below decks. She must surely have been listening in to this conversation because she now poked her head into the wheelhouse and pressed Quimbre for more information. 'These beings you speak of, how is it you know so much about these cannibals?'

'As I assured Eefa, they are not cannibals. I've encountered cannibals and have no fear of them. These beings are not so predictable. I doubt they would relish human flesh. If rumor be true, they don't eat the flesh of any animal. The Isle of Mists is abundant in the fruits of tree and shrub, which are more to their taste. More pertinent is the suspicion – nay the certainty – that they detest humans and will not countenance our presence among them. Logic dictates that, since we have nothing to gain from heading there, and everything to gain by not doing so, we should keep well clear of their misbegotten island.'

Eefa shook her head. 'But surely, Quimbre, humans are everywhere in the Sea of Stars. Surely, even if these eldritch folk are so very different to you and me, they must at least be somewhat curious about us?'

Quimbre laughed. 'Mayhaps they already know all they want to know about us.'

Bird Woman frowned. 'You sound as if you know them better than you pretend. Have you ever set foot here?'

'Once. When I was but a rig-monkey, aboard the flagship of my buccaneering father. Those same confusing winds we face today caused us to drift off course. So lost did the fleet become that the water butts ran close to dry. At the same time the worst sandstorm I ever encountered blind-sided us so that we hadn't seen landfall for a month. Desperate situations called for desperate measures. My father put me in charge of a small band, instructed to explore ashore. We hove to in a boat with some empty butts, in what we took to be a minor cove of that eldritch shore. I have never forgotten the experience. I recall to this day every moment of our visit, finding my very instincts immediately overwhelmed by a feeling of threat.'

Magio had come helter-skelter down the mainmast, full of curiosity about what Quimbre was telling them. 'What was it like, Quimbre?'

'Oh, the isle was comely enough to the eye, Kiddo – rich in fruit-laden trees. Aye, to tell you the truth, it was elfin beautiful, with waterfalls that tinkled like crystal so you felt an overwhelming desire to bathe in them and forget your worries.'

Magio laughed aloud. 'Weren't you tempted to help yourself to that fruit?'

'I was so tempted – as were my companions. But my father had given us strict orders not to taste a single rosy-red apple or luscious purple berry. Alas, our orders were clear. We were to load up our barrels with fresh water and get out of there.'

'Oh, Quimbre!'

'From your face, you are guessing the folly of our quest. Of course, we filled our barrels from the first creek we came to. But then when we hurried back to the cove some eldritch force took command of winds and waves, ripping the anchor of our boat out of its mooring and driving it out to sea. We found ourselves trapped, unable to leave the forsaken place.'

'Oh, Jinxy!'

Quimbre bunched his lips. 'Jinxy, indeed! We had no option but to wait there, on the sandy shore, and hope for rescue. But that same eldritch force, controlling winds and wave, thus prevented all efforts at rescuing us.'

'What did you do?'

'What could we do?' Quimbre shook his head. 'Daylight faded to dusk and all we could do was to sit there and shiver in that darkening night, praying for things to change in the morning. That wait was the most terrifying experience in my life. Worse even than the maelstrom that sunk me later. I dread to think of it even now.'

Magio had joined Eefa in sitting on the deck next to the wheelhouse.

'Quimbre – you can't stop there!'

'I can and will.'

'Oh, you have to tell us what happened – you really have to.'

Quimbre's head fell. Eefa could see the distinct lump in his throat as he swallowed. He tightened his grip on the wheel. 'Well, there is something I do recall. It was just as the following night was falling . . .'

'C'mon – c'mon – you've got to tell us!'

'I recall eyes . . . just eyes, all about us, glowing in the dark.'

'Eyes?'

'Eyes – brightly shining eyes, like the reflection on water of the full moon. There were thousands of them, those glowering eyes, all afire with malice in the surrounding dark. They were closing in around us. We couldn't bear to face them. I confess, Kiddo, that I shut my eyes and simply trembled.' Quimbre paused, closing his eyes here and now, as if caught up in the memory. He kept them closed for several moments. 'Any further memory of what happened is lost. I do believe that terror simply blanked it out. All I can tell you is that, as morning broke, the winds and tide did turn, allowing my father to get a boat through to us. We grabbed the water butts and fled from that eldritch nightmare, never to return.'

That night, Eefa tossed and turned in her bunk, half-asleep and half-awake, her imagination fired by Quimbre's tale. She wondered if Quimbre had just been spinning a yarn, much as Gran loved to do back home in Warren. But then she recalled the way his eyes had closed in that prolonged blink and that memory now unsettled Eefa. She thought – no, she was convinced – that Quimbre had been telling them the truth. At the very least, the truth as best he recalled it. Yet there was something in the tale that even Quimbre himself had not appeared to fully grasp. The eldritch folk, whatever they really were, had allowed him and his companions to leave. Not only had they allowed the normal winds and tide to return and thus enable them to escape, but they had even let them escape with their hard-won barrels of fresh water. Why would eldritch folks who were said to be so evil and antagonistic to humans do that?

Lulled by Quimbre's story, Eefa found herself drifting into one of those half-awake dreams she had experienced since earliest childhood, even though a sensible part of her was already warning her that to do so was a mistake. But that same sensible part of her failed to stop the drift of her dream as it wandered from what started out as her memory of the friendly beach at Warren to take her back to the very different and terrifying beach at the tower where they had found respite for the night on that first night of their flight from Warren. And now, against all common sense, she was back there, again, shivering and terrified on that beach with its eerie rock sculptures and circles, the beach where she was tricked into walking into the perilous sea . . . and that lying, alien, voice inside her head insisting that she wade deeper and deeper . . .

You're right to highlight the all-important question in the old salt's story.

'Who are you?'

Please regard me as a friend, Eefa.

'I don't know who you are, or what figment of my imagination, you come from. But I want you out of my mind. Leave me alone.'

The owner of the voice laughed, but it was a gentle laugh. *Let me reassure you, at the very least, that if Quimbre was remembering it true, the guardians of the Isle of Mists were not the evil sheeoguers he alluded to.*

Eefa shook her head. What was she doing, imagining voices inside her head? The situation was ridiculous.

'Stop that! If you genuinely exist, which I very much doubt, then I beg you to stop whispering inside my head.'

Abruptly, Eefa turned over in her half-sleep-half-awake state, and she woke up. She was relieved be awake, pulling her body into a seated posture, then hauling the blanket up to her chin. Her eyes, still sticky with sleep, were blinking owlishly in the dark.

She spoke to herself in a whisper, so as not to wake Magio, or Bird Woman. 'What in the world is happening to me?'

Was it all her fault? Had she brought it on herself? How odd to imagine that some voice from out of the dark would talk to her. Even worse, why would it go to the trouble of explaining events, as if making real something so utterly bizarre? She wished that Quimbre's story had not invaded her dreams. Did the Isle of Mists even exist? Or was the old pirate spinning a yarn because he sincerely believed that, for reasons he couldn't fully explain, they really needed to keep their distance from something else?

Sitting there in the dark, her back against the hard oak timbers of the bunkroom, she felt her throat go bone dry and her heart throb wildly in her chest. She was unable to shake the curious sensation that her thoughts really were being invaded by someone . . . or even some being.

She resisted the urge to clench her eyes tight shut. 'What's going on? Who are you to be talking to me inside my mind? If you really exist – if you are really here in this room with me – then show yourself.'

Where she expected silence, the voice replied, again softly, kindly,

You have confronted the enigma, Eefa. What, really, amounts to truth? Can any one truth be absolutely confined? Or

is truth a confabulation of mere words that enter the ear or some brave intention caught up in a thought? If truly what you are encountering is a lie, what then is the intention of the lie?'

That weird voice inside her head just confused her all the more. Was she awake? Or was she still lost in a bizarre dream?

'I'm no longer certain of anything.'

Abruptly, she was overwhelmed by what felt like the deepest of conviction. In a new dream, if truly it was a dream, her attention was drawn to a lonely figure, seated on what appeared to be a stump of stone. She could make out a man, with long bedraggled graying hair, his head bent. His face was fallen within the cataract of his hair, so she could not see who he might be, only that she was certain it was a man because she could make out an equally bedraggled beard.

But then, equally abruptly, his head lifted. He spoke to her.

Hello, Eefa.

Even as he spoke, she caught a glimpse of his eyes as they gazed through the grey cataract at her. His eyes were shining white.

Those eyes utterly startled Eefa. She realized with shock that they must be the eyes of a blind man. But if so, why were they directed at her? There was an overwhelming feeling that those eyes were aware of all that was happening about him. How calm they appeared, utterly tranquil and unblinking. Eefa was too terrified to continue to look into those eyes. She had to close her own eyes to that remorseless gaze.

She sat bolt upright in her bunk, breathing heavily, her every sense preternaturally alert.

She deliberately closed her eyes.

But even with her eyes clenched shut she could still see that figure, his blind gaze upon her, touching every inch of her skin. There was no chance that she would be able to go back to sleep. She just couldn't shake that image from her mind.

Who was the blind man?

Why in the world was she so magnetically drawn to him, to those blind yet all-seeing eyes, incarcerated in some dark prison, seated on that stump of stone?

GHOSTS

Awake at first light, all aboard the Scuttlebutt were feeling skittish and jumpy, following Quimbre's reminiscences of the Isle of Mists. Magio, his own head in a whirl, was intrigued to hear that Quimbre had also suffered a disturbing night. They were gathered, as usual, around the wheelhouse, allowing Quimbre to navigate while contributing to the conversation. Eefa told them about her strange experiences during the night, anticipating skepticism from the commonsensical Quimbre. But he surprised her by nodding his head regarding her with a thoughtful expression.

Eefa pressed him, 'Do think I'm going crazy?'

'That I most certainly do not. I have a confession of my own. Over the last day or two my own sleep has been somewhat disturbed by nightmares.'

Magio shook his head in sympathy with Quimbre. He knew that he had nightmares involving the tsunami that had sunk his fleet, tormenting him with the screams of injured and drowning sailors that had been his companions. But today Quimbre, bunching his cheeks in the way he did when embarrassed, confessed that his recent nightmares had been different from his usual.

'I will admit that I'm beginning to wonder if this ancient brig is haunted.'

'What in the world are you prattling about?' An angry Bird Woman shook her head at Quimbre. 'You were surely in your cups on that hooch you've been hiding.'

Quimbre bristled. 'I was not drunk. I declare, Woman, that when you were nice and comfortable in your bunk during the night, I saw what looked like a ghost in the shadows of the foredeck.'

Magio found himself laughing in wonderment at this heated conversation between Bird Woman and Quimbre. But, later that same night, when he was hunkering down in his bunk, he found sleep difficult to come by. It was as if the disquiet among them was catching. He pulled his blanket tighter around his throat, to protect himself from the wind that was now sweeping through the cabin from the colder southern waters they were sailing through. There appeared to be a shift in the weather. A squall had blown up, hardly enough to call it a storm, but it was enough, added to that bad-tempered debate between Bird Woman and Quimbre, to keep him fitfully awake. After an hour or two, tossing and turning, he decided to take his blanket from his bunk and go join Quimbre in the wheelhouse.

'Hey, Kiddo, what's up?' Quimbre was smoking his pipe, in the light of a single lantern, and he had a glass of amber liquid at his side.

Magio hesitated. He knew Quimbre well enough to suspect that something was still bothering their Captain, even as he also knew him well enough to think there would be no further explanation. Magio made himself comfortable sitting on the small cupboard beside the entrance, wrapping himself up in the blanket. Quimbre eyed him thoughtfully, meanwhile asked him to take the wheel while he stepped out to the rail to tap the embers from his pipe.

'You know, a thought occurs to me, Kiddo – but it's one we should keep to ourselves for the moment so as not to worry your sister.'

'What's that?'

'Well, let me say this much. What Eefa describes are nightmares of a kind? Do you agree?'

'Yeah, I do.'

'Well, if so, these nightmares have only come about since we sailed close by the Isle of Mists.'

Magio held the wheel steady while gazing at the shadowy bulk of Quimbre, now leaning out over the rail, his features limned by starlight.

'You know me. I'm a simple mariner. A man who trusts his instincts more than his eyes and ears. And now those same instincts tell me that, when we passed so close by that accursed place, something came aboard.'

'Hey! What do you mean?'

Quimbre nodded, tamping fresh tobacco into his pipe.

'You think something came aboard from the Isle of Mists . . . something eldritch?'

Quimbre took a few puffs, to get the pipe alight, then exhaled sharply. 'Problem is, I don't rightly know what manner of wight might have crept in while we slept, or for that matter, why it might have come aboard.'

Shivering in the cold night air, Magio hunched his shoulders tighter together under the blanket. 'What is it, Quimbre? What are you thinking?'

'What am I thinking?' Quimbre took back control of the wheel. 'Well now, I will admit that I have a notion, Kiddo. One that lingers in my mind, like a shadow.'

Magio was finding it hard to breathe. 'What kind of a notion?'

'Methinks something eldritch has come aboard this ship. We harbor a thief – or mayhaps even a ghost.'

'A ghost?'

'I know full well that it is easy in the dark for specters to arise from a fevered imagination. Pah! I am Quimbre, son of Baccal. I ask myself if I, son of Baccal, have grown fearful of the superstitions common to simple mariners, those very notions my father would have laughed at.'

'You are your father's son, Quimbre. You survived the sinking of your fleet. You even survived the Isle of Mists.'

'Thanks for reminding me.'

'You don't believe in ghosts any more than your father did.'

'No, I don't.'

'So why are we talking about them?'

'Why?' Quimbre suddenly exploded into laughter. 'It brings to mind a shanty the crew would sing as they hauled through the worst of storms. It concerns the lonely sailor whose heart was broken by a love untrue . . .

Quimbre sang the shanty, slapping the wheel in time to its rhythm,

'Ne'er mind the specters that torment your sleep
Ne'er mind the horrors of the ocean deep.
Pay heed in your heart to the dreams of your sleep
Be afeared of the doe-eyed lover's deceit'

Magio clapped his hands and laughed aloud at Quimbre's hearty singing. 'But no-one's heart has been broken here, Quimbre.'

Quimbre bellowed a laugh himself. 'True enough. But I have a bit of a confession to make.'

'What sort of a confession?'

'A small one – my secret, you might say. It's a prize I've kept from that inquisitive witch who is ever poking her nose into a man's business.'

'Bird Woman!'

'You've hit that nail on the head.'

'Come on, Quimbre. You've got to tell me. What's your secret?'

'A discovery I made in my inspection of the mess of wrecks that had foundered on the Beach of Bones. It was in a cupboard of some old Captain's quarters, in what was left of some fancy galleon.'

'Hey – what did you find?'

'An unopened cask of brandy.'

'Brandy?'

'I'm no ordinary tar, lad, to be sated with grog. I'm a Captain. The captain's table bears a goodsome selection of comforts.'

'I bet you were pleased.'

'Cock-a-hoop, more like. All the more so since in the same ruined quarters, I also found a tin of baccy. Let me tell you, Kiddo, that captain of old, aboard his fancy galleon – he knew how to keep up his spirits on a voyage.'

'Can I taste it?'

'Well, it's not intended for the palates of rig-monkeys. But maybe, with a little added water, you might.' Quimbre went and poured Magio a small glass, watered it, then handed it to him, and held out his own glass.

'Let us celebrate that unknown captain's foresight.'

They clinked glasses.

Magio was still laughing aloud, as Quimbre ruffled his hair.

'Where did you hide it?'

'Stashed under my bunk, nice and convenient for those sleepless nights spent keeping this old brig afloat.'

Magio wasn't altogether surprised at Quimbre's story. It was exactly the sort of thing he would do. 'Wow, it's fiery stuff, this brandy. But what has this to do with ghosts coming aboard?'

'Well, now! A seasoned salt pays attention to his hoard. Thus, when I found the cask no longer quite as I left it, I marked the level. This I did no more than a night back. And all too soon I found it down by a finger's width. So, as you might imagine, my suspicions were duly raised.'

'So – it had to be a thief among us?'

'A thief is more likely than ghosts in the night.'

'Because ghosts don't drink brandy?'

'Enough of such talk for now. Go back to your bunk, Magio – get some rest. I'm a trifle tired of this endless watch. If the weather holds fair, you'll have to replace me at first light. Are you up to that?'

'I am.'

Quimbre patted his head. 'Good lad.'

'Good night, Quimbre.'

Magio left the wheelhouse, clutching the deck rail to steady himself as a sudden squall heaved the Scuttlebutt to port. He waited, eyes closed, for it to right itself, meanwhile shaking his head with amusement at the game that was now afoot. If he knew Quimbre, he would have marked the level in that cask anew after Magio had left.

Like Quimbre and Magio, Eefa was a victim of sleeplessness. She had lain on her bunk listening to the conversation between Quimbre and Magio, whose voices must surely have carried to everyone on board. Eefa suspected that

Bird Woman would also have overheard them, and she would not be pleased by Quimbre's comments about some ghost on board who had been helping itself to his precious brandy. While Eefa couldn't help laughing at the thought of Quimbre hoarding his brandy, she found herself wondering about Quimbre and his father dismissing the notion of ghosts.

'You might not be so sure, Quimbre,' she whispered, 'if you shared my dreams.'

A dream shared is a fear halved.

'Who spoke? Who said that?'

A friend – if you will allow a friend to share your burden.

This was a different voice than that of the imprisoned blind man. It seemed altogether a friendlier voice.

'Are you Quimbre's ghost come to haunt me?

The voice laughed. *I assure you that I am no ghost.*

Did ghosts laugh? Eefa supposed that, perhaps, they did. She wondered if the ghost was somehow a figment of her own imagination.

You cannot sleep?

'I daren't sleep. I don't want to dream. I couldn't bear to see the blind man again in that terrible place.'

The one you fear is not your enemy. On the contrary, his aim is to thwart your fate. Be careful, Eefa, to distinguish friend from foe.

'Who are you? How do you know my dream?'

Eefa shook her head at yet another enigma, suddenly coming to haunt her. She sat bolt upright in her bunk. 'What does it all mean? Oh, I must talk to Bird Woman.'

At that moment she heard a rustling sound underneath her bunk that caused her eyes to widen and her heartbeat to rise into her throat.

Eefa leapt out of her bunk and she grabbed the oil lamp dangling from its hook on the post. Then, lighting it with the flint box, she peered into the dark space under the bunk. There was something strange there, skulking in a corner. She reached in and grabbed hold of it, hauling it out into the light. It was a worn old leather boot, like those she imagined the pirates wore in Gran's fairytales. The calf of the boot was curled over, so it looked like it had two wrinkly ears. Eefa was about to throw it back under the bunk when two huge green eyes blinked at her, from within the space between the ears.

'Eeek!'

She dropped the thing, with her heartbeat throbbing right up into her skull. She dived back under her blanket, her eyes clenched shut, gasping for breath. She clenched herself into a tight ball within the blanket, too terrified to move until she could see through the fabric of the blanket that dawn had broken. Only then, hearing Quimbre's heavy tread on the boards above, did she uncoil herself and peer out from under the blanket, and even more slowly emerge once more from hiding to dash a lightning-fast squint under her bunk.

The space was empty.

Flopping onto her pillow, she wondered if she had really dreamt it all, the boot, the whispering voice, that disquieting mind-to-mind conversation. She couldn't help but peer more confidently down under the bunk again, confirming the emptiness. It occurred to her to more closely examine the accumulated dust to see if there was the slightest impression to confirm that the boot had truly been there. But she found nothing.

Was it possible she had imagined it all?

Eefa refused to believe it.

Sitting up with her back against the wall behind her bunk, her head pressed against the rough oak planking of the hull, she listened to the neverending buffeting and pounding of winds and waves.

Voices inside her head! And now a boot under her bunk! A pirate's boot with ears and two huge green eyes between them!

Boots didn't have ears or eyes. She remembered what she saw with the utmost clarity. In that lucid memory there was a growing conviction that the boot was not a thing sprouted from her wild imagination. It had certainly looked like a boot but it surely was no such thing at all. Eefa was beginning to think that the Quimbre's, father and son, were mistaken. Perhaps ghosts existed after all.

THE WASTES OF DROMENON

In the stygian darkness of Dromenon, the Lady of the Shore searches for the faintest residue of forces that might betray a hidden power of magic. So minuscule is her being against the gargantuan emptiness that it seems, at any moment, that the enfolding darkness must engulf her. Her quest is endless and wearying, penetrating manifold veils of enchantment, yet all the while her persistence endures until, at last she senses the focus of her search. Here, she dares to speak, employing a tongue unknown to any but the few, opening the possibility of a conversation mind-to-mind.

I have come to find you, and if my search proves fruitful, to comfort you – though the pain you have been obliged to endure will have taken its toll on your spirit.

She waits in silence for the faintest stirring.

What appears startles her. An inner sense of danger causes her to wheel around to be confronted by a kneeling creature, whose arms are crossed upon its breast and whose face, under a cobwebby veil, is coldly indifferent. The face might possibly be female, but the Lady is unsure. The eyes that confront her are mirrors, shrouded in a heavy veil.

Her courage falters.

She has not entirely recovered from her ordeal on the Beach of Bones and is now in danger of losing what strength of spirit she had gathered. It was ever her nature to rush into things where wisdom would suggest caution. Emotion was her undoing. This surely is a moment when she thinks it prudent to take a deep breath, to hesitate, close her eyes and recover her composure.

She opens her eyes again to gaze directly into those silver mirrors of eyes.

Who are you?

I am a Keeper of Night and Day.

The reply, in an icy cold but perfectly lucid voice, astonishes the Lady of the Shore.

Why are you here?

I am empowered to observe the fate of the one imprisoned here. Yet such is my role, I am not permitted to interfere.

What then is the purpose of your observation?

We Keepers observe the evolution of worlds. As part of that compact, it is our purpose to observe significant beginnings and endings.

The Lady of the Shore is becoming frustrated by this conversation, yet her instincts bid her think hard before asking another question.

I believe that, like you, I know the identity of the one who is imprisoned here. We both know what power of malice saw fit to imprison her, and more importantly, why.

My Lady, I can neither confirm nor deny your beliefs.

That reply confirms the suspicion of the Lady of the Shore.

It was surely the one who so brutally tormented me?

The Keeper is silent.

Why, then, are you really here in this moment? What change are you observing?

I am currently observing your intrusion here. You have not come here by chance. Your search of Dromenon in itself signals an evolution. My role is merely to observe.

The Lady stiffens. *How do I know that your presence here is not subservient to that monster?*

The Keepers of Night and Day obey no master.

The Lady of the Shore is forced to step back in the void, baffled as to the meaning of this encounter. The ease of conversation seems odd considering the strangeness of the meeting. At the same time, she feels close to panic with the figure's recognition of who she is. Panic is unhelpful to her purpose here.

It surely is a moment to pause, to suppress her rising anger, her very bewilderment at this meeting. Despite its denials, the Keeper must have met her here for some purpose. She must regather her self control. She must think beyond the words – use her instincts to sense the purpose – think, think . . . She recalled those words: *As part of that compact, it is our purpose to observe significant beginnings and endings.*

Beginnings . . .

The lady, coldly, realizes the importance of what they are doing. In a flash, she searches the surrounding emptiness with every instinct raised to their highest levels . . . until . . . until she becomes aware of a new presence rippling through her being.

We are not alone here, Keeper, you and I.

The Keeper stiffens at her warning.

Who are you? What dread presence have I discovered? Aaarrrrrggghhhh!

The exclamation is followed by a cackling peal of laughter.

The Lady opens up her every sense, in an attempt to discover the source of the laughter. There is a shaded figure nearby, a figure cloaked with veils of darkness, but this is no Keeper.

Who – or what – are you?

The figure cackles again, poking her in the ribs and muttering to herself, in a voice that sounds like the shoveling of gravel into a pit.

You would know me as a raven.

The reply, lost in another cackle of laughter, sounds vaguely familiar. It rings a bell, a memory lost in the distant reaches of her memories.

Keeper – please assist me. Who is this strange presence?

Her name is one you should fear – it is Mórígán.

She recalls it now. The fell goddess who gathered the souls of the dead on the battlefield.

She remembers stories – tales of war from another world, an ancient history in the cosmos of magic.

How did you come to be condemned thus?

The figure snarls, then abruptly turns her focus on the Lady, openly confronting her. The Lady glimpses a seething restless energy in the heavily lined brow, and at the same time she witnesses those eyes clearly for the first time. They have neither white nor iris, but are all black, liquidly glistening, and as fierce as an eagle's. The Lady's gaze falls from those eyes to the voluminous rags of her dress, which shifts as if something quick and horribly alive is living there, a ferment in which minuscule limbs and jaws writhe and gambol.

The Lady's heart hammers against the cage of her chest as she realizes the true nature of the dress. It is woven from cobwebs. The diamond lights that scrabble and twinkle in its lacy depths are the eyes of the spiders spinning the weave.

Great One – I know you now. Yet still, our meeting is vital to both you and to me. I must know – why are you here?

Foolish Lady – beloved of the shore – but think you twice before tormenting me.

She cannot speak. It takes several moments for her palpitating heart to settle, her mind to rise above the anguish of her need.

I have no intention of tormenting you. I would rather free you if it were in my power to do so.

She is confronted by silence.

She is obliged to think again, to think long and hard, harder than she has ever thought in her troubled existence. Then, her heart pounding once again against her ribs, her jaw stiffened with dread, she calls out again,

I beg you, even though I could not begin to know what torment you have endured, if you still harbor hope – if even a mote of your spirit yet endures – give me a sign.

She waits again, in the nothingness for a reply. There is a protracted silence in which her fears multiply. She waits for what seems ages . . . But this is too important an occasion to abandon it through impatience . . . She tries a final time, even as the torment of waiting has exhausted her optimism, and it becomes increasingly difficult to keep the light of her being aglow beyond a silvery ember, all but extinguished by the enveloping darkness.

I can wait no longer . . . if this fails . . . I know that the monster who so hurt me has found a way to destroy your heart.

The Lady of the Shore hears the familiar clanking of rusting chains in fathomless Dromenon. If what she senses is truly a response, it is something other than an answering word. What then? An inhalation? An inhalation followed by the hushed release of a single breath that lasts no more than a moment, and yet as she senses it, she knows there is a harkening mind still there.

Who . . . who are you? Has my tormentor returned in another guise?

I am not your tormentor. I was another of his prey.

Liar! Trickster! You are ten times as duplicitous as Loki.

I was his wife.

There is a pause, in which her heartbeat rises to a crescendo.

Do you truly possess the power to free me?

Not alone. But it might yet be possible through our working together. I would take your plight to the Council of the Dragons of Aeonia.

The Dragons – they would do this for me?

They have done as much for me.

Who are you – a minor deity who claims understanding of the Lore of Dragons?

I know that accursed usurper better than most. I am one who has escaped his wrath. I would know why he would subject you to a fate even worse than my own. Are you one of his many lovers?

How gratuitously you offend me.

If not a lover, what reason could he have to so torment you?

What reason? The voice of Mórígán breaks into a thunder of laughter. *He tormented you through hatred. He torments me through envy.*

He envies you?

He envies my power over death.

Then I would earnestly implore you to let us work together to stop him.

What could I do, entrapped as I am?

All I ask is that you search your memories for some tidbit of knowledge. A secret that might appear trivial to you, but perhaps not trivial to me.

Would you confront me with trickery?

There is no trickery. I solemnly promise that I shall use that knowledge to set him back.

What secret do you seek?

Give me something – a single weakness I can explore in order to confound his ambitions.

A new silence grows monumental between them. But the Lady of the Shore has grown accustomed to patience. She waits in the infinite void of Dromenon for an answer. At last, the answer comes, in a voice husky with bitterness:

I know of only a single secret – one that is of the least importance to me – yet might be of some use to you . . .

What is it? Tell me.

The one you consider dearest – the same one he most fears – yet lives.

A Spy in their Midst

It was Eefa, only barely awake, who first heard the howling. Waking her from sleep, she followed the sound to emerge from her cabin as the first light of dawn was breaking over the Scuttlebutt. Peering about the deck, she discovered that the bizarre caterwauling was coming from a small cupboard where they kept the rags to swab the deck. Consumed with curiosity, she twisted the iron latch to open the cupboard door only to jump back with a screech.

'Eeeeek!'

Blinking in shock, she was confronted by a melee of body and limbs within the gloom, everything looking impossibly jumbled up, with a contorted face that was covered with wrinkles and folds of skin. She watched, panic-stricken, as long, tapering fingers and toes appeared to pop out of the misshapen mess, the bits and pieces extricating themselves by degrees from the awkward jumble, like a spider reassembling itself out of a hidey-hole. Then a man-like body emerged from a space so cramped that it should never have accommodated it. With her hands clapped to her mouth, Eefa saw the gradual unwrinkling of the face to be confronted by those same green eyes she recalled from the scary apparition under her bunk. The creature was panting for breath, with those eyes as wide as a cornered deer. Then she spotted the cask of brandy in one of those long-fingered hands.

Eefa shrieked and tried to slam shut the cupboard door.

But the creature started howling again.

She saw that she had trapped one of those long fingers in the door, which she promptly released before taking several steps back.

'Oh!'

Then her heart thudded with fright as the creature spoke to her. 'Please do not blame yourself, dearest lady. The fault is entirely my own.'

'Whaaaat?'

The creature drew itself erect, groaning all the while, until it loomed above her, a good foot and a half taller than Eefa. It now revealed itself to resemble a man, albeit a very tall man, with an olive complexion and skin that was as smooth as ivory. He blinked his eyes several times, as if getting used to the light, before addressing her again.

'Might we, somehow, begin afresh?'

Immediately she recognized the voice. It was the second of the two that had invaded her thoughts the evening before, the gentler, more reassuring voice.

'Who – or should I say, what – are you?'

'A thousand apologies for so startling you. For such an unwanted intrusion, I most humbly beg your pardon.'

Eefa backed away towards the wheelhouse in a growing panic as the stranger continued to straighten bits and wrinkles of himself. From behind her she was relieved to hear Quimbre's approaching roar, 'Get back from the goblin, Eefa. And look at what we have here. Is that my missing cask I spot in its paw? The thieving monster – that's who's been helping himself to my brandy.'

'I am no goblin, good Captain. Wychera Gallant is my name. Readily do I plead guilty to a swig or two of that excellent hooch. I stand before you, good Sir, contrite and ready to earn my keep.'

'I'll give you a lesson in contrition, you scoundrel.' Quimbre tore the cask out of the stranger's hand, meanwhile reaching for his cutlass.

'Hold on, there.' Bird Woman, who had been attracted to the tumult, stayed Quimbre's sword arm. 'I think we need to know more of what is going on. Who the devil do we have here? And how in the world did he come aboard?'

'Surely you folks will have heard of Wychera Gallant – adventurer and soldier of fortune? Now at the ready of your most gracious service.'

Quimbre snorted. 'No, we most certainly have not heard of you. What we have here is a thief – aye, and what would also appear a braggart and liar.'

Eefa exclaimed, 'You frightened the very life out of me, coming out of that cupboard. And now I suspect you've been aboard the Scuttlebutt for several days.'

'Aye!' Quimbre roared. 'He's somehow sneaked on board under the cover of those mists when we were perilously close to that accursed isle.'

Eefa's eyes widened, staring with open curiosity at the stranger.

'Oh, I admit it. But you see before you no ghoul or goblin – but merely a doughty adventurer, offering his experience in your good service.'

Bird Woman was now eyeing the stranger with a puzzled frown. 'Wychera Gallant, you say is your name. But you're not human. No human would be capable of contorting his body to fit into that cupboard.'

'More like a goblin Tricky-the-Loop,' Quimbre growled.

'Tricky-the-Loop – that's hardly fair.'

'Hmmm!' Bird Woman was now examining the stranger more closely. 'Judging by those ears, you're at least part elf.'

'An elf!' Eefa studied the stranger with a renewed astonishment.

Bird Woman nodded. 'Yes! It would appear that an elf has spirited himself on board the Scuttlebutt.'

'Aye – and the question now is why?' Quimbre was pacing to and fro before the tall stranger. 'To what fell purpose would an elf sneak aboard my ship?'

It was all so very astonishing that Eefa couldn't help studying the stranger from head to toe. 'Are all elves able to contort their bodies like that?'

Those green eyes were confronting Eefa's again.

Bird Woman nodded. 'You're absolutely right, Eefa. An ordinary elf wouldn't be capable of such contortions. But an elfin changer would.'

Quimbre's hand tightened once more on his cutlass. 'Hah – I knew it. A weirdling among us, bred to lie with every fiber of his being.'

'Let's not be too hasty.' Wychera Gallant lifted his gangly head aloft.

Bird Woman once again put her hand on Quimbre's arm. 'This is a new situation – one that must be closely examined. Let us examine the facts. A stranger has mysteriously boarded our ship. He claims to be an adventurer. Now we see that he is not merely an elf, but also an elfin changer. Changers are themselves exceedingly rare, if the folk tales are anything to go by. But I have never heard of an elfin changer.'

'Wow – britzy!' An excited Magio had joined the discussion and was gazing at that gangly head. 'Hey! Are you really an adventurer?'

'Adventurer and warrior! Wychera Gallant at your service, young Sir.'

'Wow – britzy!'

The stranger bowed to Magio, with a flourish.

Right then a scary new thought occurred to Eefa. Was the elfin changer, or whatever he really was, capable of changing his appearance to look like a pirate's boot?

The possibility made her feel distinctly queasy.

The changer was now grinning at Magio. 'You demand to know if I truly am what I claim to be. You see before you Wychera Gallant – famed throughout the Sea of Stars, come to join this intrepid company and readily equipped for such a quest.'

'What quest?'

Quimbre waved back Magio with a hand that was still clutching his cask. 'What I see is a skulking thief, drunk on my brandy.'

'While I cannot deny the charge, good Captain, I beg you – just think it through. Why would I come among you? You, who are presently engaged in a desperate flight to goodness-only-knows-where. We meet through happenstance. Yet my experience of adventure, far and wide, would surely prove useful in such circumstances.'

This elicited a confusion of glances among the company.

Quimbre laughed, disdainfully waving his cutlass in the changer's face. 'Will you deny that you came aboard from that accursed isle?'

'Why would I deny it? My wandering nature did lead me there – but through nothing more than morbid curiosity.'

'You liar! Who, in his right mind, would visit the abode of monsters out of curiosity?'

'An adventurer, Captain Quimbre. But, I admit, it was a somewhat foolish endeavor. However idiotic in retrospect, does not the very fact I managed to escape that lair stir the curiosity of each and every one of you?'

'Hey, what did you find there?' Magio's eyes round with excitement.

'What I discovered there, young Sir, was a veritable nightmare made flesh.'

Quimbre sneered. 'Over the side with you, you lying scoundrel. You can go spin your yarns to the fishes.'

Wychera Gallant fell to his knees, yet he was still so tall that this brought his face on a level with those of the twins. 'By my troth, I have spoken the honest truth. But you might like to know that before we were done with one another, the Isle of Mists was glad to be rid of me.'

Magio was all the more spellbound. 'Oh, britzy! Tell us more.'

Eefa piped up, 'Quimbre once escaped from there too.'

'Ah! Then the wonder is we both lived to tell the tale.' Wychera laughed. 'And as for you, Madam – had it not been for you releasing me from that ill-chosen cupboard, I would, in all likelihood, have ended up jettisoned with the bilge.'

Quimbre was unimpressed. 'You're a charlatan – but one who is clever with words. We both know that you're just hiding the fact that you're a thief.'

'I have already pleaded guilty to the charge, good Captain. I offer my earnest apologies. But, what can one expect of a desperate warrior who comes across a cask of good brandy? In recompense to you, and to all of the present company, I now offer my protection drawn from a lifetime's experience of adventuring.'

Bird Woman intruded into the conversation, shaking her head. 'Quimbre is right to be suspicious of you, Wychera

Gallant. From what little I know about changers, they're not to be trusted.'

The changer plucked a wide-brimmed green felt hat from the thin air. It had a broken purple feather poking out from its ribbon, and now the same crumpled hat was swept before them, in a flamboyant salute.

'To present company I must appear somewhat eccentric.'

'More like dissolute,' Bird Woman retorted. 'You hide deception in a cloak of eccentricity. How can we believe a word you say?'

'My dearest lady. . .'

'I'm not your lady, Mister Gallant. Quimbre is right. You have all of the hallmarks of a trickster, and more. Admit it, Sir – you are an elfin changer.'

'Madam – you are perceptive.' With a flourish, the stowaway brought the hat down over his head, as if to conceal the pointed ears, then contemplated Bird Woman with a dimpled grin. 'I, Wychera Gallant, do so acknowledge my kinship.'

'Well then, I think I am speaking for the entire company when I demand a more honest explanation of your arrival here.'

Those eyes opened wide as saucers. 'My dearest madam – if I might address all of present company – such an explanation would take more time than you might think.'

'Indulge me.'

Gallant laughed, opening wide a mouth of perfect white teeth. 'You would really demand to hear all? I would struggle even to begin.'

Eefa, who had recovered herself enough to confront the changer again, stared with open curiosity into those green eyes. 'Magio and I, we have never met an elf before. And now we find that you are not merely an elf, but some kind of elfin changer? What in the world does that mean? Oh, for goodness sakes, can you even change into a bird or a fish?'

Wychera Gallant hooted with laughter. 'Eefa – if I might speak honestly to both you and Magio – do you not both share my undying curiosity to discover all that is wonderful in this entire world?'

Magio piped up, 'Oh, yes – we do.'

'Well, then! What better adventure than to join such splendid company in sailing the Sea of Stars aboard the jolly Scuttlebutt.'

With an impatient grunt, Quimbre put himself between the twins and Gallant, his cutlass fully drawn. 'Stop this tomfoolery at once.'

'Consider it stopped entirely, good Captain. I confess. I am, as the good lady said of me, a changer – and of the elder blood. I make neither apology nor denial.'

Quimbre's jaws clenched, his posture adopting a fighting stance.

But Bird Woman once again stayed him. She peered very closely at the changer, inspecting his face, his eyes, his teeth, the very nature of the skin in the webs between his fingers. Finally, she withdrew from her examination and nodded.

'I believe he has told us the truth. He truly is both elf and changer.'

Wychera Gallant heaved a sigh. 'Thus did the specters on that accursed isle confirm. In truth, they were only too delighted to be rid of my company.'

'Pah!' Quimbre was more furious than ever. 'A changer does not arrive among us by chance. We need to know why you're here.' He pressed Gallant with the curve of the cutlass pressed against that overly long neck. 'Someone has assuredly sent you to spy on us. Who sent you? What the devil are you really up to?'

Bird Woman nodded. 'I agree with Quimbre. Wychera Gallant – will you admit that you were ordered by the inhabitants of the Isle of Mists to spy on us?'

Wychera Gallant laughed. 'You so little understand.'

Bird Woman pressed him. 'Will you now admit you came among us with a purpose? Did those ghouls torment you, to make you serve them?' Bird Woman closed her eyes, breathing deeply. When she reopened them again, she asked, quietly but insistently, 'You really must admit it.'

Wychera Gallant shrugged his shoulders. 'Very well – I admit it. The truth is that I was sent by them to spy on you. I was to insinuate myself through being useful to your company. I was to pretend to help you, all the while actually spying for those beings of evil, whose every intention is to roast you in a big black pot and eat you.'

Quimbre hissed through clenched teeth, 'Liar! I shall do you a favor by ending your miserable existence.'

'You are mistaken in that word, miserable. I am by nature given to joy. I see the humor in all that is about me. I even attempt humor, though it is my fate to be the worst comedian in all of Tìr.'

'I would find amusement in slitting your throat.'

'Go ahead, then. Test my mettle. See if you can put a scratch on me with that oafish excuse for a blade.'

An alarmed Bird Woman put her hand on Quimbre's forearm. 'Restrain your anger. An elfin changer might prove dangerous in combat. Besides, I am curious to know more. If Wychera Gallant was tasked by anyone to spy on our every move, we need to know who they were and why they were so interested in us.'

Quimbre was not convinced.

But it was Eefa who now held Quimbre's hand. 'Stop this, both of you! There's a question Wychera needs to answer – one that puzzles me.'

Quimbre looked askance at her.

'What I want to know,' she confronted Gallant, 'is what is really going on here. I sense that you are not evil. When you spoke to me in my dreams your voice was kind. Please tell me the truth. Who are these enemies who hounded us back on Moon? Why are they still so desperate to kill us?' Eefa's eyes confronted Wychera's open-eyed stare.

'I confess that I truly do not know.'

Bird Woman confronted the changer, eye to eye. 'You are a very tricky and likely dangerous being. Consider the fact that you have now been exposed. What would your controllers do to you if they discovered that you failed them?'

His eyes widened in their sockets. 'I confess that I would rather not contemplate that fate.'

'So, let's forgo the lies and get to the truth. Will you answer me so now?'

'Madam – you are right. I am no liar by nature. Thus am I glad to confess that all I have so far told you has been a litany of lies. But I did so on instruction not from your enemies but from those who care for you – being instructed that the truth was even more worrisome for you to contemplate. Now, having failed to convince you of such lies, it will likely be even more difficult to persuade you with the true purpose of my arrival among you.'

Quimbre roared, 'I wouldn't trust you any more if your very life depended on it. I would be doing you a favor to draw my cutlass across your throat.'

Wychera Gallant ignored Quimbre and his threat. Instead, he gazed first at Eefa, and from her to her brother Magio.

'My dear Eefa and Magio, you have long wondered what it is all about. Why were you hunted for your very lives back on Moon? Let me then tell that your true enemy back there on Moon was the same enemy who is now hunting you upon the Sea of Stars. She is an inhuman monster in command of an Ursascogan army, which is already at sea with the express purpose of destroying the human hegemony in these islands.'

Quimbre harrumphed. 'Don't make me laugh – those brutes declaring war on humans!'

'Brutes you call them, yet they are more learned of nature, aye, and some of the minor lores of magic, than any human.'

Bird Woman interrupted their argument. 'What you say seems altogether implausible. Why in the world would the Ursascogans declare war on humans?'

'They are misled, in mind and spirit, by the same she-devil who sought to kill the twins back on the Isle of Moon. She calls herself Lustfera, the Star of Mourning. It was she who hired the hunter with the wolf hounds, who was so determined to kill you.'

Bird Woman fell back, her eyes blinking rapidly, as if not only assimilating his words, but considering their significance in relation to their present situation.

'But why in the world. . .? There must surely be a reason. Why has this monster chosen the twins as her arch enemy?'

'She is the servant of an undying. The same undying that imprisoned your beloved Lady on the Beach of Bones.'

'Oh, merciful heavens!'

'Madam, I hear fear in your voice. I earnestly hope you are afraid. The forces against you are formidable. I – Wychera Gallant – am not your enemy. I am sworn to protect the twins, and will continue to do so with all of my heart and soul. I would henceforth be honored to join the purpose of this company without need of coercion. I was born for adventure. And, if my instincts serve me right, no greater adventure has ever confronted me.'

Wychera looked from one face to another, until his eyes had met those of the entire company. All were astounded by his words.

Quimbre snorted. 'How can we believe a word this freak of nature says?'

With a movement so fast, Eefa witnessed no more than a blur, a rapier appeared in the changer's hand, and, with the same lightning speed, its point traced a pictograph of the same silvery light as lightning in the air above them. Bird Woman's hand stayed Quimbre's cutlass with alarm,

'Hold your cutlass. He speaks the truth.'

'What is it, Woman?'

'The sigil he chased with the point of his blade – it is the symbol of Aeonia.'

'Aeonia!' Magio squealed with excitement. 'Gran used to tell us tales of Aeonia.'

'Yes, Magio.' Bird Woman nodded. 'I'm sure that she did.'

Eefa squealed with excitement. 'Aeonia – the fabled world of dragons.'

Quimbre exchanged a look of exasperated bewilderment with Bird Woman. As he did so, Wychera heaved a great sigh, then snatched the brandy cask from Quimbre's startled hand, and, ignoring his howl of protest, spat out the cork and took an almighty swig.

'Forgive me, brave Captain. I have indeed spoken truthfully. I am Eefa's and Magio's guardian and will fight to the death to keep them safe. But I cannot deny that we face odds that even the most wide-eyed optimist might baulk at. Hence, I find myself in need of solace, being aware of the fate of optimists in this world.'

A Sleepless Night

That night Eefa was so caught up in a mixture of excitement and fear that she knew there would be no comfort in a proper sleep. She was curled up in the prow of Scuttlebutt, her knees hunched up to her chest and chin cupped in her hands. A cool breeze was lulling her into a doze when she found herself in another of those familiar awake-dream states where she was playing a game in which she was no longer in control of her own self, meanwhile some unknown force plotted her every move. It felt exciting, if also frightening, as if the game really meant something. Suddenly, she woke to find a disquieted Woll flitting about her like a maddened firefly.

Eefa climbed to her feet, wiping the sleepiness from her eyes, and taking a deep breath. She knew she should head for her bunk. But it was difficult to escape from the dreamy state. Grasping the rail, she took a deep breath, then wiped her spray-soaked hands over her face in an attempt to fully wake up.

'Woll – oh, Woll!'

I am still here, Eefa.

'Help me – help me. I feel so anxious I can hardly breathe.'

Calm yourself. Take slow breaths. Panic is never helpful.

'I'll try.'

Eefa – I know what is alarming you. In spite of your reservations, you must put aside your shock at discovering the changer, Wychera Gallant, on board.

'Did you already know he was here? I see from your stillness that you did. Oh, Woll! Is there something you're not telling me? Did you expect his arrival?'

No! I assure you that I did not anticipate his arrival.

Now she found herself unsure if Woll was telling her the truth. The changer's arrival among them had been such a shock. What was really going on?

'I thought that you see and hear everything. You must have spotted his presence among us even before we knew it. So why didn't you warn us?'

Woll was very still, clearly apprehensive.

Dearest Eefa, it is easy to become dismayed when one is aware of the unfriendly forces that surround us. But we must all stay calm.

Eefa cupped her face in her trembling hands and rocked her body within the triangle of the prow. 'That isn't easy to do.'

No – it isn't!

Eefa heard the sigh of the frost sprite queen, like the faintest curl of music in a dying swirl of wind. *Oh, dear! Perhaps it is time you were educated in matters you might never have given a moment's thought to.*

Her heartbeat rose. 'What matters?'

In sailing the Sea of Stars, we have entered a world where normal logic must be abandoned. In these waters, experienced sailors, the likes of Quimbre, are long used to the unpredictable threats of current, wind and storm. Generations beyond count have endured that same unpredictability, a whim of the weather capable to destroying everything out of the blue. The islanders who inhabit this world have been so influenced by such changes that they have constructed altars to chance, in the hope that these threats might be mitigated. Quimbre will confirm my words. He will also tell you that, as his people have been sailing this tormented sea for centuries, the strangest of happenings are liable to befall them. Balls of lightning will appear on deck and wander with no apparent clear direction. But there are times when the phenomena that appear random in nature are under some malign direction.

It was the longest explanation Eefa had ever received from Woll. But she wasn't sure she understood her message.

'But what has that to do with Wychera Gallant?' Eefa shook her head.

There was no immediate danger. And, besides, I had reason to keep silent and observe what might emerge.

Eefa's eyes widened. 'What emerged was a pirate's boot appearing below my bunk.'

She heard a tinkling sound. It took her a moment or two to realize that it was Woll laughing at her.

'How can you be so calm?'

I can assure you that even the master of surprise, Wychera Gallant, is not capable of metamorphosing to a boot.

'What then?'

There is more to a master changer than mere physical change. My goodness, but I duly confess that I too have sometimes delighted in playful imagery.

'Woll?'

Oh, do not protest so! Wychera is clearly capable of impressing some dream-like image on the mind of . . . oh, let us say, a naïve observer.

'What? He put the image of a boot into my head?'

So, we must assume! But let us not over-react. It is likely to have been his foolish attempt at humor. Whatever, it is my conclusion that, even pirate boots considered, he represents no threat to you.

This was hardly reassuring. Eefa walked back along the deck to the stairs down to her bunk, and soon, back under her blanket, she remained somewhat resentful of the fact that Woll was so relaxed about it all.

'Who knows what else he is capable of? He can adopt any appearance he fancies. We can't even be sure he's any kind of warrior?'

Oh, on that score I can reassure you.

'I'm no longer sure I believe anything about him.'

Dearest Eefa! Wychera Gallant is most assuredly a warrior of some renown.

'Well, I still don't trust him an inch.'

Nor, perhaps, could you be expected to, given his silly behavior. He got drunk on Quimbre's brandy.'

True!

'But, don't you understand – this creature is now free to do what he wants aboard the Scuttlebutt?'

Let us say that I have reason for believing Wychera Gallant in all that he claims. I can assure you that he is, as he claims, a renowned adventurer and warrior.

Eefa fell back in her bunk, astonished that Woll was refusing to take her worries seriously. An adventurer and warrior – but also a changer. How could Woll be so calm about this? How could any of the company accept that some unknown, and the powers only knew, possibly dangerous being, was now at large among them?

'Oh Woll, I'm frightened. But even more than that, I feel that we're caught up in forces we don't understand.'

Your fears are understandable. My mistress had hoped that, with her release from the Beach of Bones, you would have been of no further interest to her enemy. But now, judging from the words of the changer, her hopes are confounded.

'What does that mean?'

It would appear that her cruel and relentless enemy is not finished with her, and thus very likely not with you.

'Your words terrify me.'

Unfortunately, we face a new turn of events, one we should keep to ourselves for the moment. It will change our plans. And yet, we cannot allow fear to dominate our every action. We must employ cunning to match our adversary.

Eefa's eyes widened. Just how dangerous was their adversary? She was no longer sure of what they were really facing in this voyage through the bewildering Sea of Stars.

She lifted her eyes to Woll. The spec of golden light was the only visible presence of the queen of the frost sprites, and she appeared to dance in a zigzag, as if she herself were lost in thought.

'Oh, Woll, is there something fated about me? I was born invisible. And now I have such strange dreams – dreams when I am awake.'

You are not fated. It's the circumstances we find ourselves in, dear Eefa, that make it feel strange. I fear that I must at least attempt to explain what will be difficult for any human to understand.

'I don't think I can bear the explanation!'

Now you're being silly since I have little choice but to explain if I am to help you. The words of the changer have shaken me and thus make it necessary for me to at least try.

'I'm not sure I want to hear.'

Oh, Eefa, my words will not just apply to you. What I say must be passed out to all the company. But, given its gravity, it should be at the right time and place. Your companions are not yet sufficiently prepared. There are such terrible forces at large in this world.

Eefa had clamped her hands over her ears. 'Don't say any more.'

You, above all, must be aware.

'I don't want to know such things as might inflame my imagination.'

Dearest Eefa, despite your doubts and worries, you have been hardened by endurance of the burden of invisibility. You are stronger than you think.

Eefa didn't believe this for a moment. She didn't like to be reminded of that burden. And now, all of this seemed to be some kind of misbegotten trick to boost her confidence. But the pounding of her heart in her chest and the panting nature of her breathing told her exactly the opposite. When she now tried to do the simplest thing, like climbing up out of the bunk, her muscles felt so jittery she flopped back down again. It exasperated her that she lacked the courage to rise to action. Yet all of this – all the strangeness that was increasingly surrounding them – was too frightening even to grasp. How could she, a mere girl, be expected to think logically when her heart was in her throat and her muscles had turned to jelly?

When she spoke again, she did so in a whisper. 'Your words are hardly reassuring.'

The queen of the frost sprites rose high into the air, then performed a dizzying series of curves and circles too fast to witness, as if confused within herself and attempting to find a resolution.

It would appear that I can conceal no troubling thought from you. I can understand that you are upset. You demand explanations but at this moment I cannot in truth find a way of shielding us from the growing darkness in this world. I so wish I could. There are intimations of a growing danger. I must report such matters back to one who is vastly wiser than me. In the meantime, I must beg your patience.

Nothing of this conversation soothed the growing panic in Eefa. She was struggling to breathe, her heart pounding in her throat. She gripped her face in her clammy hands, her hair trailing over them.

Woll made tinkling sounds, as if to comfort her.

Eefa, you must understand that there is a miasma moving through our world – an evil unconfined by any known bounds. It has the same feel as the evil that caused the chaos long ago. I worry that it might, in effect, be the offspring of the earlier calamity, only more terrible. That same evil caused both calamities. And it would appear that its potential for evil is even greater.

'Oh, Woll, I thought the chaos was over! Now your words frighten me. They make me feel that we are caught up in malign forces we do not understand.'

Your fears are reasonable. But I cannot explain the complexities of how we might combat the darkness. I'm not sure I know what to expect.

'Has this anything to do with Gallant?'

I doubt it. I would imagine that he is merely caught up in it, as we are.

Eefa fell back in her bunk, uncertain what to believe. She could see that Woll was distracted by strange events that were somehow linked to the chaos. It was hardly surprising that Woll would have felt more urgency in examining signs that might herald a new threat. But in Eefa's opinion, the most vital problem was the arrival into their midst of Wychera Gallant. Why couldn't anyone other than her see that none of the questions about Wychera Gallant had been answered.

Why in the world would a changer, who also claimed to be some kind of adventurer-warrior, have been sent to help them?

Quimbre had been highly suspicious of his arrival. There had to be a really important reason why Wychera Gallant was here among them, and nothing he had said about himself, including that business of professing to be here to protect them, made any kind of sense to Eefa.

'I'm struggling to understand.'

You are not alone.

Eefa's heart had never left her throat in all of this conversation. 'Then please explain to me what is going on. Why is he here?'

There was a distinct pause in the reply from Woll.

Eefa! You are perceptive. Your instincts are ever right. The arrival of the changer would appear to be highly significant.

'I knew it.'

Yet, in so far as I can judge, he is speaking the truth.

How could Eefa possibly explain to Woll how confused Gallant had made her feel about him? Was it really true that she had not really been scared by his presence? More taken by surprise – even astonishment – than scared? Oh, she didn't quite know how to explain to Woll what she truly felt.

She took a breath and gathered herself before replying. 'Woll, I'm so confused. You must explain everything you think I need to know.'

Everything is rather a big word. We are confronted by mysteries. Mysteries that, as yet, I cannot fully explain. I can only suggest that we remain acutely vigilant.

Eefa was suddenly aware of how cold she was feeling. She buried her head under the blanket, her teeth now chattering with cold. But no matter how she attempted to hide from it, the uncertainty refused to go away.

'Woll! Are you still here?'

I am always here, Eefa.

'Then . . . so what are you really saying? Are you truly agreeing with me that the changer's arrival among us is highly significant?'

That question is now at the very heart of the puzzle.

That same night, with her mind still restless, Eefa attempted to find solace in sleep, but found herself listening to her brother, Magio, snoring loudly. She muttered aloud,

'I cannot sleep.'

There is no time for sleep.

The first voice, that most terrifying voice was back.

She tried to suppress the voice with her fingers in her ears, and through curling her body up like a shrimp. But her efforts were useless. The voice was too powerful to suppress.

No . . . Nooooo . . . Noooooooooo!

That voice was invading her mind, overcoming her every resistance. Her being was melting into a mote of light in a universe of nothingness. The experience was both shocking and exciting. She felt curiously free to move at will through this nothingness, even as her instincts told her it would be an extremely dangerous nothingness to explore. Every instinct for survival switched on. She tensed, sensing traps, which she must somehow skirt by without falling victim to them. She was aware, at the very limit of her consciousness, that any failure here would be the end of her.

A familiar vision shocked her to the core. She was gazing at the same scene she had witnessed in her earlier dream, the man with the blind eyes and bedraggled hair, seated on a rock. But now she was even more startled to discover that he was surrounded by a bustling throng of the strangest beings. Eefa blinked her eyes open and shut several times, hoping the vision would go away and let her sleep.

How she wished that Woll was here to advise her. Woll would know how to erase these strange visions. Eefa gritted her teeth, resentful that such fearful visions were being imposed on her against her will. Why were such terrifying visions invading her mind – visions she just did not understand?

Even though a chill of foreboding was now invading her being, she couldn't help but stare at the lonely prisoner on his stump of stone. As the dream pulled her closer to him, that same sense of danger caused her heartbeat to rise up into her throat. Terror caused her to clench her eyes shut.

She thought about Magio's daft expressions. She whispered his stupid expression of woe inside her head, *Jinxy, jinxy, jinxy . . . JINXY!*

The dream remained.

For some incomprehensible reason, she felt strangely guilty – as if she had attempted to abandon the imprisoned man to his fate. Eefa found herself wiping tears from her face. It took all her courage to look at that awful scene, to look at the man with her eyes wide open, despite the fact that her throat felt bone dry and there was a prickling feeling running down her spine. Then, all of a sudden, her senses were flooded by a feeling of expansion, which felt like . . . like she was on the verge of understanding something really important.

But what did it mean?

Was the figure trying to tell her something?

If so, the meaning was lost on Eefa. Even as she continued to watch him, she saw that he was surrounded by what appeared to be shifting shadows – beings that, as her vision expanded, she recognized as the very specters Gran had described in her fairytales. Specters that appeared in all shapes and forms, ghosts, wraiths and ghouls, and more. Yet the blind man was unmoved by their presence.

That was the most intriguing thing about him. How could he sit there, so calm and peaceful in this place of horror?

Her mouth was wide open, a scream rising in her throat. But no scream emerged. She didn't know how, or why, but her instincts told her that, somehow, the blind man had stopped her scream. He had done so because it would be disastrous to draw attention to her presence here.

Don't be frightened. I'll protect you.

Eefa heard the soothing words in her head. But she was far too terrified to believe them. Where was this place? How had she come to be here?

Calming her breathing so she wasn't panting with fear, Eefa looked about her. There was nothing here other than what appeared to be that prison chamber – with encircling specters that she now assumed were guards. Who in the world could this blind man be? Why had he been condemned to this awful place? What terrible crime had he committed to merit such a punishment?

Eefa couldn't help but study anew the strange figure of the man, just quietly sitting on the stump of what must once have been a stone pillar, in the ruins of what might have been something grander – perhaps the crypt of a castle or palace.

Suddenly Eefa was panting for breath.

She had the strangest notion that what she was seeing here was vitally important to her and her brother, Magio. It was as if she were on the verge of a secret, a very profound and dangerous secret.

'Nothing makes sense. . .'

Eefa woke abruptly from her awake-dream. Sitting bolt upright on her bunk in the rolling cabin of the Scuttlebutt, she found herself blinking much too fast. She clenched her eyes shut to stop the blinking. Was she behaving irrationally? Just a child frightened by an unpleasant dream? There was no blind man speaking to her from some dreadful place. Just the familiar sounds of winds and sea. She reassured herself that Quimbre and Bird Woman knew how to deal with the Sea of Stars. They would take her and Magio to safety, far away from all the madness that had overwhelmed their lives.

But when she closed her eyes, she was still unable to relax into sleep. Instead, she sensed myriad forces rushing through her. The vision, the unwanted dream – the nightmare – it was still there at the back of her mind, refusing to let her go.

'What's happening to me?'

Eefa refused to re-enter that terrible dream. She had no desire to examine it in more detail, she didn't want to think of that desolate place, the neverending scurry of those terrifying specters that inhabited it, and the figure seated on the stump of masonry, his face shrouded by that cataract of lank hair.

Eefa closed her eyes, hunched her body into the tightest knot she could make of it and she screamed,

'Oh, for pity's sake, let me be.'

Now – now! I am with you, dearest Eefa.

'Oh, Woll – dearest Woll – is it you?'

I am here.

'Oh, thank goodness! I have had such a terrible dream.'

The golden wisp of light pirouetted rapidly about her.

Tell me . . .

'I found myself in . . . in what appeared to be a sort of prison.'

Tell me all – everything you recall of this prison.

'There was a figure, a man with lank, bedraggled hair, imprisoned there.'

Describe everything you remember to me . . .

'It felt like . . . Oh, it felt like a torture chamber . . . a place of infinite pain.'

Let me enter your mind and help restore your calm.

'Oh, yes – do so, please!'

Immediately, Eefa felt a soothing sense of tranquility flood her senses.

'Oh, thank you!'

There is no need to thank me. I'm here to help you.

'Did you see what I have seen?'

Yes, I saw.

'What in the world did it all mean? Who was that figure, sitting on the stump of stone? Why was I taken there?'

Those are the same questions I too am asking myself.

'Tell me – tell me, please – what you make of it.'

I have a vision of a vast wall of stone rearing out of a sea of nothingness. I sense a place that once was the embodiment of almost infinite power. But now it is entirely lost in chaos. Yet there remains a suggestion of what it was once . . . a hint of majesty . . . all reduced to a tumble of stones. What I see is all that remains of some great edifice, now utterly lost in the chaos . . .

Eefa shivered. Woll's words were so strange, she struggled to comprehend them.

'Why was I drawn there? Who was the man with the blind eyes who was imprisoned in that terrible place?'

Hush! It will take some reckoning to find the key to such understanding. Impossible, indeed, does it appear for the moment. But sometimes, with patience, even the impossible becomes the possible. For now, dearest Eefa, what you need is rest. Lie down, draw up your bedcovers. I will stay by you and ensure you have a few hours of tranquil and untroubled sleep.

SERENITY

'Wake up, sleepyhead.'

Magio's annoying whisper. His hand was shaking her shoulder. But Eefa had no desire to wake up. She felt so cozy and warm in her bunk, tucked in tight with her blanket, her head buried in her pillow. She had no desire to wake up to the memories of that terrifying awake-dream, with that forlorn figure tormented by ghouls. She clung to a new and much more delightful dream, one put into her head by Woll, in which she was swimming underwater in a lovely coral lagoon.

'We're here. Come on, Eefa. Get dressed and see for yourself. We're arriving at the famous Isle of Serenity.'

'Serenity?'

Eefa was feeling so refreshed by a decent night's sleep that she refused to allow yesterday's terror to depress her. Suddenly she was flinging her clothes on, racing up the bare wood steps onto the deck even as she rushed her fingers through her tangle of hair.

'Oh – oooohhhh!'

She could never, in her wildest imagination, have foreseen the sight that greeted her. The sea was swarming with craft of every description, ships of every size and design, double and triple-masted, all sailing in a single direction. And ahead, the horizon was a hazy glimpse of land rising out of the thinning mists of morning.

Eefa closed her eyes to allow a painful brushing of her untidy hair, under the firm pressure of Bird Woman's hands. Bird Woman's attitude was now altogether practical. As she tugged and parted fair-haired clumps, she fussed about how Eefa's clothes had grown too small for her. Bird Woman muttered about the growing need to support her growing breasts. Eefa had to tear herself away from her fussing to head for Magio on the prow. Together, they gazed wide-eyed at the emerging panorama of the capital city of the entire archipelago, Serenity, jewel of the isle of the same name.

'It's absolutely gorgeous.'

It was as if a legend from her childhood was becoming reality before Eefa's startled eyes.

A shout from Quimbre interrupted the spell.

'Make ready all aboard! We have but a single day to spend ashore. In the meantime, keep your eyes peeled and ears alert. If I judge it right, there's something strange going on in these waters.'

Magio abandoned Eefa on the prow, speedily clambering aloft to the lookout.

'Aye, aye, Captain.'

Eefa's wonderment now turned to a frown. Why had Quimbre warned them to keep a look out? What was worrying him?

Bird Woman echoed her surprise. 'What is it, man? What do you sense that none of us can see?'

'Take a closer look at that armada heading to port. We sail in what would normally be placid coastal waters. Yet few are furling sail. On the contrary, all are set square to the wind.'

Eefa followed Bird Woman's gaze to study the melee of craft heading for Serenity. There were so many boats and ships, they filled the entire horizon. But now that Quimbre had pointed it out, she saw what was worrying him. They were all rushing ahead in what appeared to be a common hurry. She now found herself tugged in the direction of the galley, where Bird Woman made a quick breakfast for the company.

She tugged at Bird Woman's sleeve. 'What's worrying Quimbre?'

'I don't know, Eefa. I swear that old salt can smell trouble on the very wind. But we had better do as he says. We keep every sense alert. And don't forget that trickster, Gallant. We have seen neither hide nor hair of him this morning.'

Eefa bit into a shrunken apple, her eyes widening at the implications of Bird Woman's words.

The journey ashore became increasingly fraught. But Quimbre had managed to edge the Scuttlebutt out into the less-cluttered starboard. It was a nerve-jangling exercise all the while, as they slid and bumped their way out of the congestion, until Quimbre piloted the Scuttlebutt into more open water a league or so from shore. From this vantage point, the passing spectacle of the capital city of the entire archipelago of the Sea of Stars emerged into the spellbound gazes of the company.

Eefa clapped her hands to her face, enraptured by the beautiful temples of honey-colored marble, with their soaring columns and shimmering blue domes. They seemed to rise up out of the misty horizon to merge with the sunshine of the waking morning. They were so like she would have imagined the palaces of gods and goddesses.

'Aren't they divine?'

'More like the follies of self-indulgent pomposity. On your left is the Temple of the Virgins; in the center is the

Rites of Spring; to your right, the Birth of Innocence. They represent the three seasons – Autumn, Spring and Summer. Lucky Serenity suffers no miseries of winter.'

In spite of Bird Woman's denunciation, Eefa could not help but admire the graceful vistas of Serenity as the Scuttlebutt glided past.

The spell was broken by Quimbre, shouting new instructions to Magio up high in the rigging. 'Keep your eyes peeled for three black rocks upraised, like jagged teeth! When you see them, we cleave to port. Make lively, Kiddo! We need to get ready to make landing.'

Within an hour or so, they sailed into a cove a dozen leagues or so downwind from the capital, to join a cluster of fishing smacks at the single jetty in a small fishing village. Eefa helped Magio to tether the Scuttlebutt and they headed ashore to explore the village, which was built out of the same honey-colored stone as the temples in the island capital. Everything in Serenity appeared to be constructed of the same honey-colored stone, from the masoned roads, the house walls, even the shingles that slated the roofs.

Eefa listened in to the conversations going on all about her, involving fisher folk dressed in colorful costumes, gossiping about the weather, the prices of the vendors, and the fishwives selling catches straight off the smacks.

'Oh! I love this place.' She clapped her hands.

Bird Woman said very little, her attention vigilant, her eyes alert.

Eefa was startled to see that Wychera Gallant had made his appearance. He was peering down at them, over the port rail of the Scuttlebutt, his eyes twinkling in his widely grinning face.

Quimbre shook his fist at the elfin changer. 'Where have you been hiding? Recovering, no doubt, from helping yourself to my brandy.'

'I plead guilty, good Captain. But allow me to return the favor. Serenity is a place I know well. I dare say – if Bird Woman will allow it – I would be glad to introduce Eefa and Magio to its wonders.'

Quimbre merely glared. But Bird Woman sized up Wychera Gallant with her brow wrinkling to a question mark.

Eefa clapped her hands. 'Oh, please let Wychera show us around.'

Magio piped up, 'No – not me. I'm staying to help Quimbre.'

Quimbre looked from the twins to Wychera, his mouth bunched up into a pout of uncertainty.

Bird Woman took a deep breath before turning to nod to Quimbre. 'I think, maybe, Gallant has a point. You've worked yourself ragged to get us here. You deserve a visit to the taverns. Don't worry about the twins. I'll keep a weather eye on them.'

It was obvious from the look on Quimbre's face that he was still dubious about trusting the changer. But Bird Woman's advice made a deal of sense.

'I warn you, all four of you, that danger is looming. I can feel it in my very bones. We can stop here for no more than a day. Tomorrow, without fail, we sail at dawn.'

Eefa looked from Quimbre's vexed face to that of the tall changer, who had now come down onto the harbor to join them. Those green eyes, in gazing about them, appeared to change from moment to moment. She saw how the pupils grew larger, even as he nodded in Quimbre's direction. 'Let Magio stay with you. I shall be honored to show Eefa the wonders Serenity has to offer. Meanwhile, I shall protect her and, by my honor, guarantee her timely return.'

Quimbre sighed, as if doubting the wisdom of what he was reluctantly accepting. 'Right, then, if Eefa must wander the island in the company of that liar, I insist that you, Woman, keep a close eye on her.'

Bird Woman nodded. 'Be assured that I shall keep a weather eye on Gallant and his tricks.'

Quimbre still looked suspicious. But the harbormaster was now watching them from the quay. Eefa wondered if Quimbre, who had nothing to barter, had any money to buy the provisions they needed.

As if he had read her mind, the changer came up close to Quimbre, and with a wink, passed him a purse. Quimbre stared back at him, as if to question where he likely had stolen it. But Wychera grinned, that wide grin of his. 'Enough to pay your tolls and get what you need in provisions, good Captain.'

Bird Woman ignored Quimbre's glower, turning to appraise the road that wound through the village, and uphill in the direction of the island capital. Wordlessly, she opened her hand to the changer. 'The twins have long outgrown their rags of clothes. It's high time we found a market where we can get some basic needs.'

With a flourish, Wychera Gallant dropped two coins of twinkling gold into the palm of her hand.

'Oh, how brilliant!'

Eefa was marveling at the winding road, so evenly set out, as they climbed the hill out of the fishing village. Back on Moon, this would have been a simple dirt track.

'It's so lovely and smooth to walk on.'

Bird Woman patted her shoulder. 'It's just a masoned road.'

Eefa exclaimed, 'But how do they get these stones all the same size?'

'They're cobblestones. All cut to the same size in the quarries.'

'Cobblestones!'

Eefa added the new word to her dictionary. She couldn't help but marvel at such revelations as she witnessed along the way out of the village and further along the coastal roads heading in the direction of the capital. What extraordinary planning must have gone into it all, to conjure up the omnipresent sound of splashing water! Water appeared to be the magical ingredient, running everywhere in controlled streams that led to tiny fountains where passers-by could gather an icy cold drink in cupped hands. By the time they came to a proper town, she saw that same planning had gone into the culturing of lovely cascades of flowers. The scented air seemed to evoke orchestras of birdsong.

The notion of waking up each morning to such glorious scents amid such lovely surroundings! It just seemed so like heaven was supposed to be. And everywhere she looked she saw sculptures and carvings of what appeared to be minor god and goddesses, or angelic creatures, all carved out of that same honey-colored stone.

'Oh – it's all so . . . so . . .' Eefa was at a loss for words to describe what she was feeling, as she whirled about herself, her feet feeling lighter than air.

'So entrancing?' Wychera laughed.

'Yes, oh, yes!' She spun giddily. 'It's just so magical.' Eefa was feeling giddy after inhaling the intoxicating scents and odors of so many beautiful and pungently aromatic plants.

'Oh, look at the flowers! There must be zillions of flowers.'

'Welcome to Serenity.'

Wychera put one arm about her and squeezed her with a laugh. 'The isle is also renowned for its many springs. They water the blossoms all year round. It is said that once upon a time a distinguished sage attempted to count them, but was driven insane by their uncountable numbers.

'Oh, Bird Woman, is that true?'

'Serenity is certainly the home of tall tales. Yet even I can see why the locals are so arrogant as to claim that only the powers of the undying could have created such a mirror of Heaven.'

Eefa spun around, her eyes closed, sniffing the scents and taking such a deep breath it felt as if she were drawing their beauty into her lungs.

'You wouldn't be the first to be overwhelmed by the sainted isle. Serenity is known in poetry as the land of Eternal Spring. The climate here, as Wychera will confirm, is warm and temperate all year round. The priests, of course, claim it is graced by the undying – such beauty is the reward for their devotion.'

Eefa spun around so quickly, she made herself dizzy.

Wychera held her steady, laughing at her giddiness.

'If you credit the myths, Serenity was betrothed by the Lady of Flowers to her youthful lover, Ylustra, who was not only mortal but so brave and handsome that he captured the heart of the goddess.' His voice was wistful, as if imbued with some secret longing of his own. 'According to the myths, Serenity was created during a golden age, when undying and humans emerged into being from the wastes of Dromenon.'

'So, the priests, bedecked in their finery, would have us believe.' Bird Woman spoke scathingly.

Eefa was beguiled by such fantastical tales during their walk through the mountains until, at length, they arrived at the outskirts of the capital city. Here they came across a teeming market where Bird Woman could search for those essentials she talked about, including new clothes for the twins. Eefa was happy to help her, holding up samples of shorts, sandals and tops, to find the right sizes in the bright sunshine.

It was here, in the very heart of the market, that Eefa was suddenly overwhelmed by a feeling of dread. It came on her so without warning that she groaned aloud.

Bird Woman fell to her knees beside Eefa, putting her arms about her. 'What is it, Eefa? What is it, girl?'

But Eefa was unable to reply. Her body was wilting. Her hands were clamped against her skull. It seemed as if, all at once, a miasma had invaded her mind.

Wychera picked her up and carried her into the shade of a stall, from where he wheeled this way and that, looking hard about them for any sign of danger. He stiffened, as if struck with a sudden instinct, then stood erect, peering eastwards, as if to get a clearer look of the harbor area, and then, rising onto tiptoes, he squinted into the mist-wreathed sea beyond.

Bird Woman cradled Eefa as she moaned again and then slumped. She would have fallen if Bird Woman were not holding her firm against her chest.

'What is it? What's amiss with you, girl?'

Eefa's voice was frantic, 'My mind is blanking, going dark. I feel so overwhelmed. A darkness is overwhelming me . . . a great malice . . .'

Bird Woman shook her head, glancing up at Wychera Gallant. 'Whatever is the matter with her? Can you make any sense of it?'

The elfin changer shook his head. But then he cursed, staring into the distance. He cursed several times more, in a throaty growl. 'We can't stay here. We're no longer safe. Grab your purchases. We've got to run.'

Picking Eefa up, as if she were weightless, Wychera was already hurrying them back along the road they had taken, his eyes searching everywhere for some means of speeding their escape.

Eefa felt the blood drain from her face, her skin becoming icy cold, drenched in sweat. She whispered, 'Something evil is approaching. I can hear the flapping of its wings. That same monstrous being that hunted us . . . the thing that flew over us . . . back in the desert on Moon.'

'Your pupils have grown huge, Eefa. What is it?'

Standing high above them on tiptoes, Wychera's eyes peered out, beyond the wall, to the distant harbor, where a dark shape was appearing out of the sea mists.

'We must get far away from here.'

Bird Woman now running pell-mell alongside Wychera, was shaking her head in bewilderment. 'We cannot continue like this.'

'No, we can't.'

As soon as they had run clear of the town, Wychera set Eefa down in the shadow of a field wall. His voice was an urgent whisper,

'Stay by her, Bird Woman. Guard Eefa with your very life, while I search for some means of speeding our escape.'

Back in the fishing village, Magio grabbed hold of Quimbre's burly arm.

'Something is happening. I sense it, overwhelmingly. Eefa is in danger. We need to get ready to flee.'

Quimbre, who had been negotiating for fish and fresh fruit with some local traders, turned to regard Magio, 'What is it?'

'We – all of us – are in grave danger.'

'What do you sense, lad?'

A spark of gold appeared in the air about them, buzzing frantically about their heads. It darted about their heads like errant sunbeams.

Magio stared up at the frenzy of gold.

'Woll senses it too. I don't know what the danger is, Quimbre. I only know that it's really close and we need to get Eefa back here as quickly as possible.'

Quimbre clenched his fists and he struck the coping of a nearby stone wall with frustration.

'I knew it. I should never have let her go wandering with that elfin scoundrel.'

Magio grabbed Quimbre's wrist to stop him injuring himself further.

'No! It's nothing to do with Wychera. It's a peril Eefa and I remember only too well. Do you recall – that time, when we were hiding in the desert and that terrifying creature flew over us on gigantic wings, looking for our scent?'

'I remember.'

'It's that same monster. Eefa and I both sensed it back on Moon. We felt the overweening malice of its searching mind. Now it's here on Serenity. It's here and it searches for us again.'

Bird Woman, sitting with her back against the wall, stared into Eefa's eyes, now level with her own. Eefa had recovered a little of her color, here in the shade.

'Your pupils are grown less huge, girl.'

'Magio senses it too. We both feel that the danger is nearby – closer than it has ever been since we left Moon. It knows we're here.'

Bird Woman looked about them. They were perched high on the hill overlooking the capital city, with all of its beautiful masoned temples and gardens. But she could detect no danger.

'Are you sure?'

Eefa was trembling. 'Yes!'

'Come, then. Do you feel able to run?'

Even as they got to their feet, they heard a thunderous explosion. It was so loud and terrifying that they both stopped dead in their tracks. Looking back, they witnessed the calamity of destruction that fell upon the capital city. It came from a monstrous ship, if a ship it could really be called, for it was unlike any ship Eefa had ever seen in her life. It was covered in huge iron plates, and protruding from its bow was something resembling an enormous cannon, from the mouth of which flames and smoke were still pouring out over the stricken harbor.

They knew, now, what the flotilla had been running from.

Eefa screamed, 'What are we to do?'

Bird Woman appeared so astonished by the spectacle that she clearly had no idea as to what to do.

At that moment a shout caught their attention. Wychera was approaching them in a rattling hurry, whipping a donkey and cart in their direction.

'Where in the world . . .?'

'No time for explanations. Hop aboard.'

Even as the donkey and cart careened back towards the small fishing village, Eefa stared at Bird Woman, then at Wychera, frowning. She felt so utterly strange in herself.

Something bizarre was happening to her. Feelings were running through her head, through her body, her limbs – the strangest sensations. She felt faint, her head spinning. She was wilting again, her strength failing. She felt herself enwrapped by a strong arm. It held her close against a body that was hard as iron.

Supremacy

'Target in sight!'

Pittaquera watched, in a mixture of astonishment and awe, as the battleship, named Leviathan after the great weapon in its prow, closed on the capital isle. The Ursascogan queen had seen, with some trepidation, how the fiend Lustfera had surrounded the warship in a mantle of mist that had helped to cloak its presence as it hoved ever closer to the teeming harbor.

She continued to observe as Karkedinn, the burly ship's captain, roared orders to the clan commanders on board, making ready for the attack. From these commanders, further orders were being passed on to the minions, echoing on through all of the hierarchy over the vast superstructure. In this slow, yet remorseless, manner, the great ship was brought into alignment for the impending assault. Given its unwieldy bulk, the Leviathan had made steady progress in its hundreds of leagues journey here from Wart, astounding the queen, who could never quite suspend her disbelief in the viability of that ponderous hull of heavy iron. Yet the damn thing floated, even if the great weight slowed its passage and made it ten times as unwieldy as a good old-fashioned ship of oak.

And now here they were, in full view of the main harbor of the Sainted Isle, with the same captain now ordering the furling of its quadruple-masted sails. That there were dark powers involved in the impending confrontation weighed heavily on the queen. Even so, she had been deeply impressed with the formidable Karkedinn, who had plotted an accurate course, despite contrary winds and currents, to relentlessly close on the very nadir of power that her husband, the King, so coveted.

Serenity to the humans – Amotée in the deeper memory of the First Folk – celebrated in the legends of Arraghmaar. In those same legends Amotée was the very birthplace of Fairy and thus the true origins of magic, and had in ages past been a sanctuary of grace before falling to the humans.

Pittaquera's ruminations were interrupted by the captain's roar,

'Cast anchors!'

At last, then, they were here.

While Pittaquera dreaded what that terrible being, Lustfera, might decree, yet still she could not contain her excitement. She abandoned the royal suite in the stern to head closer to the prow, mingling with a cluster of senior officers who were gazing ahead through the evaporating mist, to where the hilltop temples were hoving into view. Here, at a distance of no more than a league, she could make out the details of the walls – enormous bulwarks of masoned stone, decorated with towers, and everywhere bristling with brass cannons. She had to grant it to the humans that they had their prize well-guarded. She could even see the pennons fluttering here and there among the defenders, tiny as ants in the distance, as her ears rang with the rattling of the Leviathan's anchor chains.

Pittaquera wondered if there might be a meeting of envoys, as was customary in the opening gambits of a siege. But she witnessed no preparations for such diplomacy. Instead, she saw her husband ascend the steps that brought him to a dais close to the prow. With widened eyes, she listened to his speech, addressed, without need of megaphone, to all aboard.

'I promised you, my people, to lead you in a war to end all wars. Now would I keep my word and deliver you from the age-old hegemony of the foe. How long have we been obliged to defer to their whims? Now, we are here – at the very gates of Amotée – it is our turn to humble them.'

The King's voice was drowned out by the roar of all on board the ironship, by the clatter of swords on armor and the thunder of bare feet against the decks of iron. Unlike her husband, Pittaquera did not hate humans. But she knew that her feelings towards the ancient enemy did not extend to most Ursascogans. Even the gentle Khakhov, on their journey here from Moon, had regaled the company with tales of how, after the human conquest, the arrogant victors had demanded that Ursascogan maidens sweep the floors of their blasphemous temples with their tongues.

Pittaquera wondered if such tales were bombast to fire up the warriors in anticipation of conflict. And yet, here and now, the First Folk were poised to take back sacred Amotée after a thousand years of dispossession.

All of a sudden, Pittaquera's heartbeat rose into her throat. Time, she thought, for a blessed glass of rhenum. In such tense moments the fiery red liquor calmed her nerves. She issued the order, then closed her eyes, refusing to open them again until the flagon duly arrived. It was a copious glass she now had poured by the steward, sighing as she downed the contents in a single draught.

'Aaaahhhh!'

How she welcomed that warming feeling inside her.

Her eyes blinking in an unseemly flutter, she recalled those events back in the harbor port of Wart. The conquest of the town had been intended as an example to the human enemy. It must surely have reverberated through the entire archipelago. Yet it would appear, from the haughty reaction Pittaquera now witnessed in those towers and walls, that the defenders of Serenity were not in the least impressed. Had they no notion of the calamity about to befall them?

Pittaquera harkened to her husband's speech.

'Warriors!' How that powerful voice boomed from prow to stern. 'I bid you make battle ready. Are you ready?'

The reply was a single, thunderous roar.

Slightly tipsy with the rhenum, Pittaquera wondered if, perhaps, the defenders were comforting themselves with the memory that all such previous Ursascogan rebellions had ended in abject failure.

'To your positions.'

Pittaquera watched the weaponers take their positions lining the two sides of the Leviathan. With pride she saw how the clans, all working in a measured harmony, hauled the weapon forward until the barrel protruded with the muzzle now clear of the accommodating arc in the prow. Her heart now all of a pitter-patter, she signaled to the steward, holding forth her empty glass.

The now tipsy queen watched the Wizar, Khakhov, who was wiping the holy chrism over the monstrous barrel, using his bare fingers. She was still wiping tears from her eyes with her sleeve as the first volley of cannons in the city walls belched smoke, their missiles taking several seconds to follow through their smoky arcs, before thudding harmlessly against the iron hull of the battleship.

It occurred to Pittaquera that this was surely a moment when she should be seen to be at her husband's side. She began press her way through the throng, heading for the staircase to the dais, and her proud husband.

'What is it, Woman?'

Pittaquera was too upset to speak, instead embracing Wirgnatha to the cheers of every warrior.

He roared aloud, so the very iron of the deck rang with his voice, 'How the humans must have rejoiced in stealing Amotée from our ancestors! Today, we redress that iniquity! No more is it the plaything of their arrogant priests.'

Pittaquera hugged him anew.

'You know our purpose here?'

She clutched tightly to his powerful arm. 'Now the day is come, I cannot wait to set foot on that sacred shore.'

A frown disfigured Wirgnatha's countenance. 'You know there will be no crowning ceremony.'

'What do you mean?'

'What would you have me do? Would you fetter our rightful outrage?'

Pittaquera was shocked by his reply. 'No! I would do no such thing. But given our strength, the taking of the city should prove no more than a skirmish. We can take back the blessed Amotée in all of its splendor.'

Wirgnatha's head fell. 'You know I would do so. I would have us crowned in their temples of marble. But the Star of Mourning is of a mind to make an example. There is to be no quarter.'

Queen Pittaquera gazed back at those defensive walls, and beyond them to the beautiful city, the subject of admiration in every corner of the Sea of Stars.

'Oh, no! Surely, we cannot . . .'

He glowered down at her, then embraced her close so as to whisper into her ear. 'Have a care. You know not who listens here!'

'Oh, husband!'

'Hush!'

'Can we not teach the humans a bitter enough lesson? Show them the overwhelming force of our might.'

'My Queen! Yours is a sentimental heart. But this is no moment for sentiment. An irredeemable lesson must be taught here.'

She heard the command. 'Clan of War – fire!'

Pittaquera squeezed her eyes shut. In that same moment, the very air about her exploded with thunder. The force of the explosion rocked the great ship under her feet, jarring its enormous bulk against the anchor chains. The shock of it confused her senses, causing her to totter on her feet.

At nightfall on the third fell day of the siege of Serenity, the aged Wizar, Khakhov, duly obeyed the order of his queen to represent her on yet another of these dreadful explorations – though he knew not what purpose they might possibly serve, after that monstrous weapon had repeatedly wreaked its vengeance. Yet still, duty was duty. He recalled with what sadness Her Majesty's hands had clasped his own as he had knelt before her – she, the anointed queen – and she had begged him to take this burden from her own shoulders.

'Someone must bear it, for I cannot.'

It had long been their privy secret that Khakhov and the Queen could communicate beyond the normal senses. For the Royal Highness to see what the Wizar saw, for her to hear, mind-to-mind, what the Wizar heard. It was the most confidential channel of communication within the House of Obenuf, a prized relic of their shared lineages. And so, hour after hour through these hellish explorations of the ruins of Serenity, he had informed her, vision for vision, and word-for word, all that he saw and heard, with no outward betrayal of such intimate communication, thus keeping her Royal Majesty informed of the extent and magnitude of the carnage, even to the staining of his long white beard with the tears of grief from his rheumy old eyes.

Even now, long after nightfall, Khakhov saw how specters were accompanying this latest landing party, wraiths as tall as the First Born but of sinewy shapes, with molten yellow eyes. They were led by that fiend, Lustfera, dominant over all the others, who had that familiar silhouette of entwined serpents. Lightning gamboled over the vast structure of the iron ship, moored a league or so from the shore. The enormous maw of the Leviathan still poked threateningly through the flame-scorched prow, a monstrosity for which defensive walls had proved to be mere smoke and shadows. Again and again, it had roared, wreaking havoc beyond mortal ken, beyond any meaningful sense of avarice or lust for vengeance – directed, it was now clear, at the utter destruction of the sacred isle.

Yet still that Shee-devil searched . . .

The present landing had brought them a short distance eastward of the ruins of the capital, to where the remains of a hamlet opened into a tiny cove. Here, for reasons known only to herself, Lustfera had them launch a boat to the shore. In torchlight, they confirmed that the ruins were deserted, the inhabitants dead or having taken flight. But Lustfera, sniffing like a bloodhound, was not satisfied. She now insisted that they broaden the exploration to the immediate surroundings of the hamlet.

A puzzled Khakhov was now intent on his own reconnaissance.

The party followed a winding, stone-paved road that wound upslope, clearly leading in the direction of the capital city. Taking to this road, Lustfera repeatedly sniffed at the air, as if guided by a scent that nobody else could follow. She led them through a devastated valley, illuminated by the fires of the nearby city's destruction. The fiend called a halt to their peregrination at the very edges of the ruins, close enough for Khakhov to feel the heat of the glowing pyres. Here he watched her scurry here and there, searching the charred remains of what appeared to have been a small open-air market. Here she sniffed the smoky air, as if discovering more evidence of her quarry. The Wizar saw how she stood erect and turned to gaze back along the valley they had trodden, as if tracking a lingering scent beyond any mere mortals might perceive.

Khakhov shivered in his very bones, observing how wraiths were springing from the ashes, to pick and forage among the corpses.

'What's going on?'

He heard the whisper of the Queen, who witnessed through their common gift, all that he was seeing, as if she were here by his side.

'Ghouls, Majesty. Wherever there is slaughter on this scale, and no blessing or other ceremony of protection for the unfortunate departed souls, will you discover those who prey upon the dead.'

'What does the she-devil search for?'

'This I do not know.'

'But surely even that dreadful creature must realize that such devastation is counterproductive, with gain to no-one?'

'Evidently not, My Queen.'

'*Such barbarity!*'

The Wizar found himself hesitating on his reply . . . He thought it exceedingly unlikely that the fiend, Lustfera, would waste her time on sentiment.

'*What is it?*'

The aged Wizar shook his wrinkled head. '*The Star of Mourning – she surely has an agenda that remains unknown to us.*'

'*What agenda?*'

It felt as if the Queen, his sovereign, had placed her regal hand upon his shoulder. He felt her outraged sensibility invade his mind. At the same time the Wizar froze, a thought growing large within his head.

Was it possible that the fiend might be capable of listening in to his very thoughts?

'*What is it, gentle Wizar?*'

'*I am about to risk casting a spell. Look not with your eyes, Majesty. Close them and gaze about you with your inner senses alert.*'

Khakhov was far from sure that Queen Pittaquera had any such inner senses. He must imagine she was here beside him, that she was taking his advice and closing her eyes, attempting to peer beyond the normal senses, putting aside her outrage at the audible sounds of flames and crackling stone, the rancorous stench of death . . .

'*What am I looking for?*'

The wizar hesitated, his eyes clenched with self-reproach. '*We are looking for something that should not be there.*'

Khakhov clenched his own eyes even harder shut, then peered about himself once again, closing out all of the normal senses.

'*I see nothing.*'

'*Majesty – please open your eyes again.*'

'*I sense a new urgency in your voice. It merely adds to my bewilderment. Tell me, Wizar, what should I have seen?*'

'Another fell figure is walking among us. Not Lustfera, but another of her kind.'

'*Who might that be?*'

'A figure that resembles skeins of darkness.'

'*You can see it?*'

'I can sense it.'

'*Why then can I not sense this figure?*'

'Perhaps, Majesty, it is as well that you cannot.'

'*Oh, Khakhov, now you terrify me!*' The Queen's voice faltered. '*Do you have any true understanding of what is going on?*'

'No, My Queen!'

'*But you have some idea – surely?*'

'Through accident, I found myself overhearing a conversation. One I was not intended to hear. It took place in Dromenon.'

'*Tell me.*'

'Majesty! I dread to recall the strangeness of something I overheard back there on the Leviathan as we prepared for battle.'

'*Tell me, Khakhov! I need to know what you heard.*'

She listened carefully to the secret conversation between fell beings, issued in throaty hisses, but understandable all the same, through the wisdom of the Wizar.

Why do you so wish them all dead?

They serve my enemies.

As you wish, so will it be, My Master.

The Queen grasped at once what it must mean.

'*Oh, Khakhov.*'

'Indeed, Majesty – The One she serves is here!'

A Pandemonium of Flight

Eefa was clutching the rail in the prow with white-knuckled hands, meanwhile Magio was up in the lookout screeching out warnings. The Scuttlebutt was one small craft in a sea swarming with a pandemonium of ships and boats of every size and complexity of sail, all fleeing the devastated epicenter of Serenity in blind terror. Every captain was looking for what advantage he or she could find in prevailing winds and currents, seizing on any advantage that would hasten their flight from the devastated Isle of Serenity.

Already a furious argument raged on board, involving Quimbre, Wychera Gallant and Bird Woman.

'You scheming trickster – you led us there.'

'I guided you, accurately and speedily, to where, if you recall, you instructed me to lead you.'

'You scoundrel! You're fooling nobody. You knew full well what was about to happen. You led us into their trap.'

Wychera held his wide-splayed hands aloft, those luminous eyes looking to the company, appealing for common sense. But even Bird Woman, whose face was pallid with shock, refused to defend him. 'I don't know if Quimbre's suspicions of you are correct. But I do know that none who inhabits the Sea of Stars trusts a changer. How can we trust a being whose appearance can transform itself on a whim?'

Gallant was outraged. 'At the very least, I expected gratitude rather than prejudice from what I mistook for an enlightened company. Nevertheless, putting aside your mistrust, I would point to the fact that I helped you escape. The twins are all that matter to me, meanwhile you waste energy on this useless confrontation. Can't you see that the danger all the while grows? We must stop arguing among ourselves and come up with a more practical plan of escape. In this – believe me – I have a lifetime of practice.'

'Oh, I could believe that you are more than expert than any of us in escaping the consequence of your duplicities. But the question we now need to ask ourselves is if we have any further need of you.'

'Oh, Bird Woman!' Eefa shook her head. 'Wychera is not to blame for what happened back there. We should stop fighting with one another.'

'Don't you lesson me, young Eefa.'

'Bravo, Eefa – for an example of sound common sense!' Wychera Gallant stood erect to his imperious height. 'How convenient for you adults to lecture one who, in the gravest danger, gained key information from the experience. None of you, I would wager, were sharp enough to spot what might prove vital to our survival.'

'What are you prattling about now, you wretched scarecrow?'

'So, Captain Quimbre, while you were panicking, I made my own exploration of what was really going on. In her overweening arrogance, the demon being, Lustfera, revealed something of her true nature.'

'What do you mean?'

'Hah! There are times the role of changer comes in useful, even if I must decoy myself to resemble a ghoul.'

Quimbre's face was bunched in distaste, but Bird Woman stilled him with a placatory hand on his shoulder. 'Let him speak.'

Wychera looked about all of the company, arching those big green eyes.

Bird Woman sighed. 'Please! Oh, for goodness sakes, let's cease the recriminations for the moment. We all witnessed the terrible destruction of that weapon. What are you now telling us? Are you claiming that you changed form so you could examine the aftermath of that carnage?'

'Is that not the advantage of my being a changer?'

'My goodness! I don't know how even you dared to travel there. Or for that matter, how you somehow made your way back to safety. But, if you are telling us the truth, tell us what you saw?'

'What new lies are we about to hear?' The still angry Quimbre hissed.

Wychera sighed. 'I shall come to what I saw. But first, a warning! We must abandon the course we're taking. For one thing, it's the same course taken by most of the fleeing craft – which will put us in an obvious line of pursuit. We should break company immediately with the panicking herd.'

This was enough for Quimbre to confront Wychera face-to-face again, this time with his hand on the grip of his cutlass. But Bird Woman stayed his arm, shaking her head at any continuing stupidity.

'Let him explain. There's much in what he says that makes sense. He's absolutely right. There is no safety in numbers here. Nothing really makes any sense to me. Why the destruction of Serenity? The Ursascogans were the original natives of the sacred isle. They would never have willingly destroyed it.'

'Pah!' Quimbre snorted. 'Conquering armies throughout history have liked nothing better than looting and pillaging.'

'Aye, but where did you witness looting or pillaging? What we witnessed was an abomination.' Bird Woman was shaking her thoughtful head. 'The changer is right. The attack on Serenity was a deliberate annihilation.'

Wychera nodded. 'Now you are thinking as you should. Such wanton destruction makes no sense. So, we should ask ourselves a new question. What if there was a more sinister purpose in laying waste to the sacred isle?'

Eefa piped up, 'What are you suggesting?'

Wychera's voice became soft with potency. 'Well now – let's recall all of what we witnessed. I think we are agreed that it made no sense in terms of conquest. Hence, we must assume that there was some other purpose, one more important even than the prize of taking the greatest treasure in the entire Sea of Stars?'

Bird Woman shook her head. 'What possible prize could be more important?'

'What if that Shee-devil knew that Eefa and Magio were on the island?'

Quimbre's brow was creased in consternation. 'Why in the name of the undying, would you even think such a thing?'

Gallant confronted Quimbre, with his green eyes bulging. 'Why? You really ask this of me? When, back on Moon, were not Eefa and Magio hunted with the same remorseless fury? Would it not make perfect sense that the same forces that hunted them on Moon are now determined to destroy them here in the Sea of Stars?'

Bird Woman looked from Quimbre to Eefa and Magio, all three of whom now returning their wide-eyed gazes to the changer.

The twins nodded as one. It was a trembling Eefa who lifted her eyes to the air above them and then spoke for the entire company,

'Oh, Woll . . .! Is Wychera right?'

Immediately the splinter of gold materialized in their midst.

Yes, Eefa! I have seen and heard. And I am afraid that the changer has spoken the truth. The destruction of the Serenity was wicked beyond reason. And yet the Star of Mourning does nothing without reason.

Eefa was now alarmed. 'What does that mean?'

I fear the truth is much as Wychera has suggested. The enemy knew you had arrived on Serenity. The Star of Mourning sensed your presence there. I fear that the destruction of Serenity was intended to destroy you. And that being the case, she will know by now that you have evaded her once more.

Eefa was shocked at the frost sprite's words. 'Oh, Woll, don't tell me that Magio and I were responsible for the destruction of Serenity.'

You were not responsible. The Star of Mourning was responsible – under the orders of her dreadful overlord, the undying who calls himself The One.

Bird Woman exclaimed. 'Enough! No more recriminations among us. Simply tell us then, what must we do here and now to keep the twins safe?'

Quimbre swore. 'I can figure that much, woman. We must flee – as far and as fast as the wind will carry us.'

You cannot outrun the Leviathan. No! We must devise a more cunning strategy.

'Oh, Woll! Tell us what to do.'

I am at a loss in this moment to advise you. I must seek the advice of the Lady of the Shore. But currently she has grave concerns of her own.

Magio interrupted the conversation. 'But if the enemy can sense our presence, where can we possibly hide?'

Somehow, and here perhaps the changer, Wychera, would best advise you. He must find a way to hide your presence from her probing senses.

Quimbre's whisper was barely audible. 'You are asking us to entrust the safety of the twins to that ragamuffin.'

'Just a minute, Quimbre.' Magio forestalled him. 'Tell me, Woll, this so-called Star of Mourning – is she capable of detecting the Scuttlebutt by some special means, such as our scent?'

She is not interested in the ship. It is you she senses – you and your sister, Eefa. and not through any of the mortal senses. She hunts you through a more deadly skill. She can sense your very soul spirit.

Eefa's hand rose to her mouth. 'Oh, Woll! What can we possibly do to avoid her?' Can she sense all of our spirits?'

Likely not. All other than you and Magio are of no interest to her.

Magio exclaimed, 'Then we endanger everybody, Eefa and me. We must find a way to hide ourselves from her?'

If only we could find a way, Magio.

Wychera mused, 'We all need time to think some more about that.'

Indeed, time has now become a precious commodity. Back on Moon, the problem appeared a simple one – merely to keep the twins safe meanwhile planning to free the Lady from her dreadful prison. But now the danger is far greater.

Eefa was terrified by Woll's words. 'Woll! Oh, for goodness sakes, tell us what to do. Don't just leave us with such vague advice.'

What Wychera advises would appear wise. Quimbre must take heed of his advice. You must abandon the course taken by the fleeing ships. Take a new direction that will separate you from the herd.

Quimbre expostulated, 'Are you asking me to allow that wandering elf, Gallant, to be our guide? He will surely take us aslant of every wind and current.'

I'm afraid you must swallow your pride, Quimbre, and let the changer lead you. As ever, I shall assist you, helping to cloak your passage from sight and scent – aye, and perhaps some other senses that mortals do not possess.

A visibly reluctant Quimbre complied. After that conversation, he allowed Wychera to follow alien winds and currents, avoiding any confrontations that might have brought attention to them, sailing always just deliberately out of sight of any passing islands. Quimbre assented even when Wychera's instincts meandered southernmost, when a polar chill began to cool their passage.

Nowhere Is Safe

For Eefa it was just another chilly morning, sitting in the prow, with the nightmare of Serenity on everyone's mind. She closed her eyes, taking comfort from the cool breeze on her face as the ship set sail driven by a brisk wind that would take them further southwards into an increasingly cold sea. Hunched on the time-worn oak rail, her chin cradled by her cold damp hands, she allowed her senses to freely embrace the world about her, offering no resistance to wayward thoughts as the deck swayed below her and the sky wheeled above. Her careless abandoning of caution proved to be a mistake.

'No!'

Her resistance arrived too late to prevent her from falling into a new awake-dream in which she found herself frozen within a terrible stillness, trapped in a game from which she could not escape, one in which she was obliged to surrender her will to an alien mind that piloted her every move. Right there, directly facing her, was the familiar prisoner with his blind eyes hidden by his lank graying hair, sitting on that same stump of stone.

'What am I expected to do?'

She felt the hackles rise on the back of her neck, felt the goosebumps spread across her shoulders and down her arms to her fingertips, felt them rise on every inch of the skin of

her chest and abdomen, then spread out to envelop her legs
to the tips of her toes.

There appeared to be nothing she could do to calm
herself. She must surely speak to the prisoner. Discover why
he was haunting her.

'Who are you? What do you want of me?'

There was no reply.

Terror invaded her muscles, making them stiffen up,
refusing to obey her. Her heart began to palpitate, weakening
any resolve she had left. She felt her resistance falter, as a cloak
began to envelop her consciousness, causing her to enter a
stupor. Yet every instinct suggested that to give in at this
moment would be a very bad idea. Eefa struggled with her
flagging willpower just to stay in control. She must wake up.

She breathed more deeply, forcing her lungs to take air
slowly in and out. She felt herself recover a little of her will.
But even now that she was closer to awake, the dream refused
to let go of her. Why did she have to confront that figure
seated on the stump of stone? There appeared to be something
magnetic about him . . . something she just couldn't easily put
into words. Even though a chill was still invading her being,
she felt compelled to examine him more closely. She decided
it was his stillness that somehow reached out and touched her
so very deeply.

She told herself, 'Calm down. He isn't real. You're just
dreaming. It's all a dream – just a dream.'

Nevertheless, as she watched him closely, she sensed a
prickling disquiet about him. She saw that he was surrounded
by those moving shadows of what appeared to be wraiths
and ghouls. How could he just sit there, when such awful
creatures were moving about him? And yet he appeared to
be unmoved. That was it. Yes, now she realized that that was

what was so strange about him. His lack of concern about his own safety in this place of terrifying specters.

And then, in an instant, she found herself within that same terrifying landscape as the tormented man. It caused every hackle on her body to rise and her heartbeat to surge into her throat. Frantically, she scurried under a ruined arch of blackened stone, skulking as far back as she could into the shadows.

She bit her thumbnail, her body quivering with dread. She asked herself, 'Why am I here? What in the world is happening to me?'

As ever, it made no sense.

But then, who expected nightmares to make sense?

Eefa shifted her position so she could examine the desolate place, the scurry of those frightful specters that were all about her here, and then the figure seated on the stump of masonry, his face lowered.

'Who are you? Where am I – where is this place? Why in heaven's name are you haunting me?'

The man appeared oblivious of her presence.

She watched some more . . . and then, catching her breath, she spotted something even stranger still.

There was something odd about the way the specters scurried around him. Sometimes they paused, as if attempting some communication with the figure. On a single occasion she saw how a specter stopped to stare at him, as if transfixed by him. The specter was unusually tall, with a nightmarish body made of entwined serpents, visibly writhing and changing from moment to moment.

Eefa skulked even further back into the shadows, but, though she had already clasped her ears to keep them out, she heard the specter's alien words addressed to the prisoner.

She had no idea how that sibilant hiss became words within her mind. It was as if she were listening to the forked tongue of a serpent,

Why not stop this now? You could end it. You, who were renowned for wisdom – would you rather drown in ignominy than end this wretched war.

What possible war could the creature be alluding to?

The prisoner spoke – it astonished Eefa to realize that his words, in the same alien hiss as that of the specter, also became comprehensible, as if she had been enabled to understand the alien speech of his interrogator,

There might be an end, if there were hope of redemption. But when dealing with your master, Lustfera, there is but lies.

My Master will reward those who support him – power beyond any available to them in the entire realm of the undying.

You are persistent in your debate. You lie, with the precision of a dagger. There is no honor at the very core of your being.

Eefa was shocked to hear his words so calmly and lucidly expressed. She realized that she must surely be witnessing something important. But she had no idea of what the conversation between the prisoner and his interrogator truly meant. Was it possible that this specter, whom the prisoner called Lustfera, was the enemy of the same name that Wychera had detected in the ruins of Serenity? If Wychera was right, Lustfera was likely the same monster that had hunted Eefa and Magio back on Moon. If so, she was also capable of detecting their very soul spirits.

That thought was now even more terrifying.

The same terror woke Eefa out of the awake-dream.

Was it possible that her awake-dream state might have enabled the servant of their enemy to discover the Scuttlebutt?

That same thought caused her heartbeat to rise into her skull. And yet she desperately wondered, had not the blind man drawn her here to witness this very conversation?

Had she allowed herself to be seduced into trusting the blind man?

Eefa hurriedly went over every aspect of the conversation she had overheard in that terrible place. The prisoner, despite his position, had dared to confront that terrible specter even though he and she appeared to be enemies.

Then . . . oh, then . . . surely . . . the blind man must have thought it safe for her awake-dream to witness that conversation?

Eefa gripped her own face, with her eyes clenched shut.

Had what she witnessed been some sort of a lesson?

If so, what exactly had she just learnt from it?

Her thoughts were now going around and around in her head. She had seen how the blind man did not fear the snake being. He appeared indifferent to her presence. What little of what she could see of his face, his very posture, was altogether calm . . . altogether unafraid . . .

Good! You sensed what I hoped you would sense, Eefa. But, for the moment, you must keep it secret. You can tell no-one.

Oh, goodness! His voice, the voice she now recognized to be that of the prisoner in her dreams, was back inside her head. But was this just a trick to make her trust him?

'Tell me – oh, please, tell me – what am I to do?'

For the moment you must continue to hide. Continue to bide your time. Please believe me, even if it all seems so strange, so terrifying right now . . . In time things will change . . . You will come to understand.

What was going on? What was about to change? What in the world was really happening to her and her brother, Magio?

'Why won't you explain what's happening to me?'

There was no reply.

Yet his presence, his insistence, convinced Eefa that there had to be a reason she was here. She took a deep breath, her eyes blinking with the effort of trying to understand what it might possibly mean. Whatever its significance, it felt vitally important to her, and to Magio and their friends aboard the Scuttlebutt.

It was all so confusing and strange, she desperately needed to think. It occurred to her that the impulse – the instinct – that had brought her here might have something in common with her ability to enter her awake-dreams, those same awake-dreams she shared with Magio all her life. It was so very strange that it made her wonder if . . . oh, she hardly dared to think what she was now beginning to wonder . . .

She felt her heartbeat patter uncomfortably fast, her breathing to quicken.

'Yes!'

Eefa was now sure that her ability to enter awake-dreams was somehow linked to her recurring visions of the blind man in that terrible prison.

The blind man she now felt she could trust.

Even though her entire skin prickled with goosebumps, Eefa pressed her mind, her very soul, to take her back to the sepulchral prison of the blind man. But now, when she returned there, she found that the blind man's head had risen. She felt a sense of presence that was stronger than in any of her previous visitations. The man was gazing directly at her, as if he could sense her despite those blind eyes. She was certain that he was aware of her presence with perfect lucidity.

Eefa witnessed no change of expression on his face, no attempt at normal speech. She opened her will to communicating mind-to-mind.

Eefa! Please listen to me very carefully. Heed my warning while you still can. You must abandon the Sea of Stars. Nowhere you journey there is safe for you.

Eefa felt close to fainting at what he had just told her. But she took a deep breath. She struggled to control her rising panic.

'Oh, for goodness sakes! How can we abandon the Sea of Stars?'

All I can do is to advise you. If you do nothing else, make sure you communicate my message to those who would protect you and Magio.

'Who in the world can possibly protect us now?'

You must put your trust in the changer. You and Magio must put your very lives in the hands of Wychera Gallant.

The Portal

Eefa stood on the foredeck with her back to the prow, from where she saw the tall figure of Wychera approaching her from midships. Was he now searching for her? Did he know of the message she had just received from the blind man? Her heartbeat had never slowed since her recent awake-dream. She felt it throbbing in her throat as Wychera drew near, already speaking softly to her,

'You are as pale as a sheet. You look like you are about to faint. Please take hold of my hand. Grip tight and trust me.'

She couldn't help hesitating. The words of the blind man, in that terrible place, teeming with specters, had left her feeling very jittery.

'Eefa?'

It was Magio's voice. He came running to find her staring blankly at Wychera's proferred hand. Magio looked as if he were every bit as confused as she was.

'What's going on?'

'I . . . I don't know.'

Magio turned to Wychera. 'What's the matter with Eefa?'

Wychera ignored him, taking hold of Eefa's shoulders to support her.

It was all so confusing and terrifying that Eefa felt tears come into her eyes. Her voice sounded shrill in her own ears. 'Magio, I have seen him again – the blind man in that terrible place. Oh, I don't ever want to go back there!' She took a deep breath and then she stared into Wychera's face, looked at him with widened eyes.

Magio shouted, 'What is it, Eefa? What did the blind man say to you?'

'He told me we were no longer safe anywhere in the Sea of Stars.'

'But where else can we go?'

'Oh, Magio, he told me we must trust Wychera!'

'Trust that rogue.' Magio backed away from her. 'Don't expect me to take any notice of some apparition from one of your awake-dreams.'

'Magio – please! You have to listen to me. Didn't Woll tell us to do the very same? I can't even pretend to understand what's going on. I know it isn't going to be easy to trust Wychera. But such strange things are happening – things we simply do not understand. After what I just saw, I'm terrified.'

Magio tried to tug Eefa away from Wychera's supporting hands. 'No, Eefie! Quimbre doesn't trust him. I don't think Bird Woman does, neither. Come back with me. We need to talk to Quimbre.'

Wychera shrugged, then released Eefa. He held his long-fingered hands up, the same fingers spread. 'Do so, by all means go talk to Quimbre and Bird Woman. But first, please let Eefa speak. We must hear what she was told by the blind man in her dream.'

Eefa stared up at the tall, lean figure of the changer, who gazed at her with those luminescent eyes. She took a deep breath. 'The blind man said we needed to flee. But there was nowhere safe in the entire Sea of Stars. I had to trust you, Wychera, to know where to find sanctuary.'

'He spoke the truth.' Wychera nodded back to her, then looked towards the north, to the distant horizon, as if fearful of what he might witness.

'But where else can we flee? There's nowhere left to run to.'

'Not so! There is a place, one you know nothing about.'

Magio cried, 'No, Eefa! Don't listen to him.'

'What place?' She cried. 'Where else can we possibly run?'

'Somewhere I promise that you and Magio will be safer.'

Eefa didn't know what to think. She turned her tear-filled eyes to her brother, then looked back at the changer once more. 'Although every instinct in me bids me not to trust you, I'm terrified by all that I saw and heard in my latest dream. I just can't think clearly anymore.'

Magio cried out, 'Don't trust him, Eefa.'

Eefa shook her head. 'I really don't know who else to trust. I don't know what to do. But I do sense that we are all in terrible danger. I sense it so very strongly. And one person I do trust is Woll. We need to speak to Woll again.'

Wychera nodded. 'Your instincts are right, Eefa. Do so now – do it immediately. Take the counsel of the frost sprite queen.'

Eefa called out to Woll, her heart pounding so hard she felt dizzy with it. 'Oh, Woll, I desperately need you. You have to advise me.'

It only took seconds, though it seemed like an eternity, before the golden spark appeared. Even then, it appeared to be spinning dizzily, as if Woll herself were just as shaken by events as Eefa.

'Oh, Woll – thank heavens you're here! I've been confronted by the blind man in a new awake-dream. He warned me that we are no longer safe anywhere in the Sea of Stars. He urged us to escape to . . . to . . . Oh, I don't know where! He said nowhere in the Sea of Stars was safe anymore. He told me we had to trust Wychera to guide us. But I don't know if I can trust Wychera, or for that matter even the blind man. I no longer know who to trust anymore, other than you.'

The golden spark seemed to be as confused as Eefa, metamorphosing into all the colors of the rainbow. The brilliance of the frost sprite's light engulfed Eefa in a whirling cloud, until she just couldn't take it anymore.

'Stop it! Please stop all this gyrating about! You're just bewildering me further. Please advise us. Tell me and Magio what to do.'

I have just been in conversation with My Lady. She wants to know more of your recent awake-dream. But I can see from your consternation that this is not the moment. Wychera is right. We are all in the gravest danger.

'What are we to do?'

The Lady assures me that the blind man is right. If he advises you so, you must trust Wychera Gallant. The Lady now believes that he truly is your protector.

Eefa fell back in surprise, then turned to look at Wychera, who gazed at her, his luminous eyes full of concern.

An agonized Magio demanded to know, 'What in the world does Woll mean?'

Wychera spoke softly but firmly. 'We no longer have time to debate what to do. If the dreadful being I sensed back there in the ruins of Serenity can sense your very spirits, she will find you, no matter where you flee in the Sea of Stars.'

Eefa saw how Wychera looked towards that north again. All of a sudden, she was afraid that at any moment something monstrous might come looming over that all-too near horizon.

'But what can we possibly do?'

'I must take you to another world.'

Eefa and Magio stared at Wychera, equally aghast. 'What is that supposed to mean? How can you even talk of such a thing?'

He nodded, his eyes boring into Eefa's own. 'I am, as the frost sprite queen just confirmed, your protector – both yours and Magio's.'

Both their voices questioned him at once, 'Our protector?'

'I thought it unlikely you'd believe me if I had told you so when you first discovered me among you.'

Magio exclaimed, 'I find it just as difficult to believe you now.'

'Of course you do, Magio! Yet, now that both Woll and Eefa's blind prisoner have confirmed it, you know that I am telling you the truth.'

Magio exclaimed, 'So, what are you now telling us? It was no accident that you came on board?'

'It was no accident.'

Eefa no longer dared to look at the horizon. Although she suspected she would see no looming Ursascogan warship, she was more certain now that she could sense the nearness of that terrible being. 'Why in the world . . . Oh, for goodness sakes, what is really going on? Wychera, you claim you were sent here to protect us? Who, in the world, could have possibly sent you to do that?'

'I am the servant of the same undying you care for.'

'You serve the Lady of the Shore?'

'I do! And I now freely profess that, if necessary, I would lay down my life in her service.'

Eefa was so stunned she felt unsteady on her feet.

Wychera Gallant stood erect, his hands on her shoulders. He gazed from Eefa to Magio. 'The time has come for you both to trust me.'

Magio was shaking his bewildered head. 'You – you really are an adventurer-warrior?'

'Unlikely as it might seem, Magio, I am.'

Magio exclaimed, 'Oh, I can't decide what to think! How can we know what to believe anymore?'

Eefa shook her head. 'Nevertheless, Woll just confirmed it, Magio. Wychera was sent by the Lady.'

Magio was clutching at the amulet hanging around his neck. He took a deep breath, then began to murmur under his breath, blinking hard, with no attempt to hide his panic.

Eefa scolded her brother. 'Stop that! You have to calm down.'

'How can I calm down? Neither of us knows what's happening anymore.'

Wychera placed a calming hand on Magio's shoulder. 'Your skepticism is only natural, Magio. But if you would become a warrior, you must rely on your instincts in a situation like this. Go ahead. Trust your instincts right now.'

Magio stared into the eyes of the elfin changer. As he did so, Magio's eyes became round as saucers.

'Now you feel it – you too are a warrior in the making. But we know now that things have taken a critical turn. There's less time than even I realized. That terrible battleship is close. We have very little time in which to save the Scuttlebutt, and all aboard her.'

Eefa could see that Magio was close to panic. He was clutching his dragon amulet against his breast, and staring into the changer's eyes. 'I can recall once, back on Moon,' he whispered, 'when I was as scared out of my wits as I feel now. Back then, I heard the voice of the Lady inside my head.'

Wychera nodded. 'Likely, you did, Magio. Calm your thoughts right now, so you can recall it more clearly. Go back to that time when you heard the Lady inside your head. Try to remember exactly what you did.'

'The voice in my head told me to hold my dragon-thing tight. So, I did. I held it fiercely.' Magio's fist was now white with tension about the amulet, which was now pulsating with light. Magio stared at his fist in open astonishment.

'Now, do you trust me, Magio?'

Magio looked into the changer's eyes and nodded.

It was all becoming so strange that Eefa felt dizzy with bewilderment and she could see, from his face, that Magio felt the same.

'You know more of who we are?'

'Oh, you have ever been of such importance that a great witch had to be close by at all times to ensure your safety.'

'What do you mean?'

But Eefa was already experiencing the dreadful feeling that she knew exactly what Wychera was talking about. 'Oh, you're talking about Gran.'

'A great witch was indeed your protector – from earliest childhood.'

Both Eefa and Magio were dumbfounded. Neither could come to terms with what Wychera Gallant was now telling them – that their beloved Gran, who had been the only one to care for them all their lives, had been a witch.

Magio was still clutching his amulet with whitened knuckles. Eefa turned her thoughts to their friend, Woll, Queen of the frost sprites. 'Oh, Woll, if ever Magio and I needed your advice, now is the moment.'

Immediately, the spark of gold shimmered in the air above their heads.

'You've heard . . .?'

I heard, Eefa.

'What are we to believe?'

I'm afraid that Wychera speaks the truth.

'Oh, but . . . how . . . oh, Gran!'

For your safety, dearest Eefa – you and Magio – to protect your very lives. This was all that ever mattered to those who loved and cared for you.

'It's all so confusing – so confusing and terrifying.'

I'm sorry it is so confusing. Woll whispered in both their ears. *But time is passing. I'm afraid that, right now, time is too precious to spend on further explanations. You must listen to your protector, Wychera. Follow his instructions – do exactly what he tells you.*

Magio felt the focus of Wychera's gaze on his face, those glowing eyes looking deep into his own.

'Magio, you know what to do.'

'Yes, I know.'

Eefa's eyes turned to look, wide-eyed, at her brother, who was gripping his amulet with a fierce determination. The last time he had used his amulet, they had been plucked up and borne away, out of the ordinary world of Moon and ferried to the Beach of Bones in the claws of a gigantic dragon.

'Do it, Magio – do it now!'

Magio closed his eyes and focused on the amulet, dangling on the leather cord around his neck. He held his talisman even tighter still, until his hands began to shudder.

Strange thoughts, even stranger feelings, experiences, rushed through Eefa's mind as she closed her own eyes in tandem with Magio's, adding the force of her will to aid that of her brother. In the explosive consummation of their combined wills, her senses were dazzled by a vision of extraordinary beauty, with colors merging and metamorphosing beyond anything she thought possible, and inspiring strange feelings inside her very being – feelings she had never felt before. It was as if, between them, their summed wills had borne them beyond anything their individual imaginations could ever have anticipated . . .

As they gazed, with widened eyes, an extraordinary diorama came into a clearer focus, so that they saw what looked like a beautifully clear midnight sky, with a gargantuan proliferation of stars. The stars were spread about them in every dimension, and fading off into the distance, as if into eternity.

'Oh, britzy! It's like we're rising into the stars.'

A panicking Eefa shrieked, 'Oh, Woll – are you still with us?'

I am here with you.

Magio was now screeching in delight. 'Gee . . . oh, so wonderful . . . But . . . what's happening, Wychera? Where are we heading?'

Wychera's voice came to them, sounding every bit as astonished as the twins,

'Extraordinary as it might seem, we are all still aboard the Scuttlebutt – but we are no longer sailing the Sea of Stars. We are being ferried to a very different world far away, in the grasp of a dragon that should be familiar to you, Magio. Your dragon is bearing us out of harm's way from the clutches of a malign being that would stop at nothing to destroy you.'

Eefa whispered, 'I'll never understand.'

But it was Woll and not Wychera who replied,

In time you will come to better understand such mysteries. But so endangered are you and Magio that your safety can only be assured within the otherworld of Aeonia.

'Aeonia?'

Eefa heard the startled voice of her brother, asking the same question that was now uppermost in her own mind.

The name sounded vaguely familiar to Eefa's ears. A dream world she recalled from the fairytales Gran had told them when they were little . . .

Aeonia!

The World of Fairytales

Magio whirled and turned, in useless attempts to orientate himself. How could it be possible that the Scuttlebutt was now no longer afloat in the Sea of Stars but was . . . was flying through . . . through what? Through the very air . . .? No, through what felt like time and space . . . whatever those strange words meant. It was being borne through time and space as if it had sprouted magical wings . . . the wings of a dragon . . .

'Ooooohhhh – britzy! We're just floating . . . floating through the heavens . . . floating along silently . . . floating on absolutely nothing.'

Magio made no pretence of understanding what was happening. He was in ecstasy. 'Hey, I can see nothing at all clearly.'

His left hand was still gripped tightly by Wychera's guiding hand. The elfin changer was whispering into his ear on that same side. 'Please look again. This time I want you both to look once more – not with your eyes but through my eyes. I want you to see where we are going through the eyes of an elf.'

Magio heard Eefa's exclamation of wonder. 'Oh, Magio! Do you see what I'm seeing?'

Magio was unable to reply. He had no words to say what he was feeling. Nothing here appeared familiar to him. In fact, he was feeling so very strange in himself. Things were going on he did not understand.

He heard Wychera whisper, not into his ear but into his mind,

What you are experiencing, Magio and Eefa, is Dromenon.

He heard Eefa's startled exclamation,

'Dromenon . . .!'

You have heard of Dromenon, haven't you, Magio?

Yes! Gran would talk about it in her fairytales.

Dromenon – the in-between world. The world that was everywhere and nowhere. The emptiness that separated the spheres of mortals and the undying.

For Magio, Dromenon was forever linked with Gran's tales of magical places, populated with pixies and elves, a world where magical beings did magical things, a place where time was . . . was different. The beings that lived here did not age the way humans aged. Gran had taken him and Eefa there in so many strange and different fairytales, recounting stories of giants, dragons, ogres, witches casting spells. But he had never imagined it to be a real place. How could it be real? It belonged to the imagination, to the realms of dreams and fairytales.

'Oh, Eefa – don't you see! I understand – and at one and the same time I don't understand . . . I mean, how in the world have we come here? And yet, now we are here, it feels so real. How can we possibly be here and yet we still find ourselves aboard the Scuttlebutt?'

Eefa could only shake her head.

The twins stared about them at the extraordinary panorama of what had seemed like stars. But now that they looked more closely at the glowing shapes, they could see that they were not pin-points of light, like one would expect of stars, but complex perplexing shapes.

'No – they couldn't possibly be whole different worlds!'

'Yes – Eefa! That is exactly what you are seeing.'

'I can't even begin to understand.'

'How could you? But please don't ask me to explain. I'm just an elfin adventurer – no magician.'

'My dragon has brought us here.' Magio was still gripping his amulet.

'Yes, Magio – the same dragon you met in the mountains of Moon.'

For the moment Magio just continued to clasp his amulet, lost in amazement.

Eefa was the first to come to her senses. 'But where exactly are these many different worlds?'

'They populate the infinity of Dromenon.'

'But, how . . .? How did we get here? How could even a dragon bring us here?'

'Through magic, Eefa.'

Eefa took a deep breath. 'I can't even begin to understand.'

Magio shook his head. His eyes were shining, reflecting the extraordinary panorama of worlds that were everywhere about them. 'But, hey, can we simply go somewhere – take off to some wonderful place among all these magical worlds? Hey – oh, britzy! Can we explore them?'

Wychera laughed. 'We are headed for just one of that multitude. As befits the means of our getting there, we are headed for the dragon world of Aeonia.'

'Aeonia . . .' Their two voices exclaimed as one.

'I believe you might have heard of Aeonia?'

Eefa sighed. 'We have, from so many of Gran's fairytales…'

Magio remained skeptical about this fanciful place, called Aeonia. As far as he could see, they were still floating through Dromenon on the deck of the Scuttlebutt. How in the world did that make sense? Nothing here made any more sense whatsoever. But still he found himself gazing about himself in wonderment.

'How then,' he pressed Wychera, 'do we get there?'

Wychera laughed. 'There are many avenues leading to Aeonia. But I think I might have the ideal route for you. Do you recall with what joy you and Eefa swam in the bay back on the beach in Warren?'

The twins nodded as one, their eyes aglow.

'Why, then, we shall swim there in exactly the same way you swam at Warren. We shall brave the tides of Dromenon to find Aeonia's shore.'

Eefa squeezed her brother's hand, joining him in gazing over the prow of the Scuttlebutt into the inky darkness that surrounded them. She felt every bit as excited and nervous as Magio did.

She blurted out, 'But there's nothing there, beyond the prow of the ship. Nothing other than inky emptiness. What are you suggesting we do? Are you asking us to just dive into that emptiness and hope we don't just drown in it?'

'No!' Wychera laughed again. 'The wonder of Aeonia awaits you. If you but close your eyes and believe, you will find yourself there.'

Magio chipped in, 'No way!'

'Well, now, let me show you how to do it.'

Eefa hung back, every bit as skeptical as Magio.

'Step up on the rail. I'll hold you steady until you dive. Simply close your eyes and imagine you are back facing the tide at Warren. Don't question it. Just close your eyes and imagine that you are diving into those familiar waters. Close your eyes and dive in, as so many times before.'

Eefa did as Wychera instructed her. She closed her eyes. But she couldn't resist blinking them open again, fretful even as Wychera released her and her feet lifted off the rail. With a squeal of astonishment, she saw her brother dive beside her, with his eyes tight shut. With a panicky trepidation, she joined him in plunging into the pitch-dark void . . .

There was a vague impression of falling. It wasn't as unpleasant as she had imagined, just a peculiar sense of translocation, without the impression of actual air rushing about her skin, or past her panicky ears. After all the stresses of recent days, she even felt a strange, liberating sense of letting go, of abandoning every need of caring. But abruptly a powerful olive-skinned hand had taken a grip of her left wrist, a reassuring hand that was hauling her up and out of the darkness, to emerging into freezing cold water. Her heart was still in her mouth, and she felt a strange reluctance to abandoning that cloying excitement of falling.

She heard Wychera's voice penetrate her sluggish mind. 'Total abandonment is a seduction in itself. Do not allow yourself to become ensnared by it.'

'I . . . Oh, I just wanted to escape. I had felt so overwhelmed by everything.' She was struggling to understand whatever it was that she had coveted. 'It felt so liberating to just let go.'

'Beware the beguilement of Aeonia!'

She sensed his guiding hand release her wrist.

'Swim with me a little further, Eefa.'

She felt him release his grip on her wrist. He was trusting her to get a grip on her feelings.

She took strength from Wychera's presence, from his patience with her, from his belief in her. She was already swimming resolutely through a tide of utter peace and harmony, her being carried along with powerful strokes of her limbs, her mind increasingly suffused by such profound feelings of joy. Only now did she realize that her eyes were still closed. Opening them, up ahead she saw the lithesome shape of Wychera Gallant, cutting through the glimmering streams of water with occasional strokes of those long powerful arms, his body as sinewy as an eel. She was inspired by the grace of his movements, the power of his confidence.

Magio was now coming up close beside her. They glided together, all three in one coordinated graceful undulation of their beings, allowing themselves to be intoxicated by the same shared ecstasy of movement and being. All three of them emerged, gasping for breath, on a beach of warm pink sand, where Wychera's strong hands helped them, trembling and shivering, to their feet.

'Hey, Eefie!' Magio's eyes were opened wide, gazing all about them at the beautiful beach of red sand and boulders, bounding a vast landscape of rich grassland. Doesn't it feel so strange to find ourselves in a new world? I mean, doesn't it feel like we were always intended to come here?'

Eefa laughed, knowing exactly what he meant, while sitting on a boulder and grasping fistfuls of the sand and letting it trickle through her fingers.

'Yes – oh, yes, Gio! It really does.' Eefa whispered back, her own eyes wide with astonishment.

Wychera clapped his hands and laughed. 'Welcome to Aeonia!'

'Yeeeeehaaaaah!' Magio shouted out gleefully as he twirled about on the sand. 'It's even more beautiful than Warren.'

'Calm down, Magio.'

But he was already running about, exploring. Eefa could see now, just watching her brother, how he had grown taller since they had left Moon, more manly. It intrigued her even as it disturbed her a little at the same time.

Wychera gazed about them, from the sea to the shore. 'Perhaps you would also like to do some exploring?'

'Yes, I would.'

'Please allow me to be your guide. For those who have never come to Aeonia before, it can be a little daunting.'

Eefa spun around in a complete circle, gazing wide-eyed at the turquoise pools and the luxuriant deep green grass and the multi-colored foliage of the scattered shrubs and trees.

'Oh, it's enchanting!'

'Yes, you're right. It is enchanting. Even the birdsong here appears to play more beguiling tunes. In all of my wandering, it remains the most beautiful place I have ever known.'

'So that's why you wanted to come back?'

'My purpose was more dutiful – and even I must confess now that we are here, I am glad to see your joy at being here.'

'It so reminds us of our beloved beach back in Warren, although the rocks there were black, and beset with dark pools.'

'Tell me, Eefa, did you ever look at your reflections in those black pools?'

'Gran forbade it. She even forbade mirrors in the house.'

'She didn't want you to see your reflection?'

'She had such strange notions. She thought reflections could steal your soul spirit and replace it with that of a changeling.'

Wychera laughed, shaking his head. 'Did it not occur to you that it is more likely that she did so to protect your feelings, since you were invisible?'

'Perhaps she did.'

Wychera's lips bunched up, as if he were reluctant to say what he was thinking.

'Oh, come on – out with it!'

'Even aboard the Scuttlebutt, I saw no mirrors. Such circumstances – the fact that, for most of your life, you were invisible – hid something from you.'

'What did it hide?'

'Why don't you look for yourself? There are pools here, still waters among the leafy plants and reeds, the surface of which would make perfect mirrors.'

'Why do you talk about pools and mirrors?'

'Because, if you looked into them, you would see yourself for the first time.'

Eefa's heart was racing. She wasn't sure that she wanted to see herself for the first time. 'Gran told us, Magio and me, that all of the bad thoughts and deeds we had committed would be reflected in our faces.'

Wychera shook his head and laughed. 'Perhaps you might be pleasantly surprised by your own reflection.'

Eefa allowed herself to be led to a pool, where a mixture of shadows and greenery were embedded in stillness. She felt the reassuring arm of Wychera around her shoulders as she gazed into its limpid reflection.

'Oh – whose reflection is that?'

'It's you, Eefa.'

'But the face I see is so strange, rather like the face I would have imagined of a fairy, or even perhaps a princess.'

'It's the real you.'

'I'm no princess.'

'No, you are not a princess.'

'What then are you trying to say?'

'We get used to our reflections, so much so we do not see them as they truly are any more. Reflections are a superficial vision of us. The wholeness is more complex – not perfect, perhaps, but to my mind more beautiful.'

'Why do you say such things?'

'Because it's time somebody did.'

Eefa shook her head. 'I'm no longer a girl.'

'You're a young woman.'

'I cannot help being myself.'

'No, you cannot!' Wychera held her gently by the shoulders, looked at her, face to face, and smiled. 'We need to dry our clothes. While they dry, we could go for a swim in these wonderful pink and azure lagoons?'

'That would be lovely.'

When Eefa removed her clothes so they could dry in the warmth of the rocks, Wychera looked at her naked body strangely.

'You're so innocent.'

Eefa looked back at him too, his muscular olive-skinned limbs equally naked, with a similar curiosity. She found herself blinking far too rapidly.

'Are you absolutely sure we're safe here?'

'You're right to remind me. We shouldn't forget the reason why you're here. I can see how much you need to understand all that has happened to you and Magio. But I must confess that even I don't pretend to understand everything. But I can assure you that the dreadful Lustfera could not follow you here.'

'But, as you explained back there on the deck of the Scuttlebutt, Lustfera is merely the servant of a terrible undying. She obeys the same dreadful power that imprisoned the Lady, back on the Beach of Bones.'

'Yes, it's true.'

'Can you promise me that we're safe even here? That Lustfera's master cannot hurt us anymore?'

Wychera hesitated, gazing for a moment in the direction of the horizon. 'For that reassurance, you must talk to the powers who called you here.'

'What powers? Are you speaking about Woll?'

'I am speaking of the dragons, Eefa. Aeonia is the world of dragons.'

Eefa was so taken aback, she felt close to fainting. She reached out to take a tight hold of Wychera's hand. He gazed at her, and in that same moment she saw a melting in his eyes.

Abruptly, he gently reached down and he kissed her.

Eefa froze with shock.

The kiss had been so unexpected, so lightning fast, it left her confused. Her heartbeat had risen into her flushed throat. Her lips were still tingling in the parts that had touched his lips, parts she now touched with her fingers, in outright wonderment.

Their eyes met again.

She didn't know what to say.

He reached down, his wide-open eyes gazing down into hers, and he kissed her again, a longer kiss that seemed to go on and on, until she felt positively breathless.

He laughed, gently. 'I have wanted to kiss you from the moment I made an exhibition of myself, pretending to be a boot under your bunk.'

Eefa felt too jittery to stand. She just looked into his eyes, feeling so stunned and confused she didn't know what to do or say.

'Do you know, your eyes change color with your emotions. First, they are blue. But then the blue was invaded by gold when I kissed you. And now they twinkle with blue again, though I cannot say whether in delight or terror of me.'

Eefa dropped her head, not knowing where to look.

Did her eyes really change color? Oh, now that her entire face and neck had turned crimson in embarrassment, she recalled how, back on the beach at Warren, Magio would laugh at her when she wanted to know the color of her eyes.

'No-one has ever kissed me before.'

'Oh, they certainly would have – if they had but seen you.'

Her heartbeat was still racing as she insisted on walking on, not knowing what to think. In that moment she saw a strange gangling creature rise up out of the ground beyond a hillock, and with a heavy flapping of wings, beat its way into the air.

'Ooooh!'

'Don't be alarmed. You will encounter many creatures you might not recognize here in Aeonia.'

'Are there giants here, such as in the fairytales?'

He laughed aloud. 'Giants there are – and likely every variety of being you would have heard about in Gran's tall tales.'

'Giants – and fairy folk?'

'Yes, all you might ever have imagined.'

It was Eefa's turn to laugh. 'What – even elves?'

'Oh, I do believe you will even find beings as curious as elves. We all get by, if with a little rowdy banter with the dwarves, when there is cause for celebration.'

Eefa laughed. 'I feel so ignorant.'

Wychera smiled. 'Come, then! Let's put on our clothes again and go join Magio in exploring Aeonia.'

She dressed and took his proferred hand, glancing up at his friendly face. 'What other surprises are we likely to encounter?'

'Oh, I think you and Magio have had more than enough surprises for today. We need to throw up a warm and comfortable tent of branches atop the beach where we can make a berth above the tide for the night.

Eefa was still holding Wychera's hand when a cry from Magio up ahead caused her to stare in the direction of her brother, some small distance ahead.

Wychera continued to hold her hand as they hurried forward, and she was glad of it, for the world about them was rapidly changing. Even as they now broke into a run, daylight faded with unnerving rapidity into evening. As they neared Magio, the friendly landscape changed. Black mountains reared up out of a barren world, with a sky of wheeling dark masses of clouds that seemed to herald the coming night.

'Wychera, what's happening?'

'It is a sky of ominous portent – a sky of warning. But it is not addressed to you. If I read the portents, it's a summons from those concerned about your safety.'

Goosebumps were invading Eefa's skin. 'I thought we had left all of that behind us in the Sea of Stars?'

'If I judge it right, the dragons are about to announce themselves.'

Eefa was startled out of her wits. 'But what does that mean? What do Magio and I have to do with those dragons?'

Wychera Gallant smiled at her fondly.

'Everything – as you will discover.'

An Unexpected Warning

Everything . . .

For a frantic moment or two, Eefa was speechless, staring into those smiling green eyes. Had Wychera really said what she thought he said? That here on Aeonia dragons meant everything to her and her brother, Magio?

'Why – I mean – what are you really saying?'

'Please calm down.' He reached out and held her gently by the shoulders. 'I'm telling you the simple truth, Eefa. Aeonia is the world of the dragons. They rule it. They decide everything that happens here.'

'And that's why you brought Magio and me here? You brought us here to meet real living and breathing dragons?'

'I brought you and Magio here because the dragons of Aeonia instructed me to bring you here. The dragons and the Lady of the Shore were concerned for you and Magio. They knew the danger you faced. It was under their instruction that I searched far and wide for you, aboard the Scuttlebutt. My sole and exclusive mission was to bring you, the twins of Moon, to this sanctuary.'

'And then what?'

'Well then!' He gazed about him, at the sea and the sand dunes, and then up into the summery sky above them. 'Then we simply wait on the dragons of Aeonia to tell us what we must do.'

'Oh, Wychera!'

Eefa felt so jittery, she thought she would faint. She gazed about herself in a panic, looking for Magio, who had gone ahead, intent on his own exploration.

'I think we need to talk'

'Then let us talk.'

Eefa was so bewildered by what Wychera had told her, she was hardly conscious of the fact they were still walking. 'This world – Aeonia – it's so very strange.'

'I can see that you might think so.'

She was aware that he must be deliberately slowing his long-legged gait to allow her to keep up with him.

'I can see now – that swim – when we abandoned the Scuttlebutt. It felt so very strange. So . . . so dream-like.'

'Magical, is that what you mean?'

'Yes – oh, yes. It felt positively magical.'

'Aeonia can take some getting used to.'

'Yes!' Eefa spun in a full circle, her head feeling dizzy. The very notion of a magical swim. Oh, but I'm beginning to see things clearer. How else but through some powers of magic could we have found our way aboard an old clinker ship to a new world in the sky?'

Wychera paused in walking to gaze at her enraptured face.

'And you, Wychera, you really were sent by the dragons – by the dragons and the Lady – to find me and Magio?'

'Yes, Eefa. Magic was involved from the very beginning of your journey.'

'Real magic! Oh, I simply cannot believe it.'

'I'm afraid that it is true.'

'I know now that you, somehow – I don't know how – used magic to bring us here from the Sea of Stars to Aeonia. You opened up some kind of door into here?'

'A portal, Eefa. Portals are everywhere here.'

'There are portals that open out of Dromenon into many different worlds?'

'So, the mages tell us. Some say their number is infinite.'

'Oh, my goodness!'

How was Eefa ever going to understand such extraordinary things?

Aeonia was proving to be very different from her home world of Tír. In fact, the more she thought about it, the more she realized that Tír was a very ordinary world. Compared to Tír, Dromenon, with its many portals, was so shocking . . . shockingly extraordinary.

'We – me and Magio – we don't know anything about magic.'

'Don't worry about that for the moment. I think you've had more than enough on your mind just getting here.'

Magio's trail led them inland, arriving at a grassy meadow, with scattered coppices of trees. Eefa was glad to catch up with her brother, who was sitting in what looked like ordinary green grass, sprinkled with tiny yellow flowers.

'Oh,' she murmured, 'it's beautiful here. It reminds me of those wonderful flowers and waterfalls back on Serenity.'

Magio looked up into her face. 'Hey, Eefie! Are those tears I see in your eyes?'

'Poor Serenity!'

Wychera shook his head at the twins, inhaling the pine-scented air. 'Perhaps we should rest soon. You both have been hunted and harried for so long. I do so hope you will find comfort here at last.'

Eefa blinked away her tears.

'How strange it all seems. We have come half way across the Sea of Stars on a wrecked old clinker ship to find ourselves in a world of magic through a portal in the great nothingness that is Dromenon.'

All three of them continued their stroll through the yellow-speckled meadow, under a lovely summery sky. Eefa could not help but wonder about all that had happened to her and Magio since the death of Gran back on Moon. So much had happened to them – so many strange and frightening experiences – that she hardly dared to reflect on them. Yet now they were here, on magical Aeonia, which, if Wychera was to be believed, had been their true destination from the very beginning. As far as Eefa was concerned, all they had done since Gran's death was to run for their lives. But now she suspected that there was another, more mysterious, purpose that had brought them to Aeonia.

Right now, she sensed a stillness in Wychera, something that made him to bring a finger to his lips, as if to hush her, meanwhile nodding towards the broad sweep of meadow ahead, with small stands of trees here and there, like islands in the sea of grass. Eefa turned her head to follow his signal and her mouth fell open, arrested in a gasp of wonderment.

'Is that what I think it is?'

'Yes, Eefa! It's a unicorn.'

It was the most beautiful creature Eefa had ever seen. Although it resembled the body of a horse, it was far more elegant, with fleece of the purest white, a tall arched neck, regal in its curve, gazing back at her with violet eyes. In its brow she saw its long and delicate horn of ivory, an enchantment straight out of Gran's fairytales.

'Are there many unicorns here in Aeonia?'

'Only this one, as far as I am aware. The unicorn is the symbol of this world. But it is rarely seen. Your arrival here would appear to have provoked its visit.'

Magio whispered, 'It looks so proud and haughty . . . and I do believe it is studying me back with the same curiosity I feel for it.'

But even as they gazed at it, the unicorn suddenly whimpered, before abruptly vanishing.

'What happened? Where did it go?'

Wychera shook his head. 'Unicorns are creatures of magic, Magio. They are said to signal good fortune to those graced with seeing them.' But he hesitated, frowning and staring hard at the place where the creature had vanished. I have heard rumors that it likes to sleep under a particular wishing tree.'

'A wishing tree?'

'It's a thorn tree where folks – well here in Aeonia these might be any of the great variety of fairy folk who live here – but what they like to do is to tie up little messages that they then affix to the branches of the tree, messages in which they express their feelings and their love to those close to them who have departed. It's a very ancient custom. But then Aeonia is a very ancient world.'

Magio inhaled deeply. 'Oh, Wychera, I feel like sleeping under the wishing tree myself tonight.'

'I know what you mean. You'd be surrounded by all manner of prayers and pleas, messages sent to forbidden lovers, or, perhaps tales of woe wrung from hearts bitterly wronged.'

'I have no intention of reading the messages. I merely want to lie down for the night where the magical unicorn has also chosen to rest.'

Wychera laughed. 'Wishing trees are wells of wild magic, Magio. Places where the inexperienced heart should be very careful what it wishes for.'

Eefa cajoled her brother. 'Oh, take no notice of him, Magio. Wychera is merely pulling your leg. We're allowing our imaginations to run away with us. Given our experiences in the Sea of Stars, it's hardly a surprise.'

Magio nodded. 'But I still have kind of an itch to sleep under a wishing tree. It's like something is telling me to do so.'

The others decided to leave him to his idiosyncrasies. Wychera and Eefa walked on a few hundred yards, where, in the falling dusk, Eefa felt ready for sleep. Wychera was standing on tip-toe, peering ahead to find a likely shelter in an area where the lush grassland broke into several wooded coppices.

Even as Eefa curled up in the shade of a pine tree among the long grass, prepared for sleep, she heard her brother scream.

Magio hadn't noticed the fact that he had lagged so far behind Eefa and Wychera. No more had he taken much notice of the sudden change in the weather. He had wandered off into a snowy landscape in which a stream was cascading over a tumble of rocks, the scene surrounded by undulating hills, dense with trees. Every twig, every blade of grass, every flower was coated with hoar frost.

'Oh – it's freezing cold!"

It was also icily beautiful. Blinking with delight, he lifted his head to discover that he had arrived at an enormous tree, with a dense tangle of thorny branches, decorated with all manner of rags and small glittery offerings tied to the branches.

Magio laughed. 'It's the wishing tree.'

How marvelous to come across the setting from one of Gran's fairytales. In the twilight he could see the myriad tied-up bundles of rags, dangling from its thorny branches.

'Oh, britzy!

Magio took several steps closer in the pristine snow, then halted.

'But where's the unicorn? It should be sleeping here, under the shelter of the branches?'

He heard Gran's cackle inside his head.

Foolish Magio, asking too many questions! Could it be that he just has to make a single wish and his wish comes true?

Magio piped up, his face pink with embarrassment. 'Oh, Gran! Now I think that, maybe, it was you who led me here to the wishing tree. And now I ask myself why. Can I really just wish for anything I want – anything at all?'

As if in answer from the tree itself, he heard Gran's answering cackle all about him in the wind . . .

You should know by now how to ask a question of me.

Magio scratched his head, astonished to find himself in this strange conversation. But then he tore a sliver of cloth from his sleeve and he whispered his wish into it and tied it around a thorny branch. There had been no hesitation in his arriving at his most desperate wish. It was the same wish he and Eefa had harbored in their hearts forever.

'I want to know what happened to our mum and dad.'

Somehow Magio's heart felt lighter than air. The snow all about him was crunchy under his feet and the sky was deepening to crimson, with the birds still singing in the trees. Magio had no idea what birds would be inclined to sing so sweetly with the fading light, but the birdsong was the sweetest he had ever heard. At that moment, something came flying out of the ground – something much bigger than a bird – something with huge gossamer wings. It rose up out of the snowy ground, lightning fast, and then it just disappeared in a flash. Magio wondered if what he had just seen had been something to do with his wish.

In the silence that now reigned, Magio peered about himself into the crepuscular shadows. Even though the evening was fast fading, he could make out that familiar sweep of meadow, albeit now snow-coated, with those yellow stars of flowers poking through the snow. The air was becoming busy with moving shapes. Some creatures were taking to the air on what might be delicate wings. Where at first he might have thought them will-o-the-wisps, he saw that some were changing form, even blinking into and out of existence.

'Hey,' he asked the voice of Gran, 'are these ghosts?'

They're not ghosts, child.

'What then?'

Beings of magic have no sense of gravity and so are able to float and move through the air, as they wish.

'You mean fairies?'

Gran laughed. *Do you find it so very hard to believe?*

Magio pursed his stubborn lips, as he would long ago when Gran used to chide him. 'Hey – are you saying that here in Aeonia fairies are real?'

Gran sighed. *Perhaps it's time we closed those grumpy little eyes for one night.*

At that moment, Magio heard a strange screeching coming out of the branches of the wishing tree.

Schree—schree—schree!

His hand reached to his mouth in shock. 'Oh, Gran, it sounds so very familiar.'

Yes, dearest Magio – altogether familiar.

'What is it?'

It's a storm rider, child.

'Oh, jinxy . . . I think it might be the mother creature.'

Magio's eyes widened in shock as he stared up into the shadowy branches. 'But what's a storm rider doing here on Aeonia?'

Well now, we appear to face another mystery, child.
Schree—schree—schree!

Magio realized belatedly that he had already been warned about the wild magic in the vicinity of the wishing tree.

His sense of dread was overwhelming. Every instinct urged him to grip his amulet as tight as he could, to be comforted by the forces of magic pouring into him through the flesh of his fingers. But already he sensed that something was already desperately wrong. He felt the power spreading through him, rising up through his wrist and forearm, into his upper arm and shoulders, his neck, his head . . . He had no control over it. He had no idea what it meant. Gasping for breath, his heart pounding out of his chest, he felt the throb of every heartbeat rising in his throat and temples.

He screamed, 'Woll – Woll help me.'

For what seemed like an age, unwanted visions were passing through his mind. Whispers were invading his consciousness . . . arcane understanding rushing through him. He was so overwhelmed by what he was feeling, he screamed, over and over.

At last, he heard his sister's voice close by.

'What is it, Gio?'

His moaned through gritted teeth. 'Aaarrrrrgggghhhh! I can't control it, Eefa. There are numerous voices whispering inside me . . . they're running through me . . . coming from what feels like everywhere.'

At last, Magio felt the strength of Wychera's hand on his shoulder, Wychera's voice dominating above the invasive cacophony of voices. 'I shouldn't have let you wander off.

Something is terribly wrong. I hear and feel all that you do . . . I'm sharing it with you . . . I'm feeling it, heart and soul.'

'Ohhhhhhhhhhhhhh!'

There were myriad messages pouring into his mind from every direction. Ominous visions of terrifying places, the feeling of losing oneself in enchantment . . . everywhere the overwhelming feeling of magic.

He heard Eefa's scream. 'Oh, Magio! I feel what you do – the same enchantment – I'm fighting to constrain my giddy senses.'

Magio tried to speak. He struggled to control what was taking over him, body and spirit. He gritted his teeth until they felt they were cracking, blinking furiously, taking several deep breaths, then slowly he tore his senses out of the overwhelming enchantment, tore his spirit free from the strange visions . . . But to do so brought him close to fainting with dizziness. At that moment, he felt the changer's arms around his shoulders, then hold him steady, so he didn't collapse.

He heard Eefa exclaim, 'You felt it. You felt it, Wychera?'

'I felt it.'

'Then you know more about what we have just experienced? You know more about what is going on right now than we do?'

Wychera shook his head. 'Believe me, Eefa, I am as astonished as you and Magio by the strange visions. I think we are close to a very powerful source of magic. I don't think we're alone in our bafflement.'

Indeed, you are not!

A spec of gold twinkled in the air between them.

'Oh, Woll! Thank goodness you're here.'

Watch out, Eefa. Strange forces are afoot. The Oonarie were as excited as you and Magio to journey to Aeonia. We too have heard so many legends about the enchanted world. But be warned. It is said to harbor lacunae of wild magic.

A bewildered Eefa and Magio had many questions they wanted to ask. Eefa whispered, 'Woll – will you stay with us?'

Be assured – I am here with you. But it would now appear that your presence here has not gone unnoticed. Powers far more powerful than the Oonaree are coming into play.

Magio took to his feet. 'What's going on, Wychera?'

Wychera shook his head at them. 'Please, don't be alarmed. I should never have allowed you to wander off on your own, Magio. A source of wild power has awoken. We must be very careful that the same mistake does not cost us dear.'

Eefa demanded to know, 'What do you mean? I thought you said Magio and I belonged here?'

'You do belong here. But we may have relaxed too early. We should have waited until you were presented to those who shelter and protect Aeonia.'

'I don't understand.'

'What's done is done. It was my fault. But we cannot afford any further carelessness.'

'But I thought you said we belonged here?'

'You do belong here.'

'But we're not magical.' Eefa's eyes turned to her brother, now demanding his support. 'We're just ordinary people.'

Wychera opened wide his hands. 'It is understandable that you're feeling puzzled. But I assure you that all will be fine. We must be more patient – and more careful.'

But Eefa was far too frightened by what had just happened to her brother. She turned to face Wychera and demanded to know, 'What's really going on? What will happen to Magio and me?'

Wychera sighed. 'This world, all you see about you, is threatened by the same undying who wanted you dead. Power over all that exists is his sole desire. Yet, for reasons I know not, you would appear to be a threat to him.'

'But, if he is so powerful, won't he hurt us even here, in Aeonia?'

'He wouldn't dare to risk a direct confrontation with the dragons.' Wychera sighed. 'Please, trust the forces that have brought you here. Soon now, you'll get to know more. For the moment, please accept my reassurance that you are safer here than anywhere else. But now we have opened up a source of wild power, we must assume that the danger is not yet over. As to you, Magio, no more wandering off on your own. Is that agreed?'

Wychera's eyes were fixed on Magio's. 'I mean it. From now on, keep well clear of that wishing tree!'

Magio was sheepishly nodding his head.

An Icy Blade

As the new day dawned, Magio and Eefa were sitting against one of the pink rocks that lined the shore, enjoying the warmth of the morning sun. They were still struggling to understand all that had happened to them since leaving their home on the isle of Moon. Some mysterious enemy, someone who called himself The One, was determined to kill them. They struggled to understand why this enemy hated them so much. Magio laid his head back against the pink rock, now warming in the morning sun, his fingers clenched into fists.

'I mean, why us? I can't help wondering. I need an answer, Eefa. Why is he so determined to kill us?'

Eefa sighed, gazing out to sea.

She felt the reassuring hand of Wychera on her shoulder. 'Oh, Wychera! Do you have any idea why he hates us so?'

'I don't even pretend to know the answer. Only that he hates you with a single-minded ruthlessness.'

Eefa patted that reassuring hand on her shoulder. 'Thanks for all you have done to protect us. I'm sorry about Magio's mistake yesterday. But you must always tell us the truth. Are you sure, right now, that this evil being cannot reach out to harm us even here? Can he get to us even in Aeonia?'

Wychera squeezed her hand. 'It's a question that I've been asking myself since yesterday. Only those who rule Aeonia can answer it with certainty. But I can assure you that nowhere is safer for you.'

'But even here, in Aeonia, he just might come after us?'

'There are forces here that would readily overwhelm Lustfera, if she dared to attack. But as to The One himself – if he risked an attack . . .?' Wychera held her fondly. 'That would confront him with a major risk. It would bring him into open confrontation with the Dragon Council. I doubt he would risk that. But nevertheless, it would be prudent to remain vigilant.'

Magio, whose head had flopped back against the stone, now sprang to his feet, intrigued by Wychera's words.

'You talked about a dragon council?'

'I did.'

'What is this council?'

Wychera looked back at Magio, eye-to-eye. 'Aeonia is ruled by a council of elder dragons, all of them distinguished mages.'

'And this enemy who wants to kill us – he fears this council. That's why you believe he wouldn't dare attack us here?'

'That's right, Magio. But yesterday's experience with wild magic illustrated that, even here in Aeonia, unforeseen events can still happen. I cannot put my hand on my heart and assure you that there is no possible danger here. Only that it is far safer than sailing the Sea of Stars aboard the Scuttlebutt. All worlds, even Aeonia, harbor the demons of chance. Do you recall Eefa's strange awake-dream back on Moon, when she was lured onto the haunted beach with its beguiling circles of stones? I can only insist that you and Eefa stay close to me and trust my judgment. Even in Aeonia we must hold tight our defenses and all the while keep a weather eye on the unpredictable.'

Magio nodded. 'Agreed!'

Wychera's eyes now lifted to gaze into a sky of the purest morning blue to watch what looked like a large and cumbersome bird fly closer. He mused aloud, 'It concerns me when we encounter a situation we cannot control.'

Eefa climbed to her feet and confronted Wychera. 'There's still something on your mind, isn't there? Something to do with what happened yesterday?'

'Yes, Eefa.'

'What is troubling you, Wychera?'

'Something I cannot shake from my mind, Eefa. It's that storm rider's warning. I keep hearing it, "Schree—schree—schree!", inside my head.'

Magio was suddenly very interested. 'You do fear that the storm rider is warning us that something is about to happen?'

'Yes, I do, Magio.'

'Then, shouldn't we find out what it is, before ever it happens?'

'Yes, we should. But how to go about it – that's what I have been pondering over and over in my mind.'

'You want to go back there, don't you? You think there is something important happening in or around the wishing tree?'

'Yes, Magio. I do think exactly that. But I would have to go alone. I cannot risk taking you with me into a situation that might involve new risk.'

Eefa shook her head. 'If you go there, we go too.'

'No, Eefa.'

'Eefa is right,' Magio insisted. 'If one of us goes, all three should go. If something happened to you, Wychera, who would be left to protect us?'

'I doubt that the Lady would forgive my taking you into a situation of potential risk.'

'We can ask Woll to go with us.'

'It will not matter whether Woll accompanies us or not. I still cannot agree to it. I must go alone.'

Eefa took Wychera's hand and held it tight. 'We'll be safer if we take the risk only as part of an awake-dream. You know that Magio and I can share such dreams. We will take you with us into our dream. All the while our bodies will remain here, safe and sound, by the cove.'

'No – I dare not.'

'Magio – close your eyes with me. We must go back to that moment yesterday when we heard the warning cry of the storm rider. Here – take my left hand. I shall keep a tight hold of Wychera with my right. Please close your eyes, both of you, and keep them shut. Do not reopen them until I click my fingers.'

Magio joined Eefa in closing his eyes. Once closed, he had the curious feeling that he could not refuse his sister's request. Then, immediately, he was in the dream . . .

Magio's entire being was filled with a breathless astonishment, finding himself transported back into yesterday's snowy landscape in which a stream was cascading over a tumble of rocks, the scene surrounded by undulating hills, dense with trees. Every twig, every blade of grass, every flower was coated with hoar frost, which shone in the crisp morning light as if he were gazing into a world constructed of diamonds.

Magio threw himself onto the ground, dipping a single forefinger into the snow, then transporting it to the tip of his tongue.

'Oh – it tastes so real. This really is the same place as yesterday. It's where I found the wishing tree."

'It's certainly a very strange feeling to be here again.'

Wychera joined the twins in gazing around, so they could examine the landscape in all directions. 'How truly extraordinary!'

'But it is also perilous – if we interpret the cry of the storm rider as a warning.'

Eefa lifted her face to the wintry sky and called out, 'Woll – have you been watching? We have urgent need of your protection.'

In a moment a sprinkling of frost sprites was spiraling about them, twinkling in the morning light, just as they had witnessed at that extraordinary meeting in the Valley of the Raptors back on Moon.

We are here, Eefa.

Eefa was too thrilled to question Woll further. She just spun herself around in a full circle, her heart pounding with excitement.

Wychera stood erect, gazing about him at the wooded landscape 'There's one more ingredient that is still missing.'

Immediately they heard it, that same screeching in the air above them, as if the very air were being ripped and torn to ribbons

Schree—schree—schree!

Magio said quietly, 'I'm certain now that it's no ordinary storm rider. I think it's the Mother of Storms.'

Wychera lifted his face to stare high into the rapidly darkening sky.

The storm rider screeched again, this time even louder. Magio tensed, his gaze rising into the shadows overhead. Assuming the mother creature had somehow made its way to Aeonia, how had she managed to locate them here? Was she really warning him – or was she now threatening him? Even as he racked his brain in attempting to figure it out, he heard another deeper sound, a low-pitched moaning. It seemed to come from some unfortunate creature racked by torment.

Lowering his gaze, Magio crawled, using his hands and feet, so that he could get through the undergrowth to peer deeper into the shadows. The moaning came from the thickest, deepest shadows beneath the very heart of the wishing tree. There, he glimpsed something bulky and restless, something that appeared to be writhing in agony. This had to be the reason for the storm rider's warning. Drawing closer, Magio could make out a blur of white, and now the unmistakable stink of animal sweat. He could clearly see the outline of a creature that had fallen onto its side and was threshing at the ground with its limbs. Magio hesitated as realization dawned. Then, taking a few steps still closer, he confirmed what creature was lying there, in a dreadful agony. He saw huge violet eyes looking back at him out of a sweat-sodden snow-white head – eyes that were widely staring at him in panic.

'Oh, Eefa – it's the unicorn!'

That alarm was much louder inside his head . . .

SCHREE—SCHREE—SCHREE!

Magio clasped his hands to his ears again, trying to block the horrid warning from his mind. He heard that same guttural gargling and hissing he had heard before in the rigging of the Scuttlebutt in the midst of that dreadful storm. And then, as if rising out of that alien throat, the voice of the Mother of Storms again . . .

So! Now will the young mage be tested! But will he accept the challenge? With this warning is my debt repaid. Let him be judged in the forge of destiny . . .

With a clattering of scaly wings, the storm rider rose out of the branches of the tree and took off into the gathering night.

He heard Wychera's shout of caution, 'Watch out, Magio. Beware the presence of wild magic. Even in an awake-dream, there is still danger. This is a thorn tree. Its spikes are sharp and highly poisonous.'

The wishing tree proved to be even more entangled than Magio had realized. Now he was within its branches, it was the strangest tree Magio had ever seen, with a thick scaly trunk, somewhat like alligator skin, and with leaves that tinkled like metal as they shivered in the breeze. Magio pressed his way deeper into the shadows, trying to get closer to the tormented animal. As he did so, he felt Eefa's hand clutch at his shoulder.

'Can you see why it's making that awful moaning sound?'

'I can see that it's wounded. That's why it's threshing about in the shadows.'

'Oh, Magio!'

Magio negotiated his way closer still, reaching out to lift a branch as he peered deeper into the shadows. The poor creature was whinnying and moaning through dilated nostrils. As he moved a step closer, there was an explosion of golden sparks everywhere about him. It was a storm of frost sprites, illuminating the shadows with their light. He heard the voice of Woll,

Be exceedingly careful, Magio – you must avoid those thorns.

Magio froze to a halt, causing Eefa to bump into him. Wychera was behind her, those long arms reaching out to grab to hold both of them back. 'We need to be exceedingly careful. I sense very great danger here.'

'Oh, Wychera, can't we help the poor thing?'

Eefa cried out, 'Oh, Magio – look!'

'Yeah! I see it.'

In the light of the frost sprites, they saw that there was an enormous blade, like a dagger made out of ice, buried deep in the Unicorn's chest.

Magio's voice trembled. 'I can't bear to see the poor creature like this. We can't just turn away and do nothing. We must do something to help it.'

But Wychera was more thoughtful. 'Remember – this is still an awake dream!'

'But it's still a heartbreaking sight. And the poor beast is close to death.'

'Nevertheless, we should ask ourselves – what possible force of darkness could have put such an arrow into its chest? I don't trust the winged monster that drew you here. Come, Eefa and Magio. Step back, the both of you. We can do nothing to amend this outrage.'

Wychera had already taken a step backwards and was attempting to draw the twins away from the sight.

'Come away. Do so quickly. I sense a trap.'

Eefa grabbed Magio's shoulder. 'I think you should listen to Wychera. He's right. We need to get away.'

But Magio refused to do so.

He began to edge his way nearer to the unicorn, until he was close enough to touch the icy blade that was buried in the creature's chest.

'Magio, let's go.' Eefa tugged at his shoulder, urging him back.

In that same moment, Magio heard the voice of Woll inside his mind. *Beware, Magio! The icy blade is no natural weapon. You are in no position to defend the unicorn from the venom of that blade.*

'I don't know what to say, or how to explain it. But I don't agree with Wychera about the storm rider.' Magio laughed, a nervous bark. 'I might be wrong. Hey, jinxy – maybe I am. But I feel it in my bones that I am not here by accident.'

'Oh, Magio, stop this foolishness!'

Magio gazed again at the wounded creature. He saw that the icy blade was buried so deep, it must surely be close to the poor creature's heart.

'Oh, jinxy! I know how hopeless it looks.' Magio wiped both his hands over his perspiring brow. 'But I just can't abandon it.'

Eefa screamed, 'Magio! Let's go! Now!'

He knew she was right. But there was such a storm of determination growing in Magio's head, a dogged stubbornness that was compelling him to take hold of that terrible arrow. At the same time there was a rival common sense that was telling him that he should heed the warnings of Eefa, Wychera and Woll. There surely was no way that he could pull that icy weapon out of the unicorn's breast.

Magio felt a deepening sense of dread. His will faltered, causing him to take a deep breath. But in that moment, the air about him filled with those wonderful golden splinters of light. Frost sprites were alighting on every thorn, as if to guide and protect him from their poison. Magio took new courage from their presence. Closing his hands about the deadly shaft, he gripped it tight and then dug his heels in the frozen ground, hauling with every inch of his strength. Even as he did so, a vicious shock of cold invaded his hands, and with terrifying speed, ascended his arms. As it spread, his muscles began to spasm and weaken.

Gritting his teeth, Magio ignored the agony of the freezing cold and he pulled again with all of his might.

The icy numbness had already ascended his hands, his wrists, his forearms. The venom tore through his shoulders and into his chest.

But still he refused to release his grip on the icy arrow and, with teeth still clenched, he continued to haul it out of the unicorn's breast. He felt the venomous shaft slide back, though it was no more than a finger's breadth.

A fearful darkness descended on him, a storm of malice whispering threats into his mind, spreading everywhere throughout his being. The icy cold was closing down his lungs, so he felt unable to take a breath. It was invading his heart. Magio knew that he was dying. Yet still he fought back against that storm of malice. He could no longer take a breath. The cold of the grave was now invading every limb and tissue of his body, causing his senses to fade, and his very mind to falter.

You miserable brat! How readily will you die for this beast!

Whose voice was speaking to him? The words were spat out of a hateful mouth. Their spite lacerated his consciousness, somehow leaching like acid at his mind, determined to undermine his resolve.

'No!' he cried. 'I will never surrender to you.'

Magio felt his resistance faltering, all but done. The dreadful cold of the icy spear had filled every crevice of his being.

But then a new vision entered Magio's mind, a figure in a place seething with demon-like figures, a head masked by a tangle of matted hair now rising, as if to gaze back at him with blind white eyes. Magio heard a calm voice invade his faltering mind . . .

Be brave, Magio. But a moment longer.

The love in that voice swelled within him. It opened wide his lungs so he could take a deep breath. It expanded, like an explosion of daylight within his mind. Desperately, he redoubled his grip on the icy arrow in the unicorn's breast. His pulse was bursting in his skull from the effort of pulling at it, and his entire body was tensed to breaking point, a stage when he knew he could pull at it no harder. Tears entered his eyes at the certainty that it would not be enough.

Magio was trembling so badly, he could not speak. He felt the malice resurge within him to an unbearable crescendo. He felt the awful fist of cold squeeze his heart. All about him the creatures of fairytales were gathering. He could hear their excited chatter. Dark winged shapes were descending out of the heavens and alighting, with a fluttering of gigantic wings, to create an enormous protective circle around him. He could hear their thunderous roar . . .

Magio thought he must be dead. He was unaware of a heartbeat within his chest. There was a presence kneeling beside him, a gigantic being dressed in shimmering silver, with corn-gold hair and, cerulean eyes, whose hand now fondled his face. He felt the tenderness of consummation, being to being, that came from the kneeling presence. Other forces were coming to his assistance. He felt the rising power of a great consummation overwhelm him. It was becoming one with him, with his heart and mind. Their overlapping hands took a fierce grip of the icy spear. With a roar that came from the deepest part of him, Magio felt power grow huge in him and in that moment their combined strength tore the deadly arrow out of the unicorn's breast, to hiss and melt away to nothing in the surrounding snow.

He sighed even as he was enveloped by darkness.

The Dragon King

Magio tossed and turned exhaustedly, struggling to open his eyes. He screamed with terror. 'I've gone blind.'

'Please be assured you're not blind. Your eyelids are still frozen with icicles.'

Whose voice was that? It wasn't Eefa's voice. He struggled again to open his eyes and failed. Panic soared in him. His heartbeat was throbbing so powerfully, it felt as if it were about to burst from his chest.

'I'm still trapped in the awake dream.'

'Calm yourself, Magio. You are back with us. You are safe and sound. I am breathing on your eyes to melt the icicles. You are not blind.'

Now he recognized the voice. It was the changer, Wychera Gallant. He was rubbing at Magio's eyes with something warm and moist. With a sudden sharp stinging pain, Magio's left eye opened. He could see.

'There you are. We'll soon have your other eye open as well.' The face of the elfin changer was now filling Magio's vision. He was gently dabbing Magio's right eye, which was fighting to clear itself of the icicles.

'I . . . Oh, heck, Wychera!' He struggled to control his breathing. 'I'm not even sure that I'm still alive?'

'Of course, you're alive!'

Wychera helped Magio to sit up in the snow, pricked through by those same tiny yellow flowers. Eefa threw herself around him, holding on to him tight.

'You terrified me.'

'I'm sorry, Eefie. Am I really alive?'

'Oh, Magio! You . . . you . . .!'

'I need to get up. I need to stand on my feet.'

'No, you don't. There's no hurry.'

'What happened?'

'The One attacked you, here in Aeonia.'

Magio shook his head, struggling to recover his senses. 'I saw him, Eefa. I saw the man from your awake-dreams. He spoke to me, while I was trying to save the unicorn.'

Eefa clung to Magio, shaking her head. 'Stop it! I can't bear it. Have you any idea how worried I've been?'

Wychera's voice interrupted their conversation 'Eefa – Magio . . . Time is pressing. Magio, you've barely escaped with your life. We need to get you away from here. We need to find somewhere safer – and warmer.'

Magio's felt the life return to his stiff neck and shoulders. He shook his head in bewilderment. 'Oh, jinxy! I can remember that awful cold . . . the horrible malice invading my heart.'

Eefa was in tears. 'I thought I'd lost you. You were just lying there, covered in ice. You looked like you were dead. And then . . . and, then . . . Oh, Magio, something changed. Something magical appeared to be happening all about us . . . and you came back to us.'

Magio lifted his head to look up at Wychera. 'Was it you who saved me?'

'No, Magio. I have many tricks but countering death is beyond the ability of an elfin changer.'

'Who then?'

'I think you already know.'

Magio recalled the strange presence . . . the glowing being. 'Oh, Eefa! It was the Lady of the Shore. She came to me when all of my strength was gone. It was her hand that enfolded mine and helped me tear the icy spear from the unicorn's heart.' His eyes spun from Eefa to Wychera. 'The unicorn . . .?'

'Look for yourself.'

Magio, now shivering with cold, gazed out over the snowy landscape to glimpse the distant white figure, with head erect, and that extraordinary single horn. The unicorn was gazing back at him, and snorting contentedly.

Magio sat there for several more minutes before he accepted Wychera's help to get him back onto his unsteady feet. Just standing up made Magio's head spin. It was only Wychera's arm that stopped him collapsing back into the snow.

'Take your time.'

'Yeah, I will!'

Gazing into the sky, Magio thought he saw the strangest sight, as mysterious winged shapes were circling high above him.

'Am I imagining things?'

'No, Magio! You are not imagining things.' The changer gripped Magio's shoulders, to help steady him in taking his first tentative steps.

Magio blinked, to help clear his vision. But the winged shapes were still massing in the sky. They appeared to be gathering from every direction.

Wychera joined him in looking up. 'The dragons of Aeonia are coming to welcome you both.'

'Dragons?'

'Yes, Magio – this really is the world of dragons!'

Magio was startled by what Wychera was telling him. 'Why are they coming? Why are we so special to them?'

'Your amulet – do you think it accidentally found itself in your path on that beach, back in Moon?'

Magio touched the amulet. He reassured himself it was still there. 'There's so much we still don't understand. I know I used it back then on Moon. I know that it somehow called a dragon to help us. But I never really understood how or why that happened.'

'How could you understand? There was neither time nor opportunity for explanations while you were still in Moon.'

'I don't understand, even now.'

'The enemy was so dangerous, with Lustfera on your trail. Every effort had to be taken to protect you and your purpose.'

'What purpose?'

'Both you and Eefa were vital in the rescue the Lady of the Shore. Here, today, your purpose has grown even more vital, Magio.'

'But the Lady is now free. What more can we do? We're just orphans, from the small town of Warren. We're not adventurers like you. We know nothing of this world, other than the fairytales Gran told us.'

Wychera's voice softened. 'Gran saw to it that you were safe – and, in so far as I can judge, kept you happy throughout your childhood.'

'Oh, don't talk like that about her!' Eefa agreed with Magio. 'We can't believe that she was anything other than our Gran.'

'You have no idea of the threats she warded off throughout your childhoods. She hid you well and shielded you from malice.'

'Wychera – what's really going on?'

'You deserve a better explanation than I can provide. Soon, you will meet others more capable of explaining all that presently baffles you. In the meantime, be comforted by the fact that Aeonia has long been expecting you.'

Magio glanced at Eefa, whose sigh of bafflement matched his own.

Wychera laughed. 'Let's all three of us sit down and rest a short while. Let's see if we can clear some of the confusion.'

He plumped himself down in the snow and waited for the twins to copy him before speaking.

'Now – let's try to appraise the extraordinary situation we find ourselves in.' Wychera placed those long arms around his crossed legs and clasped those long-fingered hands about his drawn-up knees. 'I know that all that has happened since Gran's death has made no sense to you. So, if you are nice and settled, I want you, Magio, to take hold of your amulet with your free hand. Hold it good and strong and close your eyes.'

Magio did as Wychera asked him.

'What do you now sense?'

'I sense nothing at all.'

'No more do I,' exclaimed Eefa, whose eyes were also clenched shut.

'Magio, just keep on holding your amulet tight. Please keep both your eyes closed and try to allow your imagination to roam free.'

Suddenly Magio's eyes jerked open in astonishment. The peaceful landscape, with the yellow-flowered meadow, was transformed into a volcanic caldera. In the near distance waves of red-hot molten rock were billowing out of a central pit, in wave after wave, as new eruptions burst out of it.

'Eefa – open your eyes. Tell me what you see.'

Their faces were lit up by a nearby volcanic explosion. As every eye turned to the fiery skyline, the entire mountainous landscape in front of them was torn apart by erupting fields of red-glowing lava. Eefa was sitting there, staring at what was happening with her eyes wide with shock.

'Yes – I see it. But I don't even begin to understand.'

Magio exclaimed, 'I see it too. Wychera, what does it mean?'

'I want you to use your imaginations. The same landscape that is naturally terrifying for you, as for me, might not be uncomfortable for Dragons.'

Magio and Eefa allowed their eyes to roam over the incandescent volcanic landscape, spitting molten rock and huge geysers of debris and smoke.

'What's happening?'

'Please keep patient.'

Eefa exclaimed, 'Oh, Magio, look! There are shapes out there. Strange shapes moving about everywhere – they're all around us.'

It took Magio a little longer to see what Eefa had spotted. There really were creatures, almost invisible at first, in spite of the fact they were truly gigantic in size, monstrous shapes that were almost invisible because they had the same craggy shapes, and dark hues, as the terrifying landscape of molten rocks and fire.

'Hey, Eefa, I see them!'

'I do too. What's going on, Wychera?'

'Patience! Maintain the circle. And remain perfectly calm. They will not hurt you. Magio – I want you to keep reaching out through the amulet. What you are witnessing would have been invisible to the eyes of ordinary mortals.'

Magio and Eefa did their best to clear their minds of terror. Slowly, as their inner vision began to recognize patterns in that same dark landscape, the shock of what they were witnessing thrilled them with a mixture of delight and wonder.

'Oh, Eefa!'

'Yes, I see them clearly. Look at their eyes. Do you see those enormous golden eyes! They're everywhere.'

'Well done, both of you!' Wychera's voice was hushed. 'The dragons of Aeonia are delighted to welcome you to their world.'

Eefa and Magio now witnessed the gigantic creatures drawing closer, to form a great circle about them, and they saw, from much closer now, how those huge golden eyes were split by crescents.

'Please don't be frightened. The dragons intend you no harm. My task is at last complete. I have brought you to your destiny.'

Eefa whispered, 'What do you mean?'

Magio also whispered, 'What is to happen to us?'

Wychera released his knees to put his arms about both their shoulders. 'The attack on the unicorn has not altered our plans. It has merely given them a greater urgency. It is worrying that the enemy felt emboldened enough to attack the very symbol of Aeonia. Even as we speak, the Lady is calling for a gathering of the Council.'

Magio looked up into Wychera's face, his eyes widening.

'The Lady of the Shore is here?'

'Yes, Magio! She is here.'

Eefa joined Magio in gazing at Wychera with widened eyes. 'I don't understand – what is to happen to us?'

'The dragons have come to greet you.'

'But why in the world would the dragons of Aeonia be interested in us?'

'Perhaps you should ask them that same question?'

Magio's chest was suddenly so tight he felt barely able to breathe. He was bewildered by Wychera's words. And looking at Eefa, he could see that she was feeling exactly the same.

It was Eefa who now found her voice. 'Wychera, you told us you would explain. But all you have done is to confuse us even more.'

'The unicorn was a baited trap, Eefa.'

'A trap?'

'Aimed at your brother, Magio.

Eefa shook her head in bafflement. 'What do you mean?'

'The enemy knew Magio would take the bait. The trap was set to kill him. And I think Magio knows how close it came to succeeding.'

Eefa paled.

'Now you have a better idea of how serious the situation is. You face an enemy that is as cruel as he is malicious. The Lady brought you to safety here. She sent me as her emissary to protect you from that malice. Now I have served her bidding and brought you under the protection of Aeonia's guardians, you must be prepared for the demanding struggle that lies ahead.'

Wychera's words had confirmed both their fears. While Magio was still pondering Wychera's words, Eefa confronted the elfin changer.

'Don't you just abandon us here without answers. Please explain, Wychera. Tell us what more is expected of us.'

'I'll do my best. You know I shall remain here with you. I shall protect you as long as you need me.'

'Britzy!'

'Britzy, my eye.' Eefa smacked Magio's shoulder with annoyance. 'Oh, Wychera, you could start by explaining something to me. Why us? Why are we here? What's so special about us?'

'I don't know the answer to your question. What I can tell you is that your enemy has long been a usurper among the undying. I cannot for the life of me imagine how he first gained supremacy over such powerful beings. I would have to imagine that he somehow uprooted all they assumed to be unchanging, thereby breaking the sacred rules of their covenant. I know nothing of how he managed to do this, but it is clear that his purpose all along was to gather power about himself.'

'But surely there must have been many undying who opposed him – beings with powers as great as his own?'

'My dearest Eefa, once again you demand explanations that I am incapable of giving you. I'm an adventurer, not a mage. All I know is that your enemy is exceedingly powerful, ruthless and dangerous.'

Magio piped up, 'Oh, Wychera, now that he has shown himself capable of attacking the unicorn even here in Aeonia, how can any of us stop him?'

Wychera agreed. 'We're not immortals. But he has not yet succeeded in conquering Aeonia.'

But before they could put yet more questions to the changer, a new voice entered the conversation, a voice that was gentle to the ear as a breeze, yet one more resolute than hardened iron.

Indeed, he has not. There is a key arena that the usurper has not conquered. The very great and most mysterious of all arenas that is capable of leading to all worlds.

Eefa whispered, 'I think I know what you mean. You're talking about Dromenon?'

Yes, Eefa! Blessed Dromenon.

Magio took a very deep breath. It was as if he were awakening from one dream state into another even stranger still, a place in which everything that he had ever known, or believed to be true, was mistaken. The thought was already sinking in that from here on in, his world – and that of his sister, Eefa – would never be the same again.

'I . . . I can't say that I understand. I'm really trying my best to understand. But . . . oh, britzy! My mind is just a confusion of crazy thoughts.'

Perhaps, young Magio, your thoughts are not as crazy as you think.

Eefa and Magio's eyes met, more bewildered by each passing moment. Suddenly there were big questions that needed answering.

Tomorrow, I promise, we shall be properly introduced to one another. Then you will have the opportunity of addressing your questions directly to me.

Eefa and Magio exchanged bewildered glances.

It was Eefa that asked the question. 'Who are you?'

Oh, I believe we have already met. You, Eefa, might recall our meeting in the Valley of the Raptors. On that occasion I brought you a gift.

'You . . . oh, my goodness! It was you – you were the dragon who brought the soul spirit of the Lady to me on the Beach of Bones.'

I was!

'But . . . but . . .?'

You wonder who – and perhaps what – I really am? Why, I am Orebiquinos, ruler of this somewhat unruly world.

'Oh, I recall how Gran would tell us stories of Aeonia! Magio, do you remember? There was a dragon king in Gran's fairytales.'

Magio's eyes widened.

Eefa meanwhile clenched her own eyes shut, her jaws and fists clenched equally tight before asking the obvious question,

'Are you the dragon king?'

I am Orebiquinos, King of Aeonia.

Magio and Eefa gazed at one another, dumbstruck.

A Mystery Explained

The twins were so warmed by the furnaces of their volcanic landscape that they slept soundly with no need for a camp fire. Eefa woke at dawn, rousing her sleepy-headed brother so they could talk.

'How,' she demanded of him, 'do we come to terms with the fact that our whole lives have been a lie?'

'Your lives have not been a lie,' Wychera countered. As far as the twins were aware, their guardian had not slept at all, but had stood guard patiently over them all night long so they could get some rest. 'It's just that a key part of your history was concealed from you.'

'You mean, the meaning of our lives – our link to this world – was deliberately hidden?'

'Exactly.'

The changer looked about them at the still-glowing embers of the rocks about them in this extraordinary dragon-world landscape.

Magio sighed. 'It's hard to believe.'

'I can imagine it is.'

'I mean – did we really save the life of the unicorn?'

Wychera nodded. 'Yes – but it was not we who did so, it was you, Magio.'

How very strange everything now seemed in the clearing light of morning.

Eefa shook sand from her hair. 'I don't think I shall ever feel entirely clean again.' But then she shook her head, blinking slowly in disbelief. 'Wow! Did we really have that conversation with a dragon?'

Magio laughed. 'Yeah, we did! And it was no ordinary dragon. It was the dragon king. And, now I recall, there was a dragon king in the tales that Gran told us about the world of the fairies. Makes you wonder if fairytales can come true.'

Eefa smiled. 'Makes me wonder if she was talking about a place she actually knew.'

Magio was dumbstruck for a moment by Eefa's words, pausing as he washed his face in a stream. Even the water here was almost too hot to touch, from the heat of the volcanic landscape. He took a deep breath, and then exhaled with a guffaw. With a squeal of excitement, Eefa joined him in washing her hair in the stream, combing it with her fingers and allowing it to dry in the heated air.

After that all three of them sat among the black volcanic stones strangely quiet, while also restlessly excited.

'Were we dreaming, Wychera? Was what I recall from last night another awake-dream?'

'No, Eefa – you were not dreaming.'

Magio stirred, unable to keep still. 'What are you saying? You're telling us the dragon is really coming here?'

Wychera shook his head. He put his arm around their shoulders. 'Please don't be frightened.'

Magio whispered, 'How could we not be frightened? He's the dragon king! I mean – wow!'

Wow indeed, young Magio. And here I am, as I promised I would be, to dutifully keep that promise.

Both the twins were stunned into silence.

Magio's voice returned in a whisper. 'We didn't dare . . . Oh, britzy! We weren't trying to say . . .'

Eefa blurted, 'What Magio is trying to say . . . Oh, what we're both trying to say . . . we really and truly so much wanted to believe . . . We hardly dared to believe . . .'

That I was real?

The dragon roared with laughter.

I should think so. Please do not be afraid to speak your minds, Magio and Eefa. I would like to hear more of what you are thinking, now that you have heard what Wychera had to tell you.

Magio blurted out, in astonishment, 'You truly are the King of Aeonia?'

I am, young Sir. And you, young Madam – what do you have to say?

'Please forgive us. It's just that we can't believe that a dragon king would be interested in us.'

You have an inborn grasp of logic, young Eefa – inherited no doubt from your father.

'My father?'

So it would be logical to assume.

Eefa was so overwhelmed with a mixture of astonishment and curiosity that she couldn't help exclaiming,

'Where are you? Why can't we see you?'

In moments, the air over a craggy ledge in the near distance cracked and tore apart as the dragon spread his enormous bulk over the entire rocky outline.

Magio and Eefa sprang to their feet, dwarfed by the mountainous creature.

Are you happy now, young lady, so we can continue with this enlightening conversation?

Eefa struggled to control her mixture of terror astonishment. 'I . . . I didn't mean to . . . '

Desist with the apologies. You have a question you would ask of me?

'Yes – yes, I have. What did you mean? You mentioned our father.'

I did!

Magio blurted out, 'You knew him?'

I know him still!

'What do you mean?'

Why – have you not both encountered your father in your awake-dreams! Did he not help you, Magio, in your recent struggle with the enemy?

Magio shook his head, dumbfounded. 'I don't understand.'

Eefa could not contain herself. 'But . . . but how can we have met our father? He's no longer alive?'

Your father is not dead, Eefa.

Eefa felt the hot flush of excitement erupt over her face, and extend to her throat and neck. 'What do you mean? Is he here, in Aeonia?'

Alas, dear Eefa and Magio, your father is not free to speak to you. He is not here, in Aeonia. He is elsewhere – lost in the wastes of Dromenon.

Eefa wiped her face with her hands, struggling to credit what she was hearing – struggling to take such news in.

'Lost in Dromenon?'

We believe that he has been imprisoned in the in-between world from the very beginnings of the Chaos. His crime was to threaten the enemy's overweening ambitions.

'Who is this enemy?'

Such is his ambition he allows only one name. He has the temerity to call himself "The One". He is as cruel as you might expect of such arrogance. The wounding of the unicorn was altogether typical of his malice.

Eefa recoiled with horror. 'Wychera told us the unicorn was a baited trap, set to kill Magio.'

Likely it was! Through pity for the unicorn, your brother revealed your presence here. The consequences might have been very different had not the Lady of the Shore intervened.

Magio stared at the dragon, with a rising panic.

Fear not, Magio! It is unlikely he will reveal himself again in the world of dragons. Not for the present, I warrant. But you must be alert at all times from now on. Now he knows you are here, his lust to destroy you will be implacable.

'Oh, Eefa!'

'Make sure you listen to the dragon king, Magio. We can't take any more chances.' Eefa's voice sounded every bit as jittery as Magio's.

We dragons will not be taken by surprise a second time. He is more likely to spy on you – wait for a better opportunity to act. Meanwhile he will attempt to uncover our plans and, once known to him, plot to confound us.

Eefa winced to see how Magio was shaking. She swallowed hard against the lump that was rising into her own throat. 'Did you really mean what you said about our father? Is it true that he's still alive – lost somewhere?'

I spoke truly. It would appear that, however unknowingly, you have both already made contact with him – you, Eefa, in your awake-dreams – and Magio even more recently.

'Eefa – did you hear?'

'I heard, Magio. But I have no more idea than you of what it means.'

'The dragon king said you saw him in your awake-dreams?'

Eefa shivered. She took a deep breath, exhaled. 'You know I don't understand my dreams. I don't even pretend to control them. It feels more as if I somehow become entranced . . . taken to a dreadful place against my will.'

Please describe this place, Eefa – tell me what you recall from your awake-dreams. Tell me what you observed!

Eefa shivered. 'It was as if I had strayed into a nightmare . . . a terrible nightmare in which I came across an unfortunate prisoner.'

Tell me more about this prisoner.

'I had no idea who he was, other than he had grey unkempt hair that was falling about his face. His eyes were so white he must surely be blind. He was shackled to a stump of rock and tormented by horrible beings.'

Demon bots!

Magio blurted out, 'He helped me. That same prisoner. He encouraged me to take courage at the very moment I thought my heart would stop.'

Eefa's eyes widened. 'It was the same man who spoke to me from that terrible prison? He who told me we had to escape to Dromenon.'

The dragon king had come a great deal closer. Those huge unblinking eyes, now utterly dwarfing the twins, gazed face-to-face with them both. *Yes, Eefa! The man you saw in your dreams was your father. It was his timely warning that led you to safety here.*

The twins climbed onto shaky feet, awed by the closeness of those enormous eyes. Eefa took a breath, to convince herself that this was really happening – that it wasn't just another of her awake-dreams. But nothing had changed. She was gazing into the reflection of both their standing figures, which appeared minuscule in those gargantuan eyes. It was true – all that they were witnessing, all that they both were experiencing, no matter how extraordinary it seemed. The shock of it caused her to tremble, forcing her to take a deep breath through her wide-open mouth.

Her world had become one of shifting shadows and outlines, and all the while through and between them, enormous powers were flowing about the landscape, like waves circling a tiny raft in a huge tormented sea. Her nostrils were filled with a medley of acrid smells – of pitch, sulfur, molten rock, all of which confirmed that she was surrounded by volcanic upheaval, with the nearby landscape actively erupting.

It was all Eefa could do to suppress her rising panic.

Had that strange voice, so deep and yet bizarrely musical, really come from the throat of a dragon? From Orebiquinos, the dragon king, the same extraordinary creature who had just told her that . . . that her father . . . the father she could not even recall . . . was not dead, as she and Magio had long believed. He was alive out there, lost, as Orebiquinos had informed them . . . a prisoner in that terrible place of her awake-dreams.

Eefa was no longer quite in control of herself. The shock of all this had become too overwhelming. And she could see that it had overwhelmed Magio too.

Was this where all of their lives had brought them?

If so, what did it really mean? What were they expected to do? Eefa was bewildered by all the strange circumstances in which they now found themselves.

Here, in the magical world of Aeonia, things were so different from anywhere she had ever encountered. There were scents, movements of iridescent lights playing about in the craggy landscape, vague whispers in the very air about her. She no longer felt sure that she trusted anything about it. It felt to Eefa as if she were an alien presence here, always on the cusp of spells, suggestions, forces of magic that were as likely help or pretend the same while having other ends in mind.

She bit her tongue to stop herself panicking. She forced herself to stop and to take a deep breath.

It was too easy here, in the murky dark, to lose one's self of reality. Was what Orebiquinos told them really true? Was their father really alive? Was he really the blind man trapped in that hellish prison? Had it truly been their father who had warned her to flee to Dromenon?

A screeching wail from nearby made her feel faint.

'Woll – oh, Woll – are you still by me?'

I am here, Eefa. Please do not be alarmed. It is merely a waul making us aware of its presence.

'It doesn't sound like any birdsong I've ever heard.'

You must prepare yourself for such surprises, Eefa, if you are to spend any length of time in the presence of dragons. Each fully grown dragon is surrounded, and permeated within, by a vast assemblage of squabbling lesser beings, animal, plant, spirit, wraith – friendly, parasitic, or frankly disinterested other than taking advantage of shelter. Such is the nature of Orebiquinos, meanwhile his great mind might be pondering the mysteries of existence.

Woll's words were hardly reassuring. Eefa's panic was continuing to rise inside her. She felt that she was about to faint.

Nothing felt normal here. Things were happening to her – to both her and Magio – that suggested they were changing. Even the clothes she was still wearing since they had fled Serenity now felt much too small for her. It was as if she had grown some more even since her recent arrival here into Aeonia. Wychera, who had towered above her when they had first met, now seemed less lofty and gangling. She knew what Bird Woman would have said if she saw her now – she would tell her that, in what felt like a very short space of time, she had grown up from girl to young woman. And if she had matured so quickly, Magio must have too.

How she wished that Bird Woman was beside her now to help her understand what was happening.

She clenched her eyes shut and gritted her teeth: 'What are we to do?'

Her words echoed strangely all about her in the alien landscape. For a moment or two, there was no answer. But then, the great dragon carried her aloft in a gentle claw, and with a cackle of wild laughter, she found herself and Magio high in the air, above the acrid landscape of spuming volcanoes, gazing up to a vast spiky neck in the distance, the gigantic being spiraling higher still, until the air cleared of smoke and even the smell of brimstone, to find themselves flying in what felt like the roof of the world.

Eefa closed her eyes, feeling she would never be capable of opening them again.

THE LORE OF DRAGONS

Magio's world had become a maelstrom of massive forces, with the gigantic wings of the dragon king beating ponderously above them, and the enormous body bearing them to their destination, wheeling and undulating at phenomenal speed in negotiating huge mountain passes and towering tops. Eefa had taken to clamping her eyes shut with her hands so she couldn't see the terrifying ride. With his heart pumping madly in his ears, Magio struggled to keep abreast of it, forcing the words out of a mouth stiffened with fear. 'Oh, jinxy! What's happening, Orebiquinos? Where are you taking us?'

Why – to the Council, of course!

Magio screwed up his face, still at a loss as to what was happening to them. 'Why are you taking us there? What will happen to us there?'

Questions! Questions! You would test a dragon's heart with your interminable questions. Well, perhaps in time we shall duly discover the answers to at least some of your questions. Why would we otherwise trouble the elders, who are already busy enough with matters of state?

Eefa and Magio glanced at one another, their figures minute against the enormous claws that carried them. They appeared to be spiraling higher and higher, with enormous rapidity, so that the landscape below them was reduced to a blur. In mere moments, even the mountain tops were lost far below their terrified gazes.

'May I ask you, Orebiquinos, how we can breathe here where there is plainly no air. How can we still speak?'

In the domain of magic, the physical senses are not limited as they would be in the world of mortals. We are not ruled by the brevity of life and death. Fortunately, here – young Magio and Eefa – even you are not prey to such fleeting circumstances of existence. Here you will find yourselves capable of things that your mortal selves might otherwise have doubted.

Eefa refused to be cowed any further. 'Is that the explanation of my awake-dreams?'

Oh, Eefa, I hope so! But I don't really know. You would appear to be a quick learner. Perhaps, given a great mage as father, you were born with nascent gifts. But we must help you – teach you both – the control of such abilities. This will be the first and most vital lesson you both must learn for the challenge that awaits you, now that you are mature enough to face it.

Magio was intrigued by the notion of the strange powers that Wychera was alluding to. He could imagine the temptation of somehow learning how to make use of them. 'But how then, if our father was so wise, did he allow himself to be taken prisoner by the enemy you call The One?'

The Usurper was himself tutored by your father. Playing the part of a humble apprentice, he affected obedience and humility pretending to learn for wisdom's sake. He proved to be the master of duplicity. This was no mean feat in the presence of your father. Perhaps such faith was a weakness in one whose heart was fundamentally pure.

Magio exclaimed, 'I don't understand.'

To understand truth, you must beware the snares of falsehood. That is the mystery of all that was, and is, and ever will be. We mages are dedicated to that path.

'But . . . but it's . . . it's all so confusing.'

Indeed, it is, Magio! Yet the very same mystery lies at the very heart of the dimension of existence you know of as Dromenon.

'But what does that mean?'

Young Magio, you wouldn't believe the depths your simple question explores. It was conceived by the powers as a refuge from reality and thus a domain of absolute tranquility. But over the eons, Dromenon has become the plaything of every half-witted Magus who flaunted the smallest ambition of magic. Better we avoid thinking too deeply about it all, but rather focus on the specific. We, the dragons of Aeonia, will ensure that you and your sister will understand the profounder mysteries of Dromenon. We shall teach you and Eefa how, through such understanding, you will confound the avarice of The One.

'Oh!'

The dragon appeared to take an enormous breath, then grunted and swished his enormous tail, causing massive vibrations and ripples to run through his body, expanding even to the huge claws that currently held Magio and Eefa in their grasp.

I have confused the issue by saying too much about too little. Let us return to the basics. As you have only recently discovered, the enemy that now threatens all that was formerly sacred has come perilously close to destroying you, Magio.

Eefa whispered aside to her brother, 'If only we were changelings, like Wychera!'

My dearest Eefa, we are all changelings.

'But how – how are we changelings?'

The dragon king exhaled a long laugh.

I can see, perhaps, how all this must appear strange to you. But the notion of being a changeling should not trouble you. Nature cannot abide monotony. Did you not have the seasons back on Moon? Change is everywhere throughout existence – what you humans dismissively label "nature". Yet you are so embedded in change that you fail to grasp its essential nature. You take for granted the cycles of life. You think nothing of how caterpillars go to sleep in their pupas and emerge as butterflies. Do not humans begin as eggs that grow into the wonder of twin brothers and sisters? All are changelings. Wychera is no exception.

Eefa was still puzzled as to what he was implying. 'You talk about this enemy, called The One. But who, really, is he and why does he hate us so?'

Good! You are now asking the right questions. But now let us take things a step at a time. I have brought you to a corner of Aeonia, where you will discover one familiar to you.

Eefa and Magio were both stunned into silence for several moments as the dragon circled a location that appeared to be on a coast. As he descended out of the sky, they saw a cove, of volcanic rocks and white sand that reminded them of the beach in Warren. Then, as they came even closer still, they recognized a single rickety shack, built out of reclaimed planks of wood.

Magio was the first to recognize it. 'Hey – look there, Eefie! It's Gran's house. Oh, britzy – I know it is!'

Eefa peered down at the shack set amid the black rocks, and a little drawn back from the beach. It was their simple home, back in Warren. She could even make out the shuttered window of unpainted planks of their shared bedroom, with its ladder leading down into the hallway below – oh, and even rickety shed where Quimbre had set up his ferret hutch on the roof.

'But that's impossible. It can't be here.'

'Oh – look out into the bay!'

Eefa shrieked with delight to see the Scuttlebutt moored in the shallows, with the mainsail furled.

Magio shrieked with glee. 'Can't we go there? Let's go see Quimbre and Bird Woman.'

The dragon harrumphed, then sighed. *All in good time! First, there is one who has missed your company for considerably longer – one whose patience has been sorely tried, as even I, Orebiquinos, can attest!*

They saw the figure, seated among the black stones amid the soft white sand, one that was altogether familiar to them. All of a sudden, they were both struggling to free themselves from the dragon's claws, shrieking and leaping down onto the sand next to the seated figure. They were running madly towards the figure, with flailing arms.

'Gran!'

The figure was slowly lifting her head as they ran to embrace her, their eyes brimming with tears.

'Gran!'

'Oh, Gran, is it really you?'

The figure cackled. 'Of course, it's me! Do you think your eyes are deceiving you?'

'But . . . but . . . we saw your dead body. We were told we had to leave home – to flee from Moon.'

'It was all a deliberate pretense. A game of secrecy and confabulation, designed to keep you safe from an enemy who would have destroyed you.'

'We thought you dead.'

'So, you two scallywags were meant to think, though it broke my poor old heart.'

Eefa hurled herself to hug the seated figure. 'We can't believe you're alive. Oh, we just cannot believe it!'

Gran cackled, hugging Eefa back. 'It was a heart-breaking experience for me too when obliged to recognize that my very presence had become a liability, risking your discovery.'

Magio also dashed to embrace her. 'Why – oh, why, did it have to end? We were all so happy.'

'Why?' Gran's black eyes lifted to look into the tearful face of Magio. 'What lively sparks you've grown into. Oh, I admit it! I so relished your silliest pranks. Alas, all was brought to an end when we encountered a telling sign.'

'The arrival of the Ursascogans into Warren – that was what warned you of the danger?'

'Yes.'

'They were sent there, weren't they? They were sent there by that evil sorceress, Lustfera, to look for us?'

'You have figured it out for yourself, Magio.'

'But there's so much we still don't understand. Oh, please, Gran, you must explain.'

'Even I, a great witch, knew that I could not match the lore of the enemy who hunted you. He would not have rested until you were destroyed. Who do you think called Bird Woman to your rescue when the Ursascogans were gathering? Who, even earlier, saved a drowning pirate, albeit a useful one, from a briny death to have him find a berth in our ramshackle home? All the while, I was anticipating the coming threat – though I will admit his skills with the baccy and juniper juice were a bonus.'

Eefa could only murmur, 'You figured everything out?'

'A great witch has powers, but they cannot match those of an undying. We can influence the affairs of humans, but I knew I could not guarantee your protection when the Star of Mourning arrived in Warren.

Eefa's hand was to her mouth. 'We were so . . . so devastated to lose you. We didn't know what to do. We felt so lost without you.'

'I could not risk the possibility that the enemy would recognize you for what you truly were. I had to put my faith in the grey.'

Magio exclaimed, 'What is the grey?'

'Ordinariness – the world as it must appear without the color of magic!'

Magio shook his head. 'Oh, Gran – I can't believe that you're a witch.'

'A witch I am. I proffer no apologies. I am none other than the great witch, Granny Dew.'

Magio was blinking rapidly, tears moistening his eyes. 'Did you not love us?'

'Ach, foolish child! What is this love you would demand of me? Must I profess to care in mere words to convince my darling urchins of my love for you? So much has passed under the bridge, and yet here we are, reunited in the fairytale world of Aeonia.'

Magio took a deep breath, clapped his hands and shouted, 'Britzy!'

'There we go – you and your jinxies and britzies! Yet how it warms my heart to see that rascal grin again! And you too, Eefa! Don't you go a moaning and a fretting as usual. What's done is done.'

Magio sat down, cross-legged, facing Gran. 'You're right. We need to be focused. That's exactly what we need to do from now on. But there's so much we still don't understand. We've just discovered that our father is alive. But he appears to be in some terrible place.' Magio hesitated, his eyes meeting those of Gran, filled with uncertainty.

'Go ahead, irascible Gio! I know you have a question you are dying to ask me?'

'Yes, I do. I – we, Eefa and me – would like to know how it was that we were placed into your care as infants.'

'Ah!' Gran lifted a bony forefinger, with its elongated nail, into a cautionary gesture. 'Now, there's a thing to test an old gran's memory.'

'Please tell us – what do you remember?'

'Well, you didn't arrive at my doorstep tucked up in a ribbon basket. Rather you burst upon my dozing by the fireside, out of the blue.'

'What do you mean?'

'It could only have been a desperate measure by one gifted in magic. One single moment of confusion, a jumble of whispers invading my mind, and there you were. Two bawling infants a tumble on my hearth rug, naked and unannounced.'

'It was our father who sent us, wasn't it?'

'So, I have always assumed.'

'But why?'

'Oh, my dear, I asked myself that same question. Clearly, he was unable to keep you by him. You appeared well-fed and cared for, so I was inclined to think that the need to protect you was very sudden – and likely of the greatest importance.'

Eefa shook her head, still puzzled. 'He thought we were in danger if we stayed with him?'

'So, I was obliged to conclude.'

'You must have been very shocked.'

'Very shocked – and equally intrigued.'

'What did you do?'

'You must recall that the Chaos had begun. All was confusion. If fear for your safety was the driving force behind the transfer, it must have been a very great fear. At the same time, it required great lore of magic to do the sending. The smallest error – my, oh my, but it could have ended badly. Hrrrmmm! I confess I was bewildered at first – and somewhat angry too. I had concerns of my own that had little to do with nurturing swadlings. But then, as hours became days, and days became years, I grew accustomed to this new role. I was somewhat taken by the mystery of it all. And, I warrant, your arrival heralded mysteries.'

Eefa spoke softly. 'Like my invisibility?'

'That was a dander, my little chickadee!'

Magio shook his head. 'You must explain!'

'I am under no "musts" or "have-to's", young Magio. But if you ask me nicely, mayhaps I might even oblige. Of course, I searched high and low to discover your origins. I began with the obvious. Your arrival into my humble abode had to be a deliberate act of very powerful magic.'

'You tried to find the source?'

'Of course, I did! But every stratagem I could devise led ultimately to nowhere.'

Eefa sighed. 'So you gave up?'

'Not at all! I realized that the very mystery of your origins was itself a clue to the answer. It spoke volumes of the intention of the sender – who, as we now know, was your father, the Great Mage himself. I realized that he took such pains to conceal your identity because its discovery would have placed you in very great danger.'

'What did you do?'

'I asked myself, "Who are the master planners of the grandest magical schemes?"'

The twins gazed at Gran in an uncertain silence for several seconds before Magio spoke, 'The dragons – !'

'Clever Gio – yes! The dragons! Or more pertinently, their Grand Council in this same world of Aeonia!'

'So, you asked them – the Dragon Council – who we really were?'

'I asked them a number of questions.'

'And they told you?'

'It was they who had advised the Great Mage, your father, what to do in his moment of crisis. In their wisdom – or mayhaps you might think otherwise – they chose me, Granny Dew, to be your protector and guardian.'

Eefa cried, 'Oh, Gran – what about us? Did you come to care for us?'

'Ach!' Gran cackled with amusement. 'Magio was easy to love, since he was such a naughty puppy never far from trouble. But you – you, my darling Eefa – you presented a deeper puzzle. Invisible as you were to mortal sight, I had to figure you out for myself. Why this additional burden my little Eefie had to bear? I knew there had to be a reason for your invisibility. But try as I might to discover the why, I was ever confronted by a telling silence.'

'The dragons – they hid the Lady's purpose even from you?'

Gran hugged Eefa to her, with a soft chuckle. 'This they did! They kept it good and tight up to the revelation in that extraordinary exchange of soul spirits on the Beach of Bones.'

Magio shook his head. 'They used Eefa. The dragons and even the Lady of the Shore! And now we know that they sent Wychera Gallant, the elfin changer, to bring us here to Aeonia. As you have made clear, the dragons never do anything for no reason. So, they must be planning to use us once again!'

'You're right, Magio. The dragons do use people. And, right now, they have plans for you.'

'Well, I have a plan of my own. You spoke of our father, the Great Mage. And now we've discovered that he's the blind man in Eefa's dreams.'

Gran clapped her hands and her eyes opened wide. 'Go on – I know you're dying to tell me more, my clever Gio!'

Eefa stared from Gio to Gran, her eyes widening: 'But – what in the world are you saying?'

'Oh, I think your brother has already worked it out, Eefa. Go ahead – tell her, Magio!'

Magio's voice had fallen to a whisper. 'Now that we've discovered that our father is alive, we must find a way to free him.'

'Has it occurred to you that your plans, and those of the dragons, might actually be one and the same?'

'You really think so?'

'Ach! It doesn't take too much deliberation to realize that you and Eefa and your imprisoned father might all somehow come together in everybody's plans right now? Of course, that is also what the dragons want. And you can add Gran to your plans, Magio. I want to help you too! Eefa asked me if I came to care for you. Oh, my dearest children – why I have always loved you as my own! Yes, even a great witch is capable of loving – and I still love you, with all of my heart. But now you will risk your lives to free your father from his nightmare prison. This will be the riskiest adventure you could possibly face. Such perils will you face – such powers of darkness you could not even imagine!'

Magio retorted, 'I have already felt his rage. I don't fear The One!'

'No – I can see that you don't, Magio. But fear him you should! I will address myself to you, Eefa, because you are less wilful than your brother. The danger of any such enterprise will be truly enormous. It may mean war in Dromenon.'

'Oh, Gran!'

'Please take time to reconsider. Here in Aeonia, you are safe. You don't need to continue this desperate course. You could live here with me in the safety of this wonderful world of dragons for the rest of your lives, surrounded by beauty and contentment.'

Eefa and Magio looked at one another, eye-to-eye. They were agreed. 'We have to do it. We've seen our father in that terrible place.'

Granny Dew sighed. She drew the twins about her, taking them into the bosom of her embrace. 'Oh, my darling children – you are still so very naive! You little understand the perils you will face.'

'We'll face them together.'

Granny Dew spoke softly, sadly,

'Of course, you will! And I'll help you all I can, as will Orebiquinos, and his Council. But it won't be easy. You will require training in the darker arts of war. You must acquire the Lore of Dragons. I promise that I shall also do what I can to protect you with the ancient craft I bear. Thus, twice-armed, in Lore and Craft, will you be forged into the mage-warriors you must perforce become!'

THE TWINS OF MOON

Eefa and her twin brother, Magio, are on the run, hunted by a ruthless predator with a pack of wolf hounds. Until recently they enjoyed a carefree life in the ramshackle town of Warren on the Isle of Moon. Since birth, Eefa has been invisible to everybody other than Magio. But now, after the sudden death of their beloved Gran, their world has been turned upside down. Out of the blue, terrifying giants try to kidnap Eefa, who is rescued by the intervention of a stranger known to the locals as Bird Woman. And now Bird Woman insists that the twins are no longer safe. They must flee their childhood home and head for the Valley of the Raptors, high in the snow-capped mountains.

What fate awaits the twins in the Valley of the Raptors? Will Eefa discover the reason for her invisibility? Will they escape the vicious forces that are closing in around them – or is this really a malevolent trap?

For more info go to www.swiftpublishers.com and
www.frankpryan.com